"Are you ready to collect on our bet?"

The corners of Chris's eyes crinkled after he said it.

"I am." Marissa smiled and took a step closer. "Kiss me."

He ran a finger down the side of her face to brush her hair back behind her shoulder. And then he gathered her into his arms and pulled her tight against his chest. Her heart beat faster, and he hadn't even gotten to her lips yet. He lowered his head and brushed his mouth against hers like a whisper. She parted her lips to draw in a breath, and he captured her mouth. Her arms wound around his neck, bringing him closer.

How she'd missed this. The way they fit together. His arms holding her safe, his heart beating in time with hers. It was like the last piece of a jigsaw puzzle that fit into the remaining spot and brought the whole picture into focus. It was never this way with anyone else. She wanted to stay in his arms forever.

Dear Reader,

I love Christmas. I love the decorations, the food and the excitement of children as they anticipate Santa coming. In my heroine Marissa's family, Christmas is not only a passion, but a way of life. Marissa grew up on her aunt and uncle's reindeer farm in Alaska, and Christmastime is their busiest season. Her uncle Oliver is a natural Santa, with his white beard, round belly and love for children. But Oliver is sick, and it's up to Marissa and Aunt Becky to carry on.

For my hero, Chris, Christmas magic was in short supply during his childhood. Until he met Marissa, he'd never known that that sort of supportive and happy family unit existed. But a fundamental disagreement led to their breakup.

Now, as much as Marissa would like to deny it, her family needs our hero's help. Partly to annoy her, he agrees to step in. Just to complicate things, a dinosaur-loving boy in dire need of a dose of Christmas spirit ricochets into Chris's life. And Christmas starts to work its magic...

I hope you enjoy reading this story. There will be more Northern Lights romances to come. To keep in touch, visit www.bethcarpenterbooks.blogspot.com, where you can find my email, Facebook and Twitter contacts as well as the latest book news. You can also sign up for my newsletter.

Wishing peace, love and joy to you and yours the whole year through.

Beth Carpenter

HEARTWARMING

A Gift for Santa

———

Beth Carpenter

HARLEQUIN® HEARTWARMING™

Recycling programs
for this product may
not exist in your area.

ISBN-13: 978-0-373-36863-1

A Gift for Santa

Printed in U.S.A.

Beth Carpenter is thankful for good books, a good dog, a good man and a dream job creating happily-ever-afters. She and her husband now split their time between Alaska and Arizona, where she occasionally encounters a moose in the yard or a scorpion in the basement. She prefers the moose.

Books by Beth Carpenter

Harlequin Heartwarming

The Alaskan Catch

To my husband, Steve. Thank you for supporting my dreams.

I also want to thank my agent, Barbara Rosenberg, and editors Kathryn Lye and Victoria Curran for believing in me and working with me to make each story the best it can be. And thanks to Brenda, Brenda, Christy, Sue, Diana and other early readers. Your encouragement made all the difference.

CHAPTER ONE

Twenty-four days till Christmas

No snow. No Uncle Oliver. Even the reindeer weren't cooperating. Instead of following the others out, Peppermint pawed at the floor of the trailer and shook her head, jingling the bells on her harness.

Marissa scratched the hairy diva's forehead and spoke in a low voice. "Come on, girl. You'll have fun. Think of all those kids so excited to ride behind a real live reindeer." She patted Peppermint's neck until she seemed calm. "Let's go. Your public awaits." She gave a little tug on the lead, and with a toss of her antlers, the reindeer trip-trapped down the ramp. Her snort formed a cloud of white vapor in the icy air.

The last few rays of sun cast a pink glow on the oval track of trucked-in snow, breaking up the expanse of brown grass. Ordinarily, at least ten inches of packed snow would blanket the area beside the golf-course clubhouse

Grizzlyco always rented for their Christmas party, making it the perfect venue for reindeer sleigh rides. But there was nothing ordinary about this year, especially without Oliver playing Santa Claus.

It felt wrong, setting up for a party without Oliver's hearty "Ho, ho, ho," booming in the background as he warmed up for his favorite role. Her uncle barely had the energy to get out of bed these days, much less spend a strenuous evening handling reindeer and wrestling children on and off his lap.

Aunt Becky pulled one of the pop-up Christmas trees from the back of the truck and stopped to look across the clearing, where a man was attaching grooming equipment to the back of a snow machine. "The snow track looks good."

"It does. I'm amazed Grizzlyco took on the expense of trucking in snow."

"Lucky for us, this is their premier event of the year, and the sleigh rides for the kids are a big draw." Becky frowned. "And speaking of draws, have you seen the guy who's supposed to play Santa?"

"Not that I know of." A few people had been milling around the kitchen and decorating the party room when she went inside earlier, but she hadn't seen anyone who looked like a would-be

Santa. Of course, it was hard to picture anyone else in the role except Oliver.

Becky clucked her tongue. "He was supposed to be here twenty minutes ago. I'll take this tree inside and see if he's arrived."

Marissa unloaded the other tree and Santa's throne. On her final trip indoors, she found Becky pressing the cell phone to her ear, a look of panic spreading across her face. Was Oliver okay? Marissa stepped closer to listen to the conversation.

"Yes, it's today. What's all that noise? Are you in a bar?" Becky paced back and forth as she waited for the reply. "No, thank you. And don't bother showing up for the next one, either. Yes, well, I'm sorry, too. Goodbye." Becky tapped the phone and met Marissa's eyes. "No Santa."

"You're kidding me."

"That's what I get for hiring someone's nephew as a favor. He sounded half-sloshed." Becky gazed upward. "Now what do we do?"

"I don't know." Marissa thought for a moment. "I guess we'll have to draft Dillon." Although how they were going to turn their sixteen-year-old assistant, with a voice that tended to unexpectedly switch octaves, into the jolly old elf himself was hard to imagine.

"Dillon?"

"Who else? Maddy or Jasmine? All they do is giggle."

"True." Becky shook her head. "I've got one or two possibilities. Let me make some calls while I set up Santa's throne."

"All right." Marissa unpacked the tree she'd brought in. "I'll make sure the reindeer rides are ready to go."

Becky nodded, already flicking through the contacts on her phone. Marissa picked up the empty tree bags and carried them to the truck.

Hiring a Santa was never a consideration before, with Oliver so perfect for the role. He kept his white beard all year round in preparation for the Christmas season. How long had he been going downhill? It had been too many years since Marissa had made it back to Alaska to visit. Oliver had seemed fine last February when he and Aunt Becky had come to see her in Louisiana—maybe a little thinner, less energetic, but then he was getting older. Still, she should have realized something was wrong.

If she hadn't been so busy assisting Jason with that fund-raiser while they were visiting, she would have. Or maybe not. If she were any good at picking up subtle clues, Jason couldn't have conned her and left her jobless and under suspicion of fraud. Once the River Foundation closed, ending her work there, she'd come slinking back to the reindeer farm outside Anchorage where she'd grown up. She'd never expected to find Oliver so pale and weak. Why had they kept it from her? At least the train wreck in her own life brought her home, where she could help Becky get through the Christmas season.

Marissa stopped to check on the reindeer and the three elves who would lead them around the tracks. The teenagers clustered together under the light pole where children would be lining up for rides. "You guys all have your boots and costumes, right?"

"Do I really have to wear the thing with the bells?" Dillon scratched the back of his neck.

"Of course. It's all part of being an elf. You're lucky. When I was your age and doing this job, I had to wear elf ears, too. The only reason you don't is that people kept asking if I was a Vulcan."

Predictably, the girls giggled. Dillon shifted his weight from one foot to the other. "We just have to lead the reindeer and pull the kids, right? We don't have to talk to the kids or anything?"

Hmm. Not the best candidate to embrace the whole Santa Claus persona. Surely Becky could come up with someone better. Marissa gave Dillon an encouraging smile. "Just look friendly and lead the reindeer around the track. Becky will handle getting the kids in and out of the sleds. Okay?"

Dillon nodded and adjusted Peppermint's harness. At the other end of the clearing, the snow machine made a second pass along the track, leaving a packed trail with twin grooves in the snow. At least something was going right. Marissa had figured the trucks would just dump the snow, but whoever had hauled it in had taken the trouble to find a cross-country ski groomer and condition the trail. That would make the reindeers' job, as well as that of the reindeer handlers', much smoother.

Marissa walked over to the edge of the oval and waved down the driver. He stopped the snow machine in the shadow of a tall spruce, cut the engine and lifted the helmet from his head.

She stepped forward. "Thanks for grooming. It looks great. We appreciate the extra effort."

"Bo?"

She froze at the sound of the familiar voice. Great, just great. What were the odds of running into him here? If they had to meet, she would have liked it to be on her own terms, not when she was already frazzled. But it had to be Chris. Nobody else ever called her Bo, short for Rainbow, because he said her smile was like a burst of sunshine after a rainstorm. At least he used to say that, a long time ago.

She swallowed. "Hello, Chris."

"Why are you here?" He stepped out of the shadow. The light from the pole bounced off auburn hair, disheveled from the helmet. His beard was neatly trimmed, not wild and curly the way it tended to be at the end of fishing season, but he still had the same broad shoulders, the same crooked smile. Maybe a few more lines around his eyes. Darned if he didn't look even better than he had ten years ago.

"I'm helping with the party." And that's all he needed to know.

"I mean in Alaska. I thought you'd gone for good."

She nodded. "This is just temporary. I'm between jobs and Becky needed help for the busy season."

Chris studied her face. "I see."

He looked as though he did see. Scary thought. The Ponzi scheme Jason had been running was all over the networks, but Chris usually didn't pay a lot of attention to national news. He wouldn't know she'd been working at the River Foundation Jason had founded, much less that she and Jason had been dating. At least she hoped not. The fewer people who tied her to Jason, the better.

"No luck, Marissa," Becky called as she hurried toward them. When she realized who Marissa was talking to, her face lit up. "Chris!"

"Becky, how are you?" He opened his arms to hug the small, plump woman. "I thought I'd find you here. Merry Christmas."

"Merry Christmas to you. So you trucked in the snow?"

"Yes. My snowplowing business isn't doing so well this winter, so I jumped at the chance to earn a little extra hauling it down from the mountains."

Becky stepped closer to the track. "It looks great. Where did you get the grooming equipment?"

"I borrowed it from the Nordic Ski Club. They're not using it. So, where's Oliver? I'd like to say hello."

Marissa didn't want to get into explanations. "He couldn't make it today. He's not feeling well."

"I'm sorry to hear that. It won't be the same without him playing Santa."

"No. In fact…" Marissa could all but see

the light bulb go on over Becky's head as her aunt said, "We're having a little problem."

Marissa gave her own head a brief shake. No, no, no. The last thing she needed was to spend a whole evening with Chris. Not with their history. Even if it meant forcing Dillon into the role. In fact, she'd play Santa herself before she'd let Chris worm his way back into her life.

He glanced at her in time to see her trying to wave Becky off, and the lines at the corners of his eyes crinkled. Uh-oh. She knew that look.

Her aunt bumbled on, either completely missing Marissa's signals or ignoring them. "Our substitute Santa backed out at the last minute. It looks like you're about done with the snow. Would you be willing to fill in for Oliver?"

Chris raised his eyebrows. "You want *me* to play Santa?"

"Chris can't do Santa." Marissa tried to keep her voice matter-of-fact. "He doesn't like children."

He frowned at her. "That's not true. I have nothing against kids."

"But you said—"

He turned to Becky. "I'll do it. Where do I get a costume?"

"We've got everything you need. Marissa will get you fixed up." Becky beamed at him. "Thank you, Chris. You're a lifesaver."

"No problem. I just have to finish this pass and send my guys home with the equipment." He caught Marissa's eye, and there was a challenge in his gaze. "I'll be back."

She met his stare without blinking. "I'll be here."

THIRTY MINUTES LATER, Chris slouched in his chair while Marissa smeared petroleum jelly around the edges of his beard. "Is this really necessary?" he muttered.

She smirked. "Unless you want white dye all over your skin. Trust me, when I wipe it off, you'll be glad."

"Why can't I just wear the fake beard, like everyone else?" Sure, Oliver had a real beard, but then his was naturally white.

"Real is better. We might as well take advantage of yours."

"Great." What had he gotten himself into? He didn't dislike kids, no matter what Marissa said, although it was true he had little experience with them. But when he'd seen how much she hated the idea of him playing Santa, he couldn't resist yanking her chain. Besides, Becky was in a bind and he was fond of her and Oliver, in spite of everything. They weren't the ones who'd dumped him.

Marissa held a spray can near his face. "Ready?"

"I guess."

"Keep your eyes and mouth closed." With a hiss of aerosol, she started turning his beard white. A little tickle followed her progress. She paused to shake the can. "Hang on. It's not easy to cover all these red whiskers."

He scowled and looked up at her. "My beard is brown."

A hint of amusement glinted from those green-blue eyes of hers, the exact color of the Kenai River on a sunny day. "Sure it is. Close your eyes and don't talk, unless you want a mouthful of dye." She took so long he wondered if she was stretching out the process on purpose, but finally, she finished.

He reached for his beard, but she slapped his hand away. "Let it dry."

"This stuff does wash out, right?"

Marissa snickered and started smearing petroleum jelly across his forehead.

"You have to do my hair, too?"

She pushed a stray lock away from his face. "No, the wig and hat will cover that, but Santa can't have red—excuse me, brown—eyebrows." She used to tease him about his hair when they were together. She'd run her fingers through the thick waves and say she was jealous.

Her own hair was perfectly straight, a warm brown that glowed even under the fluorescent lights of the closet they were using as a dressing room. He knew if he reached out to stroke it, it would feel like satin ribbons under his hand. She'd changed surprisingly little in ten years. Only the easy smile, the confident optimism, was missing, but that might have more to do with the way they'd parted than the years that had passed.

She was still beautiful, no doubt about that. He'd been drawn to her from the first moment he saw her, laughing as she helped a group of schoolchildren release salmon fry into Chester Creek. He'd interrupted his hike to listen to her explain the salmon's life cycle. Once the teacher herded the children back onto the school bus, Chris saw his chance. He'd helped Marissa pack some gear into her car, and struck up a conversation. By the time she'd closed the trunk, he was hooked.

Smart, energetic and laugh-out-loud funny when she wanted to be, Marissa had fascinated him. A year later, she'd let him put a ring on her finger. But at twenty-four, Marissa was a woman who knew what she wanted, and wasn't about to let a little thing like love interfere with her carefully laid plans. A month before the wedding, she'd called the whole thing off.

Maybe he'd dodged a bullet. He hadn't had a relationship since Marissa that lasted even six months. Sometimes he suspected she'd done him a favor when she broke the engagement, saving them both the agony of a bitter divorce. He wondered how those plans of hers had worked out. Last he heard, she was doing some sort of research on the Gulf Coast. A quick glance reaffirmed the absence of rings on her hands, so maybe the devoted husband and two-point-four kids hadn't materialized. Not that it mattered to him one way or another. Their relationship was ancient history.

"Eyes closed." Two puffs on his eyebrows and she started wiping the grease off his skin with a tissue. "Okay, that does it for the dye. So, here's the routine. I'll organize the kids and bring them to you one at a time. You set them on your lap, ho, ho, ho a little and ask what they want for Christmas. Then I snap your picture together, you give them a candy cane and we send them on their way."

"Okay." Chris nodded. "That sounds straight-forward enough."

"Be enthusiastic, but not too loud. And if

they start screaming, don't force them onto your lap."

Was she serious? "Screaming?"

Marissa nodded and dipped a fluffy brush in a powder pot. "Imagine if somebody told you to sit on a bearded stranger's lap. It can be scary." She reached for his face with the brush. "Hold still."

Chris pulled away. "Santa wears makeup?"

"Just a little powder so your nose won't shine in the pictures. Man up." She tickled his nose and cheeks with the powder. "There. I'll leave you to get into your costume. The pants are waterproof."

"I'm afraid to ask why."

"Like I said, sometimes the kids are scared."

"So they pee? What are they, puppies?"

She gave a maniacal laugh. "You should hear some of Oliver's stories. A friend of his from Santa school had a diaper leak all over his lap."

Now that was disgusting. The only child Chris had spent much time around was his little sister, and he couldn't remember her doing anything along those lines.

He grimaced. "You know, I never graduated from Santa school. I don't want to get in trouble for practicing without a proper license or anything."

"Too late now. The children are counting on you." Her grin was pure evil. "Besides, you promised Becky. Get dressed. I'll check back in a few minutes."

Fifteen minutes later, Chris examined himself in the full-length mirror leaning against the wall. Amazing. Santa Claus looked back at him, blue eyes twinkling beneath white eyebrows. Padding filled out the plush red costume under the wide black belt. Fortunately, he'd worn black snow boots, because he never would have fit his feet into those patent leather booties.

He looked the part. Now the question was could he play the part? No one had ever taken him to see Santa when he was a kid, so he didn't have that experience to fall back on. He'd been to a few parties where Oliver was working, but never paid much attention to how he did his job. Oliver just seemed to treat the kids with the same gentle enthusiasm as he did everyone, and they adored him. He loved playing Santa. Poor guy. He must be down with a nasty flu or something to miss the biggest party of the year.

Chris wrinkled his nose and patted the stiff plastic lining of the pants, hoping he wouldn't need it. Surely Marissa was exaggerating. All those stories were just to torture him for defying her and agreeing to Becky's request. No doubt if he'd declined, Marissa would have held that against him, too. There was no winning with her. She expected the whole world to fall in with her plans. You'd think she would have outgrown that by now.

If it were just Marissa, he'd take the hint and leave her to solve the problem on her own, but Becky deserved better. She and Oliver had made Chris feel truly welcomed from the very first time they met, when Marissa had brought him home to meet the couple who'd raised her. Even after the split, Chris would run into them now and again, and they greeted him like a long-lost relative.

A knock sounded, and the door opened a crack. "Are you decent?"

Chris glanced toward the mirror again. "Only my hands and eyes are showing."

Marissa walked in, wearing white tights, a red dress trimmed with white faux fur, and a matching stocking cap with a jingle bell on the end. More bells jingled from the turned-up toes of her shoes as she stepped into the room. Chris grinned.

She shot him a look. "Don't say a word."

He chuckled. "For an elf, you're awfully bossy. Come on. Let's get jolly."

THEY'D BEEN AT it for two hours, but it looked like they'd finally worked their way to the end of the line. Chris watched Marissa climb the step of the platform and deposit another child on his lap. He'd lost count along the way, but it felt as if he'd interacted with a thousand or so little people so far. They'd had a few meltdowns, but Marissa was good at assessing whether they wanted her encouragement to approach him or just needed to put some distance between themselves and the scary man with the beard.

He smiled at the girl on his lap. "What would you like for Christmas?"

She just stared up at him, her little mouth forming an O, her dark eyes wide. Chris tried again. "You've been a good girl, haven't you?"

"Yes." She reached up to touch his beard, stiff from all the white dye. "It's real," she whispered.

He gave a gentle "Ho, ho, ho. What would you like Santa to bring you?"

A confident smile bloomed on her face. "An Elsa doll and a big elephant."

Chris's chest rocked with suppressed laughter. "You mean a stuffed elephant."

She shook her head, her eyes solemn. "No, a real one I can ride, with long tooths and a trunk."

Chris looked over to her parents for guidance, but they only shrugged. He turned back to the girl. "I'm not sure I have room for an elephant in my sleigh. Besides, where would you keep him?"

"In my room."

"Hmm. That could get a little messy. I'll have to think about it, but I'll make a note. I'm sure you'll be pleased with what you find under the tree on Christmas morning. Now, smile at Elf Marissa and she'll take our picture."

The girl beamed at Marissa, accepted her candy cane and skipped off with her parents. Chris hoped she didn't have her heart set on a live elephant. He looked to Marissa for the next child, but no one seemed to be in line.

A small boy stood to one side, peering at him from behind his mother.

Marissa smiled at the boy. "Would you like to sit on Santa's lap?"

He shook his head and ducked behind his mom. Chris got down from his big chair and sat on the step, looking toward the windows instead of at the boy. "You know, Elf Marissa, if someone wanted to give me a message, they wouldn't have to sit on my lap. They could just whisper it in my ear."

Marissa cocked her head at the boy. "What do you think? Do you want to whisper something to Santa?"

The little guy leaned out from behind his mother's legs to look at Chris, but hid again and shook his head.

Marissa pressed her finger against her chin. "Or maybe they could whisper the message to me, and I could pass it on. What do you think, Santa?"

Chris couldn't resist teasing her. "I don't know. That's a big responsibility for an elf." He glanced over at the boy. "Do you think we can trust her to get it right?"

The little boy bobbed his head eagerly. Chris smiled. "All right, then."

Without hesitation, the boy hurried to Marissa. She bent so that her face was level with his, and he whispered something in her ear. She motioned his mother over and the three of them huddled together for a minute. When the boy looked up, Chris offered him a candy cane. After a little encouragement from his mother, he crept toward Chris while she and Marissa watched and whispered.

Without making eye contact, the boy took

the candy from Chris's hand. "Thank you," he whispered.

"You're very welcome. Merry Christmas."

The boy ran back to his mom, but turned to smile and wave at Chris before disappearing into the crowd with her. Marissa came to sit beside Chris on the step. "I think he was the last."

"Good, but don't you have a message for me?"

She laughed. "Taking your duties pretty seriously there, Santa. Yes, Noah wants his dad home for Christmas, and from what his mom tells me he's going to get his wish."

"Military?"

She nodded. "A few months apart must feel like years when you're that small."

"His mom looked excited, too. I'm glad they'll be together for Christmas."

Marissa turned to him, but quickly glanced away again. Was she remembering, as he was, their last Christmas together? Snuggled up next to the fire, the air spiced with peppermint and evergreen and the light flowery scent that clung to her hair. Warm laughter and cookie-flavored kisses. Back then, he'd believed it was the beginning of a lifetime together. He was wrong.

He stood abruptly. "So now what?"

She rose and faced him. "You're done. Just

leave the costume on the hanger." She paused, and then continued in a formal voice. "Thank you for your help. Have a nice Christmas."

"Santa." Becky came bouncing toward them, her cheeks rosy above her fur-trimmed red sweater. "How did it go?"

"Fairly well, I think." Chris looked at Marissa.

She nodded. "Just fine. Everything okay with the reindeer?"

"The kids loved them, as always. At first, Dillon acted like the kids might bite, but he eventually settled down." Becky took Chris's arm and led him toward a quiet corner. Marissa followed. "So, Chris, we're going to need a Santa for a party Tuesday afternoon, and for several other appearances between now and Christmas. It's a paying gig, and there's no snow to plow in the forecast anytime soon. What do you say?"

"No." Marissa stepped between them. "We'll find someone else. Chris is busy."

Ten years ago she'd dumped him, and now she thought she could speak for him? Not likely. But why did they need him? Chris frowned. "Won't Oliver be better by then?"

Becky shook her head. "Oliver's quite ill. It's his heart."

Oliver had a bad heart? He seemed so

healthy. Granted, he carried a few extra pounds thanks to Becky's cooking, but he was strong, tossing around fifty-pound feed sacks with ease. "I'm so sorry. If it—"

"We'll be fine." Marissa locked eyes with him. "We appreciate the help, but you've done enough."

Chris's gaze shifted from Marissa's glare to the hopeful glint in Becky's eyes. He ignored Marissa and smiled at her aunt. "Of course. I'd be happy to help. Let's go find my phone and I'll put in the dates."

He left Marissa standing there with steam coming out from under her elf hat. So she didn't want him around—tough cookies. He wasn't so keen on spending time with her, either, but Becky and Oliver needed his help. Marissa was just going to have to grow up and think about someone besides herself for a change.

That alone was worth the price of a few dozen candy canes.

CHAPTER TWO

Twenty-two days till Christmas

THE BUZZING FLUORESCENT bulb in Chris's warehouse office seemed to hit the resonant frequency inside his skull. He massaged his temples while he waited for his password to reveal the balance of his checking account. Sadly, the figure was exactly what he expected. He'd have to transfer more money out of his boat fund to cover payroll.

After years of working on someone else's boat, socking away his earnings from his share of the catch, he'd almost reached his goal of owning his own fishing boat. In fact, he'd come close to buying one in September, even going so far as to sell his one indulgence, his red convertible. At the last minute, the boat owner had changed his mind about selling. Just as well, because the money from Chris's car had been keeping the plowing business afloat. Who knew this would be the winter of no snow?

He was down to two employees; the previous year he'd had ten. He couldn't cut his last two guys. They'd both been with him almost from the beginning. Besides, he was under contract to clear parking lots for several businesses, and if the weather ever turned, he'd need them. And he sure wasn't about to let anybody go this close to Christmas.

He got up from the desk and stared into the warehouse. Six trucks sat idle. He'd started with one pickup and a plow, clearing driveways, a few months after he and Marissa began dating. Before that, he'd fished in the summer and spent the winters skiing and riding his snow machine, but being with Marissa had made him think of things like down payments and IRAs. Besides, Marissa was uncomfortable with a high play/work ratio, and at that time he'd been willing to jump through fire if it meant she'd stick around.

Marissa was a grad student then, going to school in Fairbanks while Chris got this business off the ground in Anchorage. Their relationship consisted of snatched weekends and holidays, interludes of sweetness that always left him wishing for more. Maybe if they'd lived in the same town he'd have realized before he asked her to marry him just how unsuited they really were. After all, she had a master's degree in wildlife biology; he was a college dropout who fished and plowed snow. Although her parents had died when she was small, Marissa grew up as part of a loving family. Chris was lucky to get the occasional pat on the head from his father, and his mom hardly noticed him. But he and Marissa were happy together, and their differences didn't seem to matter. Until they did.

What was she doing back in Alaska? Was something going on with Oliver and Becky? Marissa had said she was between jobs, but knowing her work ethic, it was unlikely she would leave one position before she'd lined up another. Before she'd even finished her degree, she'd landed several job offers from all over the country. Hard to imagine an experienced wildlife biologist would resort to working as an elf, even if it was the family business.

Of course, he'd resorted to a job as Santa Claus. It was mostly as a favor to Becky, but looking at the weather forecast, he figured a little extra income wouldn't hurt.

Chris sighed and returned to his desk. He transferred the money into the checking account and printed the payroll checks. They were sliding out of the printer when the office door opened.

"Hey, we got all the plows waxed." Brad, his most senior employee, sauntered in. "Kenny's putting the stuff away."

"Good. Thanks." All the equipment had been waxed back in May before it went into storage, but since he was paying the guys, he might as well give them something to do. "Hang on a minute. I have your check ready." Chris signed it, then handed it to him. "Don't cash it until tomorrow, though. I just put in a transfer but it won't go through until tonight."

"No problem." Brad tucked the check into his wallet and looked up at the ceiling. "That bulb is flickering."

"Yeah, I know."

"Want me to change it for you?"

"Sure—" Chris stood and stretched "—but do it tomorrow. No need to stick around any longer today."

Brad shifted his weight to his other foot. "Actually, I might not come in tomorrow."

Chris looked at him. "Why not? You getting sick?"

"My brother-in-law has this business going, hanging Christmas lights. He wants me to run the cherry picker. And I figured since you don't really need me around here anyway…"

"I don't care if you take some time, but you are coming back, right?"

"Well, sure. I'll be back after Christmas."

"Okay." Chris shook his hand. "Sorry I can't do a Christmas bonus this year."

Brad shrugged. "Weather's a killer. Merry Christmas, dude."

Chris laughed. "Yeah. Merry Christmas." He watched Brad walk away before grabbing Kenny's check and flipping off the office lights. He'd replace that bulb tomorrow. It wasn't as if he had anything better to do.

MARISSA TOSSED A bale of hay onto the rack. The reindeer crowded past her to the food, two yearling bulls tossing their short antlers with the kind of attitude usually seen on high school basketball courts. The older bull, Blizzard, had already shed his impressive antlers, but the cows would hold on to theirs for another few months.

One of the cows, Snowflake, stopped to nuzzle Marissa's hand. She still remembered. Marissa pulled out a piece of carrot she'd hidden in her pocket just for the old girl, a tradition of theirs since Snowflake was a calf. In fact, Marissa had been there at her birth. Hard to believe it was almost twelve years ago. Chris had been there, too. He'd come by to take her out to dinner when Oliver announced Muff was about to give birth. Neither of them could bear to leave until Snowflake had arrived and was on her feet and nursing.

Many of the reindeer pulling hay from the feeder had been born since the last time Marissa visited Alaska. She'd been away too long. Becky took good care of the animals, but the farm, always so crisp and kempt, showed signs of neglect. Rusty hinges, broken boards, peeling paint… Even the sign at the road had faded. Oliver must have been losing ground for a lot longer than Marissa had realized. But it was easier to have him and Becky visit her than to come back to Alaska on her limited vacation time. And if she were honest, she was also afraid she would run into Chris.

Now she had, and it wasn't as hard as she'd thought it would be. Same old Chris, eager to pitch in, as long as you didn't try to tie him down. Never with one woman too long, judging from what she'd gleaned from social media. Chris's own page hadn't been updated since she'd set it up for him back when they were dating, but he was always being tagged in pictures, usually by some blonde bragging about the "real Alaska man" who made her vacation the "best ever." Not that Marissa was stalking him or anything. In fact, Chris barely even crossed her mind anymore. She just happened to stumble across the photos now and then when looking up other old friends from Alaska. At least that was her story, should anyone ask.

Across the pasture, Oliver's old truck bounced up the lane. Good, they were back from the doctor's appointment. Marissa had been home for a little over a week, but Oliver and Becky had been very closemouthed about his health status. Hopefully, the doctor had suggested a different prescription or treatment—something to help Oliver's heart and build up his strength—because the current medicine didn't seem to be working.

The truck circled behind the old farmhouse, which could definitely use a coat of paint. Even from where she stood, Marissa could detect spots where the white paint had flaked off, exposing the weathered wood siding. It was one of those sprawling houses built in stages. Wood-frame additions had grown up and out from the original two-room log cabin as the homesteaders added rooms to accommodate their eight children.

Even though Oliver and Becky had closed off a whole wing and added insulation, Marissa suspected the fuel bill to run the main boiler must be enormous.

After checking to make sure the heater was

keeping the water trough clear for the reindeer, Marissa made her way home.

She stepped over the broken front step and onto the porch, noticing as she opened the front door that one of the small panes in it had a crack in the corner, temporarily mended with duct tape.

In the living room, Oliver lay back in his recliner, his face paler than ever. But he greeted her with a smile. "There's my girl. How's the herd?"

"Just fine. Snowflake was begging for treats." Marissa could hear Becky banging around in the kitchen. She shed her coat and sat on the sofa. Tiger, the yellow house cat, jumped onto her lap and purred.

"Snowflake has a long memory." Oliver paused to breathe. Just walking from the garage to the living room had left him winded. "Remember how she used to try to follow you into the house?"

"I remember." Snowflake's mother had sustained an injury a week after the calf was born, and Marissa took over bottle-feeding her. Before long, Snowflake was following her all over the farm, and couldn't seem to understand why she wasn't allowed to come into the house when Marissa ducked in to grab a snack. She would stand on the porch, grunting and snorting, until Marissa returned for her.

"I thought I heard you in here." Becky bustled in, carrying a tray with three steaming mugs, which she set on the coffee table. "I made orange spiced tea."

"Thank you." Oliver accepted his cup and set it with shaking hands on the table beside his chair. His breathing slowly returned to normal.

"So what did the doctor have to say?" Marissa asked.

"Nothing much. It's all about the same." Oliver was trying for nonchalant, but his smile looked forced.

Becky's mouth tightened. "That's not what he said." She turned to Marissa. "His heart is getting weaker. The doctor says a transplant is really our only hope. He's on the list, but—"

"Transplant?" Marissa stared at her.

Becky shot an accusing glance at her husband. "You said you told her."

"I did."

Marissa shook her head. "When you called, you said you were having some trouble with your heart, and the doctor gave you medication. This is the first I'm hearing about a transplant."

"I didn't want you to worry."

"How long have you known about this?"

Oliver wouldn't meet her eyes. "Four months or so."

Marissa sat in a chair across from his and leaned forward. "You should have told me. I would have come home a long time ago."

"That's why I didn't tell you. There's nothing you can do. I'm not that sick. I'm what they call status two, which means I can stay at home and don't need any special IV meds while I wait."

"So how long will it be before the transplant?"

"Nobody knows." Becky plopped into the chair beside Oliver's and took a sip of tea. "The sicker patients get first priority, of course. They're the ones in hospitals, hanging on and waiting for a match." She left unspoken that if he didn't get a transplant soon, Oliver would be one of those people in the hospital, hanging on.

Marissa caught Oliver's gaze. "So, if I hadn't lost my job and come home, were you not going to tell me at all?"

He patted her arm, the way he used to when she was a little girl with a skinned knee. "Of course I was. But I was hoping to sandwich it in with the news that I was getting a transplant."

"Oh, Oliver." Marissa blinked back tears. "You and Becky have always been there for me. When my parents died, you were there. When Jason took off and everything fell apart at the River Foundation, I didn't know who to trust, but I knew I could count on you and Becky to take me in and love me. Don't you know I want to be there for you, too? We're family. We share the bad times as well as the good."

He gave her a gentle smile. "You're right. I should have told you, but you've had so much on your plate. I didn't want to be a burden."

"You could never, ever be a burden. Not to me." She kissed his cheek. She'd been nine years old when her parents died. Oliver and Becky had been her family ever since, and she couldn't have asked for a better one. From the very first night when they tucked her under the quilt in the cozy bedroom beneath the eaves and kissed her forehead goodnight, she'd felt cherished. She still did. "How can I help?"

Becky reached over to rub her shoulder. "It's out of our hands. All we can do is hope and pray."

Oliver gave her a wry smile. "I can't in good conscience ask you to pray for someone with a healthy heart to give up his life for mine. But if you really want to help, you could go get me some of those oatmeal cookies Becky made this morning." At his wife's pointed look he amended, "One cookie."

"All right. I'll be right back." Marissa gave him a brave smile and went to the kitchen. When she opened the snowflake-printed tin, the scent of cinnamon wafted through the air. It smelled like home. Her vision blurred as tears welled up in her eyes. She couldn't lose Oliver. She just couldn't.

Becky and Oliver were her rocks. After the fiasco with Jason and all the nasty accusations launched in her direction, it made all the difference to know there were two people in the world she could count on to believe in her no matter what. People who knew she would never embezzle money, never lie to donors and never be involved with a man who did. At least not knowingly.

Jason. Who would have thought he was capable of something like this? His philanthropic efforts had established the research center she'd worked for in Louisiana, or rather had worked for until they were forced to shut down. They were studying the recovery of a riparian ecosystem once devastated by a chemical spill, but steadily recovering. She and the other two scientists at the River Foundation were documenting the recovery, observing how the various building blocks of the ecosystem linked together. The information they'd gathered would help others trying to reestablish similar ecosystems.

But it turned out Jason was using the River Foundation as a front, part of the elaborate Ponzi scheme he'd engineered. He'd convinced hundreds of people to invest with his company, or to donate to the River Foundation. They all trusted him, and why not? Who wouldn't trust someone so friendly, and generous, and full of confidence? Which was probably why they called such types confidence men.

When Marissa first started at the center, a rumor had been circulating that Jason was getting divorced. Everyone worried that it might affect their funding if he lost too much in a divorce settlement, but it didn't seem to. Marissa had been with the center for almost a year when Jason invited her to attend a fundraiser with him. She'd asked if he wanted her to speak about their research, but no. He had a short Powerpoint presentation, but mostly he just wanted her there, on his arm. He'd explained that people didn't respond to lectures. What he wanted was her enthusiasm for the project. He said if Marissa chatted with potential supporters one-on-one, they'd line up to donate. He was right.

The evening was a huge success. They began dating, and Marissa threw her considerable organizational talent into fund-raising for the River Foundation. Jason seemed so interested, so sincere, that she believed he truly cared for both her and the research center. But it was all an act. Even the divorce was a ruse to hide money. At least it looked that way, since nobody could seem to find Jason's ex-wife, either. It caused a knot in Marissa's stomach whenever she thought of the people who had donated money to her efforts, only to have it disappear along with any sign of Jason. No wonder they hated her.

Threatening letters arrived at the center from donors accusing her of stealing their money, of knowing where Jason was hiding. The investigators were watching her passport even now, waiting for her to make a move to some Caribbean island without an extradition treaty. She'd had to get permission from federal agents to fly home to Alaska.

If only she did know Jason's whereabouts. She'd turn him in so fast he'd get whiplash. With any luck, he'd spend the rest of his life locked away where he could never betray honest people again. She would like to see him just one more time, though, to tell him exactly what she thought of him. The stories of older people losing their retirement savings, of a young couple forced to give up their home, sickened her. And it was all because of Jason.

She dabbed at her eyes with a paper napkin and washed her hands before setting three oatmeal cookies on one of Becky's reindeer plates.

Her memories of her parents were vague, only bits and pieces before they'd died and she'd come to live in Alaska. They'd loved her; that she knew. But they were gone. Becky and Oliver were the people in her life whose love was unconditional and constant. And now there was a chance she could lose Oliver. She'd known his condition was bad, had seen how weak he'd become, and yet she'd refused to believe he could die. But it was time to be a grown-up and face facts. She might lose him. And all she could do in the meantime was cherish the time they did have together.

She'd been a lucky little girl. After her parents died, she could have ended up with someone who only tolerated her. Instead, her aunt and uncle were thrilled to bring her home, as though she was a special gift. Despite having no children of their own, they'd quit their jobs and started a successful reindeer farm to provide a magical Christmas experience for other people's kids. And Marissa landed right in the middle of the magic.

Knowing it was Oliver playing Santa didn't diminish the experience at all. Just the opposite. She got to grow up on the farm with the jolly old elf, his lovable wife and his magical reindeer the whole year round.

Marissa pasted a smile on her face and picked up the plate. Santa Claus needed his cookie.

CHAPTER THREE

Twenty-one days till Christmas

"…AND A NINJA SWORD, and books, and a puzzle."

Chris glanced over to make sure the parents were able to hear the conversation. They smiled and nodded, so apparently there were no surprises.

He reached into the bowl beside his chair. "Got it. Have a merry Christmas, Sean. Here's a candy cane."

Today, they were working a party for a large group of homeschoolers and their parents at the community center. Chris was starting to get the hang of this Santa thing. Kids were just people, but without the filters. They were noisier and messier, but also more spontaneous and joyful. And they believed in magic, some more than others. But whether they were skeptics or true believers, they knew Christmas was special. And he got to be the spirit of Christmas. How cool was that?

Of course, a two-minute conversation with a kid who believed you had the power to make their dreams come true was a far cry from actual parenting. Even his own father used to feign interest in Chris's activities every once in a while. How did parents do this? A couple hours of holding the kids on his lap and talking to them left Chris as tired as if he'd been digging ditches, and yet parents did it all day, every day.

Marissa started to lead the next child forward, but another boy, maybe four or so, ran to the front of the line. "My turn to talk to Santa."

"No, it's Nolan's turn." Marissa's voice was firm. "You need to get in line with the others."

"But I wanna go now." Tears squeezed from the boy's eyes and he wailed, "It's my turn. My turn." He sobbed as if his heart were breaking, and sank to the floor.

Chris winced. So much for getting the hang of things. He'd have to remember this next time he felt cocky. The boy's mother hurried over, but made no move to pull him away. Instead, she crossed her arms and made eye contact with Marissa.

Marissa gave her a sympathetic smile and

led the next boy in line around the weeping child sprawled across the vinyl floor. "Santa, this is Nolan."

Okay, if that's how they were going to play it. "Hi, Nolan."

Chris watched the other boy from the corner of his eye while carrying on his conversation with Nolan, at least as well as he could with earsplitting screams a few feet away. Within minutes, the sobs diminished and the boy opened his eyes. When he realized no one was paying attention to him, he stopped crying as if turning off a faucet, and allowed his mother to escort him to the back of the line. When his turn came twenty minutes later, he cheerfully recited a long Christmas list, including requests for his baby brother and the dog. He gave no indication he even remembered he'd had a tantrum.

Wouldn't that be great? To be able to simply put past mistakes behind you, without giving them another thought? At what age did you start to keep track of all the stupid, thoughtless and selfish actions that you and the people around you committed, letting them build up into walls? Chris wondered. On the other hand, what if everyone just acted as rotten as they wanted, without consequences?

There was a reason people called it childish behavior. Kids were a puzzle.

How did Marissa know how to handle all this stuff? She was an only child, raised by an older couple. But somehow, she seemed to know exactly how to manage a herd of excited kids without breaking a sweat. She'd always wanted kids. Maybe she did a lot of children's outreach programs with her job. That sounded like something she would enjoy. Or maybe she had a boyfriend with kids back in the lower forty-eight, so was used to hanging around with them. Chris pushed that thought away without giving himself time to wonder why it made him feel antsy.

Once he had talked with all the twenty or so kids at the party, he and Marissa went outside to watch the reindeer rides. With no snow, Becky had hitched up a red wagon that could hold one or two children at a time. Marissa offered to take over and give her a break.

Chris pulled out his phone from inside his Santa jacket and snapped a few photos of Marissa leading the reindeer and wagonful of wide-eyed children around the parking lot. "They're having fun," he stated.

Becky waved at the little ones before turning to him. "Don't post those online without their parents' permission."

"No problem." The photos were just for him, although he wasn't sure why he wanted them. To remember the day, he supposed, and his time as Santa Claus. It surely had nothing to do with how cute Marissa looked in her elf costume, leading the reindeer and laughing with the kids.

When the party was over, Chris helped Becky and Marissa load their equipment. After waving goodbye to the last child, Becky went inside to collect the fee. Chris arranged the sections of the Santa throne in the bed of the truck. "How long until you go back to work?" he asked Marissa.

She flashed him a look of suspicion. "That depends."

"On what?"

"On when I find a job."

Chris closed the tailgate. "You didn't have one lined up before you quit? That doesn't sound like you."

"I didn't quit. The facility I was working at closed down."

"Why?"

"Lack of funds." She pushed a lock of hair away from her face. "Don't worry. I've got applications out and a headhunter looking. I'm sure I'll find something soon."

"And in the meantime, you're staying here?"

"This is where my family lives." She crossed her arms. "Why? Is Alaska not big enough for the both of us?"

"Just asking. I figured you'd need to get back to a husband, or at least a boyfriend, who misses you."

"Well, I don't." She spoke a little too quickly. "I don't have a boyfriend and I'm not looking for one. Right now, I just want to get Becky and Oliver through the Christmas season and then get my career back on track."

Chris smirked. "So, you've made a few changes to the master plan?"

"What are you talking about?"

"You know, the plan where you've established your professional reputation by thirty, and by thirty-five you have two or three children and a golden retriever. You're what, thirty-four now? You're running a little behind."

A strange expression flashed across her face. "Very funny." She spun away from him and flounced across the parking lot.

What was that all about? Marissa never backed down from a good sparring match. He trotted after her. "Marissa?" She didn't slow.

He finally caught up with her and caught her by the elbow. "What's going on?"

She spun around, her eyes shiny with unshed tears. "Nothing. Leave me alone."

"Look, I'm sorry if I said—"

She jerked her arm from his grasp and turned away. "Forget it. Just go away."

"But you're upset."

"Don't talk to me. I don't want you here. How much clearer can I be?"

"Bo, I didn't mean—"

Her head shot up. "Don't call me that. Don't ever call me that. Just go."

He held up his hands in surrender. "Okay, I'm going. Whatever it was, I'm sorry."

"Fine. Go."

Chris crossed to his own truck and got in, but instead of starting the engine, he sat there watching her. She stood at the edge of the parking lot, her back rigid, as if it was taking all her strength not to burst into tears. Which was crazy. Marissa didn't cry. She planned.

Where most people hung posters or art on their walls, she posted goals. She created notebooks full of lists, time lines and flowcharts, color-coded and with footnotes. She made contingency plans, and if those fell apart, she wasted no time on regrets, but immediately started a new plan. Chris had to admire her ability to strategize and follow through.

Even so, he'd never been able to resist the occasional urge to sabotage her daily schedule. "Sometimes you've just got to throw out the plan and follow your heart," he'd tell her. He showed her the joys of spontaneity, of ducking out of a party early to spend the evening wrapped in blankets, gazing at the stars from the bed of his truck. Of blowing off a dinner reservation in favor of an impromptu picnic. Of stolen kisses in elevators and coat closets. And she'd loosened up a little, learned to let go, while she'd taught him how to organize his business. They were good for each other. When he'd needled her about her grand plan just now, he'd meant to tease, the way they'd always teased each other. Hadn't he?

Or maybe there was a part of him that wanted to hurt her, the same way she'd hurt him when she made it clear her love for him only extended so far. That her desire for motherhood trumped her promise to marry him. Maybe he'd done it on purpose, to see her suffer.

If so, it had backfired, because he felt no satisfaction, watching her pain. Only an overriding desire to make it stop. But it was too late. The damage was done.

Marissa stood motionless for several minutes. It was only after she disappeared into the community center that Chris started his truck and drove home. There was really no reason to feel guilty. So he'd stepped over a line he didn't know was there. He'd apologized. Several times. That's all he could do. Besides, why should he care about Marissa's feelings? She wasn't concerned about his.

He parked in the driveway of the split-level house at the end of a cul-de-sac that backed against the woods in Bicentennial Park. The smell of fresh-baked cookies greeted him as he opened the front door. "Dana?" Kimmik ran to greet him, his tail thumping against the banister railing as he led Chris upstairs to the kitchen.

Wire racks full of shaped Christmas cookies covered most of the kitchen island, but Dana's bag was missing, as were her keys. Chris grinned. If she didn't want him to eat the cookies, she shouldn't have left them unguarded. He helped himself to a slightly lopsided star, breaking off a corner for Kimmik before taking a bite himself. Yum. The quality of food had improved considerably in this house since his sister moved in. He finished the cookie before shedding his Santa hat and coat. Kimmik whined and scratched at the door, so Chris let him into the back-yard before heading for the shower to wash the dye from his beard and eyebrows.

He emerged fifteen minutes later and thirty years younger. He threw on old jeans and a flannel shirt, and padded barefoot across the room to let Kimmik inside. But when he whistled, no dog appeared. He leaned out the door to look for him, but saw only an empty yard with the gate standing open.

Shoot. He couldn't lose Sam's dog. He crammed his feet into shoes, threw on a jacket and hurried out. *Let's see, where would a loose dog go first?* Probably straight into the woods. Chris would just have to pick a trail and follow it, hoping the sound of his voice would bring Kimmik home.

He shivered. Frosty weather and wet hair wasn't a good combination. He should have grabbed a hat. He was considering whether to go back for one when he spotted Kimmik up Bunchberry Street, chasing after a stick and returning it to someone Chris couldn't see behind a bush.

Letting out a breath of relief, he trotted toward them. "Here, Kimmik." But the dog didn't come. When Chris reached the bush, he spotted a boy in a baggy green jacket deter-minedly holding on to the dog's collar while

Kimmik, still holding the stick in his mouth, struggled to break loose and answer Chris's call. As soon as Kimmik saw him, he stopped struggling and wagged his tail.

"Hi, I'm Chris. Thanks for taking care of Kimmik."

The boy studied Chris with skepticism. "That's his name?"

"Uh-huh. It means dog in Inupiat. Right, Kimmik?"

The dog wiggled in agreement, but the boy didn't release his hold on the collar. "Kimmik likes to fetch sticks."

"He sure does, but he shouldn't be out of his yard unsupervised. Do you live around here?" Chris was familiar with most of the kids on the street, at least by sight, and was pretty sure he'd never seen this boy before. He was seven or so, with brown hair spilling forward from under the hood of his sweatshirt, and he was eyeing Chris with contempt, as though he could barely bring himself to answer such an absurd comment.

"He wasn't unsupervised. He was with me." Chris noticed the boy didn't answer the last question. He decided not to push it.

"Yeah, it was lucky you were there when he got out so he didn't get into traffic or anything."

The boy looked at the stick Kimmik was holding, obviously wanting more playtime with the dog, but Chris's ears were freezing. Before he could figure out how to get the kid to release Kimmik's collar, a woman's voice called, "Ryan."

The boy stiffened, but didn't answer. She called again.

Chris jerked his head in the direction of the voice. "Your mom is calling."

"She's not my mom." The boy finally released Kimmik, who ran to greet Chris. With a mighty sigh, Ryan trudged away.

Chris located the voice as coming from a woman standing on the second-story deck two houses down, and waved. "Merry Christmas, Sandy."

"Merry Christmas," she called back. "Ryan, hurry. We have to go now, or we'll be late."

With no discernible change in speed, the boy made his way toward her. Once, he looked back, the expression on his face like that of a starving man being dragged from a Thanksgiving meal.

Chris shrugged. Not his problem. He whistled, and Kimmik danced up to him, carrying the stick. He threw it ahead, playing fetch with Kimmik all the way home. He was shutting the gate when Dana's jeep turned into the driveway. She waved before pulling into the garage. Chris slipped in the back door. When he arrived in the kitchen, Dana was there, unpacking a bag of groceries.

"Hey, how was the Santa gig?"

"Not bad." He swiped another cookie from the rack and bit into it.

"If you'll wait a little while, I plan to frost those cookies."

"No need." He took another bite. "They're good like this."

"So what are you doing running around in the cold with wet hair? Trying to catch pneumonia?"

"You sound like a mom." He thought about that while he finished the cookie. "Well, maybe not our mom, but somebody's mom. Actually, I realized Kimmik had gotten out and went to find him."

Dana frowned. "How did he get out?"

"The gate was open and I didn't notice."

"That's odd. It was closed when I let him out a couple of hours ago." She rubbed Kimmik's ears and looked into his eyes. "You haven't learned to open the gate, have you?"

Kimmik declined to answer, rubbing his body against her legs. Chris went to pour himself a glass of milk to go with his cookies. "I doubt it. Must have not latched well, and blown open or something."

Dana emptied a bag of tiny oranges into a wire basket. "Still no snow in the forecast. Good thing you found this Santa Claus job."

Chris nodded. It would be, except today when Becky tried to pay him, he'd turned the check down. If Oliver had something wrong with his heart, they probably had prescriptions and doctor bills to worry about, and Chris didn't feel right taking their money. Becky had tried to insist, but he'd said he wouldn't cash the check even if he took it, and she'd finally backed down.

Dana grinned. "A friend of mine was at the Grizzlyco party the other night with her daughter and told me all about the Santa Claus there. You must feel like a rock star, having all those kids waiting in line to talk with you, and a pretty elf fawning over you."

Chris shook his head. "Believe me, the elf is doing very little fawning. I'm not her favorite person."

"You know her outside work?"

"I did, a long time ago."

Dana's ears perked up and Chris braced himself for the upcoming interrogation. When Dana was a teenager, Chris had left his family after a disagreement with their father. Nineteen years later, Dana came searching for him, and along the way had fallen in love with his roommate and best friend, Sam. Now that she'd married Sam and moved into the house with them, Dana was determined to catch up on everything she'd missed in Chris's life. "What's her name?" she asked.

"Marissa Gray." He picked up a couple cans and set them in the pantry. "You don't have anything planned for dinner, do you? Because I'm hungry for Thai. Do you want pineapple curry?"

"That sounds good." She seemed to be accepting his change of topic, but the glint of curiosity in her eyes warned him she wasn't giving up. Before she could frame another question, Chris pulled out his phone and started walking toward the stairs that led down to is bedroom. "I'll call in the order." He really wasn't up to a conversation about his history with Marissa right now. No doubt Dana would get the whole story from Sam tonight.

"Chris?"

Too slow. He stopped without turning around. "Yes?"

There was a short pause before she spoke. "Get extra rice."

BECKY STOPPED THE truck and trailer in the pullout beside the main road. A motley collection of mailboxes lined the edge of the pavement. Marissa hopped out to collect their letters. As she returned to the truck, she happened to glance up at Becky, catching her unaware. Worry lines formed deep furrows across her forehead, and the slump of her shoulders hinted at her exhaustion. Oliver's illness was taking a toll on both of them. But when Marissa opened the door, Becky turned to smile at her, banishing any trace of sadness or fatigue. Marissa smiled back. "Good party today."

Becky put the truck in gear and turned down the secondary road that led to the farm. "Yes. Chris is good with the kids."

He was. And it was driving Marissa crazy. When they were engaged, Chris had as much as told her he wanted nothing to do with children, and yet he seemed to have a natural way with them. Marissa wondered, not for the first time, if his no-kids stance was only an excuse to get out of marrying her. But she didn't need to lay all that on Becky. Her aunt had enough to worry about.

Instead, Marissa opted for loyalty. "He's not as good as Oliver."

"Well, that's a given. Oliver is the master of all things Santa."

"Yes, he is." Marissa smiled again, thinking about her uncle's constant research on Christmas traditions past and present. They drove along for another fifteen minutes, past the entrance to their solitary neighbor's seasonal cabin, and turned in beside the faded Reindeer Farm sign with a stylized portrait of a reindeer pulling a sleigh. The truck rattled over the drive, which was in desperate need of gravel and grading, and came to a stop near the barn.

Marissa pulled down the ramp on the trailer. "Why don't you go check on Oliver and let the aid go home? I'll take care of the reindeer and everything."

Becky looked relieved. "Thank you. I'll do that. Leave the truck, and I'll unload later."

Marissa nodded, although she had no intention of leaving work for Becky. She unloaded the reindeer, brushed each one, and led them into their pen. "You girls did well today. Great party." She gave each of them a pat on the rump before she left the pen.

It had been a good party. The homeschool kids were really into the magic of the reindeer and Santa Claus, and Chris was selling the whole child-loving, jolly old elf persona quite well. But, of course, it was an illusion.

And she should recognize an illusion when she saw it, having been fooled so many times. She'd been so in love with Chris. The day he put a ring on her finger, she was happier than she'd ever been. But then he'd started to withdraw, to push her away. When she tried to make plans, he'd change the subject. It all came to a head that weekend they'd skied at Alyeska. The day she'd brought up children.

Just outside the resort, they'd spied a family gathering at one of the Nordic ski trails—two boys, maybe nine and seven, a preschool girl riding on her dad's back, and the mom with a baby in a front pack. The mother transferred the little girl and the baby into a pulk, one of those small nylon tents on a sled, while the dad got the two boys outfitted with skis and poles, all involving an incredible amount of noise and confusion. But eventually, the family started off down the trail, with the dad pulling the pulk behind him and the mom chasing after the two boys, who'd surged ahead. After they'd gone by, Marissa laughed. "They have their hands full."

"I'll say." Chris looked after them and smiled as the boys raced forward, pretending they didn't hear their mother calling for them to slow down.

Marissa took his hand. "How many do you want?"

"How many what?" Chris seemed genuinely confused.

"Children. How many kids do you think we should have?"

The look of horror on his face said it all. "Kids? Oh, no. I'm not cut out to have kids."

Marissa tried to smooth over his blunt reply. "It wouldn't be for a few years. The plan is to get my career established first, and have the kids between thirty and thirty-five."

"No. Not now, not in a few years."

"But—"

"No. I know what it's like to have a bad father. I wouldn't do that to an innocent child."

"Oh, come on, you'd be a great dad. Just think—"

He stopped in his tracks. "No, I wouldn't. I won't."

Marissa crossed her arms across her chest. "What are you saying? You've just made that decision for both of us? What I want doesn't matter?"

He blew out a breath. "It's always about what you want. I've agreed to all your wedding plans. I've agreed to leave my job behind if you decide you want to move away from Alaska once you graduate. But not this."

"So, you're not even willing to compromise?"

"Compromise how? Half a kid? Children can't be a compromise. If both parents aren't fully committed, they shouldn't have children. Period." He turned away and strode toward the hotel.

She ran to catch up and grabbed his arm to stop him, to force him to look at her. "I've always wanted children. What if this is nonnegotiable for me?"

Chris shrugged. "Then I suppose you'll have to make up your mind which is more important, marrying me or finding someone who wants kids. It's your decision."

And in the end, she made it. She couldn't marry someone so deeply selfish he wasn't even willing to discuss the possibility of children, knowing how important they were to her. Pretty ironic as it turned out, but the point stood. She'd believed Chris was the one. She was wrong.

And she'd been wrong again. Wrong when she'd thought Robert would make the perfect husband and father, and so very wrong when she'd believed Jason was someone she could trust. Wrong, wrong, wrong.

So many bad choices, but she was finally taking the lessons to heart. She had poor judgment when it came to men. Much better to focus on the aspects of her life she did well, like her career and her family. Not that she'd done so well with family in the past few years, but now she would, because the scare with Oliver made her realize he and Becky meant more to her than anything else in the world.

She went back to work, taking care of the rabbits and feeding the goats and Willa, the potbellied pig. Once she'd checked that the chickens were all right, she unloaded the party gear from the truck. The mail still lay on the front seat where she'd left it.

She put the truck away and carried the letters to the house, sorting through them to see if anything had been forwarded to her. A large "second notice" stamp on one of Oliver's envelopes caught her eye. Uh-oh.

Oliver had always handled the bills. Maybe with his illness, he'd fallen behind. Marissa decided that after dinner she would volunteer to help out. The scent of sage and onions greeted her when she opened the back door. Becky was stirring the chicken soup she'd started in the slow cooker that morning.

Marissa closed her eyes and inhaled. "Mmm. I'm starved."

"Then it's a good thing we're ready to eat." Becky dished up bowls of soup filled with big chunks of chicken, vegetables and barley. Oliver sat at the kitchen table, slicing bread. Marissa hurried to wash up.

After dinner, she washed the dishes and Becky dried. While her aunt was still wiping down the countertops, Marissa slipped into the living room to talk with her uncle. "I brought in the mail today and left it on your desk."

"Okay, thanks." Oliver reached for the remote control.

"I, um, couldn't help but notice that one of the envelopes said second notice."

Oliver didn't look at her. "Humph. Must be some computer error or something."

"Do you want me to check? I'm good with paperwork, if you need me to balance your accounts or anything."

"No, no. I can handle it." He was answering too quickly.

She studied his face, at least what she could see of it, since he still hadn't looked her way. "I know you can, but as long as I'm here, why don't you go ahead and write the check so I can put it in the mail tomorrow?"

He snapped the television on to some reality show that she knew he had zero interest in. "Not necessary."

"Aren't you curious as to which bill is late?"

He shook his head and pretended to watch the show. He knew. It wasn't some computer error. Oliver knew exactly which bill was late and why. What was going on with their finances?

"Uncle Oliver, tell me the truth. What's wrong?"

For a moment, he ignored her. Finally, he clicked the TV off, but continued to stare at the screen. "We're having a little cash flow problem."

"Why?"

"I made a bad investment."

A sense of foreboding formed an icicle in her stomach. "What kind of investment?"

He shrugged.

And she knew. "You invested with Jason, didn't you?"

Jason had gone out of his way to welcome them when they'd visited in February. He'd asked all sorts of questions about the farm and life in Alaska. He'd seemed fascinated with Oliver's stories of the reindeer farm and how isolated they were with their closest neighbors a mile away, a couple who used the house only in the summer. And of course, Oliver ate it up.

Jason had never mentioned money or investing while Marissa was around. He'd obviously waited until he had Oliver alone. Of course, even if Marissa had realized he was soliciting investments from Oliver, she wouldn't have objected. After all, she'd entrusted her own modest savings with him. And now Oliver and Becky were facing old age and illness without any financial cushion, while Jason lived it up with their money on a tropical island somewhere. Damn him.

Oliver eyed her with concern. "Honey, it's not your fault. You didn't know."

"I should have known. The whole setup was wrong. It was too good to be true. He was too good to be true."

Her uncle reached for her hand. "Don't beat yourself up. Most people are basically good. So, you and I let a slick huckster take our money. Next time we'll know to ask more questions. But what would be the real tragedy is if we let him destroy our faith in people, don't you think?"

How did he do it? Here he was, sick, unable to pay his bills and yet he was comforting her. Her heart swelled with pride to be related to such a man. She hugged him. "I think you're the world's best uncle."

He chuckled. "I believe I have a mug that says so. Don't you worry about that bill. Once Becky takes today's check to the bank, we can pay it and the feed store. And the good news is we have several more parties scheduled between now and Christmas. We'll be fine."

But what about after Christmas? There was a huge gap between Christmas parties and the summer tourist season. They were going to require a regular income above their modest retirement checks just to get by, and the transplant wouldn't be cheap. As soon as she could make it happen, Marissa needed to find a job.

CHAPTER FOUR

Twenty days till Christmas

ANOTHER DAY, ANOTHER PARTY. This one was a private birthday party. Not as profitable as the big events, but every little bit helped. Marissa grimaced as she bounced the wheel of the trailer over the curb on the turn into the parking lot, no doubt jostling the reindeer inside. *Sorry, girls.* She wasn't used to driving with a trailer, but Oliver's aid was running late and Becky had to stay until she arrived. Marissa gingerly pulled the truck and trailer along the edge of the almost-empty parking lot where they would be setting up the reindeer rides.

Across the lot, the door of an old blue truck opened. Chris. What was he doing here so early? Becky had him scheduled to arrive just in time to get dressed before the party started. After her meltdown the other day, Marissa had hoped to have Becky as a buffer the next time she faced him, but apparently not.

He walked across the parking lot. "Hi. Where's Becky?"

"She'll be along in a little while. Oliver's health aid got delayed."

"Oh." He shifted his weight. "I, uh, I'm sorry for the other day. I didn't mean to upset you."

"I'm fine."

"Good. Because I—"

"So let's just forget it, okay?"

"Okay."

"What are you doing here so early?"

He shrugged. "Nowhere else I need to be. Besides, Sam is leaving for his rotation to the North Slope today, so I wanted to be out of the house."

"You still live with Sam?" She'd have thought Chris would have gotten his own place by now.

Chris shrugged. "Why not? He's been promoted to head supervising engineer at Prudhoe Bay, so he's gone to the slope two weeks out of four, and I'm out fishing most of the summer. Why leave two places sitting empty? I might be moving soon, though."

She smirked. "Trouble in paradise after all these years?"

"Very funny. No, it's just getting a little crowded, now that he's married. And since it's his last day home for two weeks, I thought I'd give the newlyweds some privacy." He opened the tailgate. "You need all this stuff carried in?"

"Sam is married?" She wasn't sure why she was so surprised. Sam was a great guy, but he'd been solely focused on his career. More than one woman had tried to tie him down, with little success. Marissa wondered who had finally won him over. "What's his wife's name? Do I know her?"

"Dana. And no. She's from Kansas." He lifted the parts of the Santa throne from the truck. "She's my sister."

"You have a sister?" Marissa stared at him. How could she not know that? She'd almost married the man, for heaven's sake.

"Half sister, technically."

"She wasn't on the guest list for the wedding." Marissa blurted it out before she thought, instantly wishing she could recall the words. The last thing she wanted to do was talk about the wedding that never happened.

But the reference didn't seem to faze Chris. He just kept on unloading. "Long story short, I hadn't been in touch with my family since I left home when I was twenty-one. Dana literally showed up on my doorstep this past summer, after my father died."

"I can't believe you have a sister." Marissa wasn't sure why she found that so surprising. Chris never talked about family, seldom mentioning his life before he came to Alaska, and she'd inferred he must be estranged from his parents. But for some reason, she'd never pictured siblings. Maybe because she didn't have any. "Any other family?"

"Only my mom. That is, my stepmother. She still lives in Kansas."

"Is your sister older or younger?"

"Dana's my little sister. She was sixteen when I left home."

"And you've never seen her since?"

"Not until this summer. Now that we're living in the same house, we're seeing a lot of each other."

Marissa tried to imagine it. "What's she like?"

"Dana? She's a sweetheart. You'd like her. She's in college right now, updating her credentials. She wants to teach math." Chris spoke about this sister he'd never mentioned with a casual fondness, like any brother talking about a younger sibling. Marissa was beginning to wonder if she'd ever known Chris at all.

"So whatever it was that made you leave your family, it's resolved?"

"Yep." He closed the tailgate. Marissa

ached to know the rest of that story, but Chris obviously wasn't inclined to share.

Not that it was any of her business. Not anymore. "And your sister is married to Sam, the confirmed bachelor?"

"That's right." He grinned. "You should see them together. It's a little sickening."

"Oh?"

He chuckled. "Way too much giggling and whispering. Sam goes around with this goofy grin on his face."

Marissa thought back to the ambitious young engineer she'd known. She'd always liked Sam. She felt a certain kinship with him, since he'd lost his parents and been raised by someone else, as well. Marissa had met his auntie Ursula, and it was clear he adored her as much as Marissa adored Oliver and Becky.

She'd like to talk to him herself, to meet his wife and offer her best wishes. But she'd seen Sam only once after she broke the engagement to his best friend, and he'd been far from friendly. He wouldn't want to talk with her now. Still… "I'm glad he's happy."

"Yeah. Me, too. I'll carry this stuff in and come back for the next load, okay?"

"Sure. And when you see Sam, tell him I said congratulations."

"Will do."

THE NEXT DAY, Chris slept in. No use jumping out of bed. No snow meant no work and no skiing, just time to kill. If he were willing to drive up to the mountains, he might be able to find enough snow to run his snow machine, but when he'd been hauling snow the other day, conditions looked poor. He finally dragged himself into the shower and pulled on some clothes. He was almost glad when he noticed his overflowing hamper. At last, something to do.

He went upstairs and poured a cup of coffee from the pot. Another perk of having Dana around. A bouquet of red carnations on the kitchen table emitted a spicy odor that blended nicely with the scent of coffee. No sign of his sister, but if the coffeemaker was on, she must be around.

A few minutes later, a door opened and Dana came down the hall, her arms full of books and Kimmik at her heels. "Good morning."

"Morning." Chris took a sip of coffee. "I'm washing. Got any laundry you want to throw in?"

She dropped the books on the island and dug in the kitchen drawer for a pen. "Maybe some towels. What are you doing home?" She tucked the books and pen into a backpack.

"Nothing to do at work, and I'm not scheduled for a party until tomorrow. I gave Kenny the day off."

"Well, if you're looking for something to do, you could check the gate and make sure Kimmik can't open it. And if you want to get the towels from our hamper and wash them, that would be great."

"Sam get out okay this morning?"

Dana's face lit up at the mention of Sam's name. "Yes, but he'll be home for Christmas." She paused. "He told me about the girl you were engaged to. I'm sorry."

Chris shrugged. "Don't be. It was over a long time ago."

"But it's her family's reindeer business you're working for, right?"

"Yeah. Her uncle always played Santa, but he's sick, so they need a sub. No big deal. It's only until Christmas."

"So there's no chance of the two of you getting back together?" Dana shrugged into her coat. He wasn't sure if she was hopeful or wary, but it didn't matter. He and Marissa were over.

"None. I've learned my lesson."

Dana stopped in the middle of reaching for her keys. "I'm getting together with some friends for a movie tonight. Want to come?"

"No, thanks. You have fun."

She threw a look of concern over her shoulder on her way out the door, but finally left him in peace. He smiled and shook his head. Funny girl. When he and Dana were growing up, their mother had basically checked out, spending all her time compulsively shopping rather than nurturing her family. In spite of that, or maybe because of it, Dana had developed a strong mothering instinct. With no other outlet, she'd focused that instinct on him. Never mind he was five years older than her or that they'd been apart for nineteen years; she was convinced he couldn't cross the street without her. Not that he really minded. It was fun having his little sister around again.

She had no reason to worry about him, at least when it came to Marissa. Chris had never had much trouble finding female companionship whenever the mood struck. He wasn't so lonely he was likely to start mooning over the one woman he knew for sure didn't want him. There were a dozen women he could call if he felt like a date. But he didn't call them.

Instead, he gathered up the laundry and started a load. Then he decided to surprise Dana by vacuuming and cleaning. It was only fair. She was busy and he wasn't. It was midafternoon when he remembered about the gate. He pulled on boots, and was reaching for his jacket when he glanced out the window to see Ryan lifting the latch and calling Kimmik outside. By the time Chris pulled on his coat and made it to the door, boy and dog were playing fetch in the cul-de-sac.

"Hey, Ryan."

The boy looked up, eyes wide and startled, but then turned his back and threw the stick again. Kimmik ran after it and galloped back, carrying it in his mouth with his head held high.

Chris trotted over to the boy. "Ryan, you can't just be letting the dog out of the yard without asking."

Ryan took the stick and threw it again. "He got out. Maybe he dug a hole."

"I saw you open the gate."

The kid raised his chin. "Well, he's lonely. You don't ever play with him."

"I do, but you're right, not as much as he'd like. Ryan, I don't mind you playing with the dog, but you have to ask first. You can't just take somebody else's dog without permission."

"If he was my dog, I'd take good care of him. I'd play with him and brush him and feed him." He patted Kimmik on the head and threw the stick again. "You should take better care of your dog."

Clever way to shift the blame. Chris smiled. "Technically, he's not my dog. He belongs to my roommate, Sam. But I think we take pretty good care of him."

"He's not yours?" Ryan looked him in the eye for the first time.

"No. He's Sam's dog."

"Is it your house?"

"Nope. Sam's house, too. I just live there." Chris rubbed Kimmik's ears and took the stick, handing it to Ryan.

The boy threw the stick and turned to him. "So are you, like, a foster kid, too?"

Chris chuckled. "Not exactly. I pay rent and help with the chores, like taking care of the dog."

"I do chores, too."

"Good. That shows you're responsible."

"Ryan?" a man's voice called from up the street.

The kid made a face. "Homework." He made no move to answer, instead throwing the stick again.

Brent, a neighbor from up the street, walked toward them. "Ryan, it's time to come inside." He looked at Chris. "Sorry. Hope he wasn't bothering you."

"No, he just wanted to play with the dog." Ryan shot Chris a look of alarm, but Chris patted him on the shoulder. "I told him he was welcome to play with Kimmik anytime, as long as he comes to ask first."

"He loves dogs. He might drive you crazy."

"Nah, he's fine. I'll let Sam and Dana know he might be stopping by."

"Thanks." Brent grasped Ryan by the shoulders and turned him around. "But right now, you need to go inside. Sandy wants to go over your spelling words with you while the baby's napping."

"But Kimmik wants to play."

"Ryan, now."

Ryan dropped his chin onto his chest with a mighty sigh, and trudged away.

Brent stayed with Chris. "Thanks for being nice to him."

"No problem. I like him."

"Do you?" Brent watched the boy. "He's a handful. Sandy and I are fostering a baby girl we're hoping to adopt. Ryan is new to foster care. His grandmother was looking after him, but she had to go to a nursing home. Sandy heard about him and couldn't stand the idea of him not being with a family for Christmas, so she volunteered to keep him until January. Hopefully, they can find a long-term placement for him by then."

Chris got the impression it wouldn't have been Brent's idea to take Ryan, but what did he know? Either way, they were taking care of him over Christmas, so kudos to Brent and Sandy. "Congratulations on the baby. And I meant what I said. Ryan is welcome to come play with Kimmik. He's not dangerous."

"I know. Labradors are great with kids."

"Yeah. So give Sandy my best wishes, too. What's the baby's name?"

"April. She's six months old." Brent pulled out his phone and started pushing buttons. Chris had been around enough new fathers to know where this was going.

"Pretty name."

"Thanks." Brent held out his phone. "Here she is with Sandy on the day we brought her home."

Chris dutifully studied the picture. The infant laughed toward the camera, her eyes opened wide and framed with dark curly lashes. "She's gorgeous," Chris assured him, truthfully in this case. Some of the babies he'd been forced to compliment looked, well…scary. "I'd better get Kimmik in. See you around."

Chris put the dog in the yard and carefully latched the gate. Maybe he should have told Brent about Ryan letting Kimmik out, but it sounded like the kid had enough trouble in his life. Chris had a feeling he might be seeing a lot of Ryan over the next few weeks. Or at least, Kimmik would.

"So, Layla, have you been a good girl this year?" Chris smiled at the pigtailed imp in his lap. Wide brown eyes looked back at him solemnly.

"Nuh-uh."

Well, he had to give her credit for honesty, even if it meant he wasn't sure what to do next. "No?"

She shook her head. "I'm supposed to sit still and pay attention at school, but it's too hard."

"Huh. What grade are you in?"

"First grade."

He nodded. "What's your favorite subject?"

"P.E."

"Oh yeah? Mine, too, when I was in school. I liked basketball."

"You went to school?"

"Of course. School is important. If I hadn't learned to read, I wouldn't be able to read letters or make lists. I used to have a hard time sitting still, too."

"You did?"

"Uh-huh. But I had a trick. I'd listen to what the teacher said, and then repeat it inside my head, and wriggle my toes."

"Your toes?" She giggled, watching his eyes as if she thought he was joking.

"Sure. You're not supposed to wiggle your body, but if you wriggle your toes, nobody sees. And it helped me remember. Say we were doing spelling words, like *c-a-t, cat*. I'd wriggle my toes, right-left-right, *c-a-t*, and I'd remember."

"*C-a-t*," she repeated, flapping her feet.

"Good, but when you do it in school, just do your toes, not your whole feet. Okay?"

"Okay."

"Good girl. Now, I've got a present for you here, somewhere." He rummaged through the stack of packages he'd been provided.

"But you only get presents if you're good."

"You are good. Sometimes it's hard to behave, but you try, and that's what matters. Here it is, a package for Layla." He handed her a polka-dotted box. "Merry Christmas."

"I love you, Santa." Layla hugged the box against her chest and flashed him a bright smile before skipping away.

Chris chuckled. The things kids said. Like Ryan the other day, asking if Chris was a foster kid. It must be hard, knowing you were a temporary part of a family, that the place you were living was your home only for a while. You could never have a pet of your own if you were moving around all the time. Chris could sympathize there; he'd begged for a dog for years when he was a kid but his parents said no. The closest he ever got was a fish.

Was it wrong for Chris to encourage Ryan to form a bond with Kimmik, knowing he'd be moving elsewhere after Christmas? The kid obviously loved dogs. Anyway, if he hadn't promised, Ryan would probably just continue sneaking Kimmik from the yard. He seemed like a strong-willed kid.

Marissa stepped forward, leading another little girl with a thick black braid. "Santa, this is Lotu."

"Hi, Lotu." And so it went. One child after another. Some were shy, barely able to verbalize one gift, while others had an entire spiel memorized, including a record of their good behavior. After a while, the requests tended to run together, but each child was unique, and Chris tried to give every one his full attention.

He used to wonder why Oliver would have

left a well-paid desk job in order to start a reindeer farm. It must have been a risk. But now that Chris had experienced the magic for himself he was starting to understand. Watching the kids' eyes light up when they touched real live reindeer, or the excitement on their faces when they talked to him. Christmas magic.

There wasn't a lot of magic in the house where he'd grown up. Sure, they got presents from his parents. His mom was a compulsive shopper, after all. And she usually had some Christmas doodads scattered around the house. But nobody baked goodies or decorated a tree. Nobody set out milk and cookies for Santa, because Santa didn't come to their house. Chris remembered feeling superior to the kids who still believed in Santa. Who would have thought he'd ever be charged with the awesome responsibility of being the jolly old man himself?

Once all the children had had a chance to talk with him, he and Marissa went outside to watch the reindeer rides. This was a mixed group from an after-school program. Some of the parents had decided to put together the Christmas party as a special treat. The kids were thrilled to get to hang out with Santa and real reindeer.

Becky and the elves had three reindeer pulling little red wagons around the brightly lit parking lot. All three elves seemed to be enjoying their jobs, including Dillon.

Near the front door, children waited for a turn. One boy jostled a girl, causing her to spill the cup of red punch she'd carried outside. Her squeals as it splashed onto her sweater and the sidewalk startled the nearest reindeer, who threw up her head. But fortunately, the elf in charge was able to control her, while Becky calmed the girl and sent her inside with a parent to clean up.

At the end of the night, Becky paid the three elves and sent them home. Chris helped Marissa load up the reindeer and pack the equipment in the truck, while Becky collected their fee. Marissa had just closed the tailgate when her aunt reappeared. She started down the sidewalk, but when her foot hit the now-frozen puddle of punch, it slid out from under her and she went down.

"Becky!" Chris rushed over and knelt beside her.

Marissa was right behind him. "Are you okay?"

Becky blinked at them for a moment. "I think so." She sat up.

Chris put a restraining hand on her shoulder. "Just take a second. Did you hit your head?"

She rubbed the back of her skull. "No. Only my bottom." She moved her legs and winced. "And my ankle."

Marissa touched it gently. "We'd better get an X-ray."

Becky hissed as she moved her foot. "No. I'm pretty sure it's just twisted. If you can get me home, I'll be fine."

Despite Marissa and Chris's best efforts to convince her, Becky refused to let them take her to the emergency room. She smiled at Marissa. "I guess you're driving."

"Why don't I drive the reindeer?" Chris suggested. "And Marissa can take you home in my truck. It's not quite as high to climb into."

Marissa jerked her head toward him, probably about to say they didn't need his help, but after another glance at Becky, she nodded. "That's a good idea. Thanks."

Chris helped Becky into the passenger seat of his truck and carefully tucked her foot onto a folded blanket. He handed the keys to Marissa. "See you there."

He climbed into Oliver's old dually and followed Marissa out of the parking lot, slowing down to make the turn with the trailer.

The truck shuddered over the joint where the concrete met the asphalt, and Chris was doubly glad he'd volunteered his vehicle. Becky's ankle would have felt every bump in the road with the worn-out shocks on her truck.

Forty minutes later, he swayed and bumped down the drive and pulled up outside the barn. Before unloading the reindeer, he walked back to the house, where Becky was sliding out onto her good foot. With Marissa on one side and Chris on the other, she hopped across the front yard. She stopped in front of the porch to catch her breath. A crack ran across the bottom step. Paint peeled away from the porch railings. When Becky grasped the handrail beside the stairs, it shifted. Marissa bit her lip and eyed the path to the front door.

"Let's not stress that ankle." Chris bent and lifted the older woman into his arms. "Marissa, could you get the door?"

Becky almost giggled. Marissa scurried ahead while Chris carefully climbed the steps and then carried Becky into the living room, setting her on her usual chair.

Oliver struggled out of his recliner. "What happened?"

"I'm fine." Becky squeezed his hand. "It's just a twisted ankle."

He settled into the chair beside her without

ever letting go of her hand, panting a little. For a moment, Chris thought it was panic, but soon realized it was simply the exertion from standing that had Oliver out of breath. He didn't look good, being thinner than the last time Chris saw him, his face almost as pale as his beard.

A middle-aged woman, presumably Oliver's health aid, pushed through the door from the kitchen. "Oh, my. What happened here?"

Becky explained briefly, while Marissa dragged an ottoman in front of her chair and plopped a pillow on top for her foot. Chris was glad to see the ankle didn't look too swollen. It wasn't until Becky was comfortable that Oliver finally looked up. "Chris. Thank you for your help. And for filling in for me."

"It's only until you're ready to take over." Chris shook the older man's hand.

Oliver gave a wry smile. "I don't quite have the energy right now. Maybe by next Christmas I'll be back at my fighting weight."

"I hope so. Nobody does Santa better than you." Chris caught Marissa's eye. "I'll unload the reindeer and the truck while you get Becky an ice pack."

"Thanks." Marissa actually smiled at him. "Just put them in the corral by the barn. I'll come out later to brush them and unload the truck."

"I can do that. Where does it all go?"

"Inside the barn, in the storage room. I'll be out in a little while."

Halfway between the house and the barn, Chris stopped and turned to look around. He couldn't see much except in the pools of light on the porch and from the floodlights on the barn, but what he saw needed work. The tidy farm he'd loved to visit ten years ago had deteriorated.

How old were Becky and Oliver now? In their late sixties? They probably should have retired a while ago, especially with Oliver's health. Chris opened the trailer and led the first reindeer to the corral. The gate groaned. He unsnapped the lead, and the big animal wandered toward the hayrack in the middle of the pen. The top rail beside the gate had cracked in the middle, and a cluster of vicious-looking splinters protruded, fortunately toward the outside of the pen. It wouldn't be easy to sell the farm in this condition. They needed help.

Chris had all three reindeer in the corral and most of the truck unloaded by the time Marissa arrived. She handed him his keys. "Becky's feeling better. I think she's right, that it's just a twisted ankle and she'll be fine tomorrow." Marissa looked up at him. "She appreciates your help."

Chris nodded and pulled out the last bundle from the truck. "How bad is it?"

"I told you, she'll be fine." At his searching look, she glanced down. "Oliver? It's bad. He needs a heart transplant."

"Wow. What kind of wait time are we talking about?"

Marissa shrugged. "It depends. He's not high priority. Yet."

Chris shut the tailgate and topper and nodded toward the sagging barn door. "He must have been sick for a while."

"Apparently. They didn't tell me anything about the heart condition until a couple of months ago."

"But you had to have seen that the place was—"

"I wasn't here." She met his eyes, allowing him to read the guilt and regret there. "I haven't been here in years. It was easier just to have them visit me, a nice winter break for them." She looked away, but not before he saw the glint of tears. "I should have come home more often."

She was right. But how could he judge her? He'd deserted his family and never looked back. Never even considered that they might need him. Marissa at least stayed in touch. "You're here now."

She nodded. "For the moment. To help them get through the party season. But then I need to go back to work."

"You're leaving them?"

"I have to."

Chris's mouth tightened. Couldn't she see that Oliver might not have much more time? Couldn't her precious career wait? Marissa didn't appreciate how good she'd had it, growing up with an aunt and uncle who adored her. She owed them, big time. But what could he do? He was Marissa's ex, not family. Not even her friend. He had no say in her decisions.

"I guess I'll see you at the next party. Let me know if Becky needs help in the meantime."

"Chris?" Her voice was tentative. She must sense his disapproval. Well, she should.

"Good night, Marissa. Tell them I said goodbye."

CHAPTER FIVE

Seventeen days till Christmas

WHEN MARISSA CAME downstairs the next morning, Becky was already in the kitchen, stirring pancake batter. A pot of coffee sat ready on the drip machine. Marissa frowned. "Should you be on your feet?"

"I told you, I just twisted my ankle. I'm fine now." Becky smiled. "Although it was nice to have a handsome man carry me over the threshold."

"He's too late. I already carried you over the threshold almost forty years ago." Oliver chuckled as he made his way to the kitchen table. "Tell Chris to get his own girl." He settled into his chair and caught his breath.

Becky set a mug full of coffee in front of him and kissed his cheek. "I remember. You carried me into our first apartment." She returned to the stove and shook a drop of water onto the griddle to test the temperature. "The one with a bedroom so small we had to jump into bed from the doorway, and a bathroom with one pink sink and never enough hot water. But I thought it was beautiful."

"You made it beautiful." Oliver sipped his coffee. "Seriously, though, I'm glad Chris was there to give you a hand. He's a good man." He sent a pointed look toward Marissa, but mercifully said nothing else.

He didn't have to. The unspoken question was there. *Why did you let him go?* But they didn't know the real Chris. Yes, he was kind and generous, when it suited him. But the occasional grand gesture wasn't enough to build a life together. Especially when they didn't want the same things.

She grabbed her coat and slid her feet into boots. "I'm going to see about the chickens. I'll be back in time for pancakes."

Marissa slipped out the back door and picked up the basket lying on the stoop. The sun wouldn't be up for hours yet, but a full moon illuminated the familiar shapes of the trees, shaggy dark spruce and pale white birch trunks. Farther back, the barn, the well house and the chicken coop formed a tiny village, while the reindeer milled around in their pen. The scene was beautiful, cozy and welcoming, until she got close enough to trigger the floodlights. Instantly, the sagging boards, peeling paint and hundred-and-one chores that needed to be done popped out at her.

She should make a plan. List all the things that needed repair and prioritize them. Get supplies and bids. That was how she always tackled problems. She'd learned early, and from the best. When Marissa's parents died in that accident, she'd been terrified, not knowing what would happen. But then Becky and Oliver came, and Becky showed her how they could move forward step by step. First, the funeral. Then packing up the house. Moving her things. Enrolling in a new school. As long as she took it one step at a time, she could cope.

But the farm overwhelmed her. If she had the time and money, she could organize it all, but thanks to Jason, she didn't have a dime to spare, and neither did Oliver and Becky. They needed to sell the place and retire, but right now it was their only source of income, except for social security and Oliver's tiny pension. Besides, the farm wouldn't bring in what it was worth, not in this condition.

The image of Chris's face last night, his lip curled in disgust, came back to her. He thought she didn't care, that she'd neglected her family. Maybe she had. But she was doing her best from now on. And why did it matter to her what Chris thought, anyway?

She stepped into the chicken coop, warm from the small heater and lights that came on automatically at six. The hens clustered around her, hoping for handouts. Within fifteen minutes, she'd cleared out the dirty straw and scattered a fresh layer. She poured feed into the trough and stepped out of the way to avoid the feathery stampede. Three warm fresh eggs waited in the nests, two brown, and a blue one from the Ameraucana hen. Not a great harvest from a dozen hens, but considering the shortest day of the year was fast approaching, not bad. The artificial light helped.

She stepped outside and checked to make sure Chris had locked the truck after he unloaded last night. He had, of course. In spite of his seat-of-the-pants nature, he always did good work. It was nice having him here last night, knowing she could count on him to take care of the reindeer. Much as she hated to admit it, it was nice having him around at the parties, too, instead of some stranger taking Oliver's place. She and Chris could still read each other. She could tell from one raised eyebrow that the child in his lap was tensing up and ready to cry. A subtle tilt of her head, and he knew the kids waiting were getting restless and he should speed up the process.

How was it they could be so in sync about the small things and so far apart about the big ones? He was the first man who really got her humor, who made her feel special. More than once, they'd noticed the sun rising and only then realized they'd talked all night. Chris made her believe in soul mates. But once they were engaged, he'd changed.

The interest and enthusiasm, the connection they'd felt, seemed to drift away. Between her graduation and job search, and the wedding to organize, there were a thousand decisions to be made, but he didn't seem to care. She tried to involve him in the planning. Where would he like to live? Which jobs should she apply for? Should they get married outdoors or in a church? Suddenly, he had no opinions. Not until she mentioned children. Then he certainly had one.

Why had a man so afraid of commitment ever asked her to marry him? It wasn't as though she'd given him an ultimatum. She wasn't even thinking of marriage until the day Chris dropped onto one knee at Thunderbird Falls. But he begged her to marry him, said he couldn't live without her. But he could, and he did. Because he felt more strongly about not having children than he did about her.

She'd emerged from her relationship with

Chris wiser and determined to get it right the next time. Relationships weren't built on kisses and laughter. Marriages endured because of shared values. Six years later, she hadn't tried to convince herself Robert Torrington Watson IV was her soul mate. But he was a kind man. Steady. They got along well. He was a wildlife biologist, too, so he understood the demands of her job. And he wanted children as much as she did. More, actually, as she found out after a rogue bull bison and misassembled squeeze chute led to a tragic chain of events culminating in an emergency hysterectomy.

It broke Marissa's heart, knowing she'd never give birth to those babies she'd dreamed of. And she'd been angry. Angry at the man who'd assembled the chute, angry at her supervisor, who'd ordered the blood tests on the wild bison out in the field, and angry at herself for not recognizing the danger in time. Eventually, she'd come to accept the reality. But she'd never quite gotten over the loss.

At first, Robert was the perfect fiancé, waiting outside the operating room while they saved her life, bringing her flowers, visiting every day. Four months later, he dropped the bomb. He felt bad, he said, but he knew she would understand. They'd talked about children, about how important it was to him to carry on the family line. He at least had the decency to wait until she recovered from her injuries and returned to work to ask for his grandmother's ring back. Because, after all, a woman without a uterus no longer met the job requirements. And Marissa did understand. But that didn't keep it from hurting.

And then there was Jason, her biggest mistake of all, because she wasn't the only one who got hurt. At least that relationship ended without another broken engagement. She hadn't fallen in love with Jason, hadn't built castles in the clouds, dreaming about their life together. She'd just seen him as a successful, charming and generous man she enjoyed spending time with, and wondered if it could grow into more. She hadn't given him her heart, only her money and access to the two people who meant the world to her so he could rob them, too.

So, where did that leave her? Three men, three strikes. Once upon a time, she'd prided herself on her ability to read people. Was she ever mistaken! She'd loved and trusted her parents, loved and trusted Oliver and Becky now, and that love was returned tenfold. What she'd thought was good judgment was just good luck. Because if there was one thing she'd learned, it was that she couldn't rely on her instincts when it came to love.

Thanks to that enraged bull bison, she would never give birth. She'd accepted that. It would save a boatload of heartache if she just admitted she wasn't good at picking men, and had long ago realized it was better to be alone. She should concentrate on her career studying wildlife, and on helping Oliver and Becky. With no ties, she could accept an assignment anywhere in the world, or change jobs whenever she wanted. It was safer that way.

She reached the back door. Inside, she heard Oliver's deep baritone chuckling over something Becky was saying. Marissa smiled. At least some loves lasted a lifetime. She only hoped that lifetime didn't end too soon.

"CAN KIMMIK PLAY?" The voice drifted to the living room, where Chris was pretending to watch sports insiders discuss the upcoming bowl games. It was Saturday, but there were no reindeer events scheduled until tomorrow, so he was killing time. What he really itched to do was to go out to the reindeer farm with some tools, but he couldn't figure out how to broach the subject without Marissa getting all defensive.

"Sure. Come on through and take him with you to the backyard." Dana sounded delighted that Ryan was there. "I got him a new tennis ball yesterday."

Chris left his chair and stood up. "Ryan, my man. What's up?"

Ryan came up from the basement and stopped at the top of the stairs to scratch the dog's ears. Kimmik reacted by thumping his tail against the back of the couch like a bass drum. "Nothin'."

Chris scooped up a bright yellow ball from Kimmik's basket of toys and tossed it to the boy. "How's school?"

Ryan shrugged. "We get out next Friday for the holidays."

"Cool." Chris grabbed his coat and followed Ryan and Kimmik outside. The sun peeked between the trees low on the southern horizon. A few clouds drifted in the sky, but none of them looked like snow clouds.

He watched Ryan throw the ball for Kimmik for a few minutes. "Hey, let's play keep-away."

Ryan narrowed his eyes in suspicion. "My teacher says keep-away is mean."

Chris chuckled. "Maybe for kids, but dogs love it. Throw me the ball." They spent the next few minutes tossing the ball back and forth while Kimmik ran between them, leaping to catch it. Finally, a wide throw missed Chris's outstretched fingers and Kimmik ran it down. He carried the ball in his mouth, prancing as he returned it to Chris. "Good dog. Shall we go again?"

They continued to play, with Ryan often stopping to hug and pet Kimmik. The kid really did like dogs. He probably liked all animals, which gave Chris an idea.

"Hey, Ryan. You have any plans for the afternoon?"

"No."

"I know some people who have a farm with lots of animals. You want me to call and see if we can go see them?"

"Really? You'd take me to a farm?"

"Yeah, if it's okay with everybody. Let me check if they're home." Chris pulled out his phone and made the call. Ryan threw the ball for Kimmik, but he stuck close enough to overhear. As expected, Becky invited them to come right out. "They'd enjoy a visit. Let's go ask your…uh, Sandy and Brent."

"Can we take Kimmik?"

"Maybe we'd better not. They have barn cats at the farm, and we don't want him to get in trouble. He can stay here with Dana."

"Okay." Ryan rubbed Kimmik's broad

head. "I'll tell you all about it later," he promised the dog.

Chris grinned. "Just let him sniff you after you've been to the farm. He'll love that."

Multicolored lights from a Christmas tree blinked in the window at Ryan's house. The sound of a crying baby almost drowned out the doorbell. April wasn't nearly as cute when she was screaming.

Sandy bounced the baby and patted her back while she listened to Chris's plan, and quickly gave her approval. "Get your seat from the car, Ryan." She nodded toward the garage. Ryan took off like a shot. She shifted the baby to her other shoulder and turned to Chris. "When will you have him home?"

"We should be back by, say, seven? Would that work?"

"Sure. Thanks, Chris. Brent's working today, and April's teething. I was trying to figure how I was going to keep him entertained all afternoon."

"No problem."

"Dana's been really nice about letting Ryan play with the dog every day."

"Dana likes him. So does Kimmik. Ryan's a good kid."

"Yeah." Sandy sighed. "He's a little wild, but what can you expect from a seven-year-old? I wish we could keep him longer, but my mom's got some health issues, and with the baby…" She shrugged.

"I think it's great you're giving him a home for Christmas." Ryan came running back, holding some sort of seat. Chris would have to figure out how to use it. He smiled at Sandy. "Hope April's better soon. We'll see you later."

Sandy handed Ryan a woolly hat from the rack near the door. He pulled it over his ears. "I'm ready."

"Then let's go."

Chris threw some work gloves, his toolbox and a circular saw into his truck. The booster seat baffled him, but fortunately, he was able to pull up an instructional video on his phone on how to install it, and soon they were on their way. "Before we go to the farm, I need to stop by the lumberyard, okay?"

"What's a lumberyard?"

"It's where you buy wood and building materials."

"Why?"

"Last time I was at the farm, I noticed a couple of things that could use some work. I thought I'd fix them while we're there."

Ryan thought for a moment. "If you had a

triceratops, he could knock down a tree so you wouldn't have to buy wood."

"Oh, yeah?"

"They have three horns on their face and a big bone thing on their neck and they're as big as a van."

"Sounds useful. Maybe I should get one."

Ryan giggled. "You can't get a dinosaur. They're extinct."

"What does that mean?"

Chris listened in wonder as Ryan rattled off a well-considered definition of extinction, along with various theories of what had caused dinosaurs to disappear. The sullen kid who'd scolded him for not playing with his dog enough was long gone, and this chatterbox had taken his place.

At the lumberyard, Ryan tagged along, touching the wood and offering opinions as Chris selected his boards and nails. Near the counter, a display of balsa wood models lined the aisle. Ryan stopped to run his finger over one of the figures. He'd stopped fidgeting and was being careful not to bump the display. Chris pointed at the dinosaur. "Is that a triceratops?"

Ryan giggled. "It's a stegosaurus. It doesn't even have any horns."

"You're right. It doesn't." The age suggestion on the box read eight to twelve. The kits weren't expensive. He looked at Ryan. "How old are you, again?"

"Seven."

"But you know a whole lot about dinosaurs, and I can help you with the instructions. Let's get one."

Ryan's eyes opened wide. "Is it the first of the month?"

"No, it's the eighth. Why?"

"Then we can't get it."

"Why not?"

"It's not the first of the month."

"You can only buy toys at the first of the month?"

Ryan nodded. "That's what Granny says. It's when her check comes."

"Oh, well, that makes sense. But this is special, like an early Christmas present from me. Is that okay?"

"Really?"

"We'll build it together. Do you want the stegosaurus or this guy with the big feet?"

Ryan laughed at Chris's ignorance. "Those aren't feet, they're fins. It's a plesiosaurus. They swim."

"Huh. I didn't know dinosaurs swam." Chris rested his hand on Ryan's shoulder. "Which one do you want?"

Ryan's eyes darted back and forth between the two. "Stegosaurus."

"That would have been my choice." Chris grabbed the kit and checked out. In the parking lot, he loaded the lumber in the back of the truck while Ryan sat inside, gazing at the pictures on the box.

Chris climbed into the driver's seat. "You buckled up?"

Ryan nodded, and pointed to the box. "What's this word?"

"*Assembly.* That means put together." He started the truck. "Who taught you so much about dinosaurs?"

"Granny took me to the library and we'd get books. She used to read to me until I could read by myself. She still helps with the hard words."

"Sounds like you have a really good granny."

Ryan nodded, still looking at the box. "She's sick now and can't take care of me anymore."

"I'm sorry to hear that."

Ryan looked up. "I go see her, sometimes. She likes where she lives, but only old people live there. That's why I can't stay with her."

Chris nodded, at a loss what to say to that. Poor kid. If he'd been living with his grandmother and then put into foster care, that meant he didn't have family to fall back on. Chris's parents might not have read him books on dinosaurs, but he'd always had the things he needed, never had to wonder where he'd be sleeping next month.

Ryan didn't seem to notice Chris's discomfort. He launched into a lecture comparing and contrasting various dinosaurs until they reached the turnoff to the farm. When he saw the sign, his eyes widened. "Real reindeer?"

"Yeah. They have a whole herd."

"I thought reindeer were supposed to live at the North Pole."

"You're thinking of Santa's reindeer. Reindeer live all across the arctic. Alaskan caribou are just another sort of reindeer, but the ones on this farm are European reindeer, originally imported from Norway."

"Caribou are reindeer?"

"Uh-huh."

They parked near the front porch. Ryan climbed out and gazed toward the pen where the reindeer were milling around. Before Chris could herd him to the front door, Becky stepped outside to greet them. "Hello. You must be Ryan. Welcome to the Reindeer Farm." She whisked them inside and introduced Ryan to Oliver and Marissa. "Would you like some hot chocolate, or save that for after you've met the animals?"

Ryan looked to Chris for guidance. He chuckled. "Whatever you want is fine."

"I want to see the animals, please."

"I thought so." Becky patted his shoulder. "Come with me to the kitchen, and I'll give you some treats for the reindeer. Then Marissa will take you to the barn."

As soon as Ryan and Becky were out of earshot, Marissa edged closer to Chris. "What are you doing with a kid?" she whispered. She looked at him as though he might have snatched Ryan out of his mother's arms.

"A neighbor of mine is fostering him. He likes dogs, so I thought he might like to see the animals."

"Huh." The suspicion on her face was rather cute.

Chris grinned. "You don't mind, do you?"

"No. I'm just surprised."

Ryan ran back in. "I have carrots and little apples."

"Those are crabapples from the tree out front. The reindeer love them," Oliver assured him.

Marissa flashed Ryan that smile, the one that used to make Chris's heart skip a beat.

"Are you ready to go? Watch this bottom step."

Chris followed them out, but when they started toward the barn, he stopped beside his truck and opened the tailgate. After a few steps, Marissa turned back to look at him, her eyebrows drawn together. "Aren't you coming?"

"Actually, I thought I might do something about that broken step."

Her glare softened into a look of surprise. "Oh. That's…nice. Thank you."

Chris nodded. He strapped on his tool belt and measured the tread. Good, he'd guessed right when he chose the board width. He rubbed his hands together in satisfaction. He couldn't make it snow, or replace Oliver's heart, or make Ryan's grandmother better, but he could fix this step.

MARISSA OPENED THE barn door for Ryan. "The goats are in here."

The boy ran inside, but before she followed, she glanced back toward the house, where Chris was industriously unloading lumber from the back of his truck.

She'd been suspicious from the moment Becky told her Chris had called and asked permission to bring a foster child out. The

Chris she knew wasn't in the habit of hanging out with anyone under the legal drinking age. He had to have an ulterior motive.

And she was right, except his ulterior motive was a chance to fix that step while making it appear Oliver and Becky were the ones doing him a favor. Who would have guessed? She closed the barn door behind her and followed Ryan to the pen. The goats left the hay she'd put in the rack for them and crowded against the fence. Heidi, the droopy-eared Swiss Alpine, pushed to the front, next to her friend Rosa, the Lamancha with almost no ears at all. The dwarf goats squeezed between them and reached through the barrier to nibble on Ryan's jeans, sending him into fits of giggles.

Willa, the pig, shoved the goats aside to claim a place up front, closest to Ryan. The goats, rabbits and chickens were mostly used as a petting zoo for summer visitors, so they were quite tame. Only the barn cats, like the one watching from the beam overhead, tended to be shy with strangers.

Ryan reached through the fence toward the pig. She pushed her head against his hand, encouraging him to scratch behind her ear. He grinned up at Marissa. "It feels funny."

"That's Willa. She's a potbellied pig, but

she thinks she's one of the goats. Or maybe she thinks the goats are pigs."

"Why is she the only pig?"

"Becky and Oliver didn't intend to have pigs, but Willa's family moved out of state, so they took her in." Marissa scooped a handful of grain pellets into a bucket and handed it to Ryan. He made sure Willa and each goat got a share, giggling as they took the food from his hand. "It tickles."

"It does, doesn't it? The goat you're feeding now is Daisy. Petunia is the black goat. She's Daisy's mother. They're Nigerian dwarf goats."

Ryan looked up, startled. "They're dwarves?"

She chuckled. "Yeah, but that just means they're little. Not like the dwarves in *Lord of the Rings*."

"Oh." Ryan wanted to know the names and breeds of every goat and rabbit. He was just as thorough with the chickens when he followed her into their coop. But he really got excited when she let him into the pen with the reindeer.

"Caribou are reindeer. Chris told me."

"He's right about that." The look on Ryan's face made her suspect that in his opinion, Chris was right about everything. "These aren't caribou, though, they're European reindeer."

"I know. Chris said."

"This is Snowflake. Do you want to give her a treat? Hold your hand flat, like you did with the goats."

The joy on the boy's face when Snowflake nuzzled him hoping for another crabapple had Marissa pulling out her cell phone to take a picture. She'd just planned to have Ryan feed the animals and let Becky stuff him with cookies, but he was so fascinated, she ended up showing him how to harness one of the reindeer and hitch it up to a little red wagon. He led the reindeer in a loop around the barn and toward the house, as confidently as any of their teenage elf helpers.

"Hey, Chris. Look. I can lead Belle."

"I see that. Good job. I think Belle likes you." Chris returned a hammer to his tool belt and picked up some sort of power tool. "Did you have fun seeing the animals?"

Behind him, Marissa noticed the strong new bottom step. They wouldn't be able to paint it until the weather warmed, but at least she didn't have to worry about someone breaking their neck. Chris had reinforced the handrail, too.

Ryan's eyes roamed over the porch and Chris's tools. "What are you doing?"

"I was just working on this step, but I'm done now. I've got an idea. I want to fix that broken board on the corral. How about if I put my tools in the wagon, you and Belle transport them over for me?"

"Yeah, okay."

They loaded up the wagon, and Marissa accompanied Ryan and Belle to the corral. Chris followed, a long length of timber slung over his shoulder. Ryan held the reindeer's lead while Marissa unloaded the tools and nails. He looked up at Chris. "I'll help you fix it."

Chris started to shake his head, then paused. "That would be great. I'll tell you what. You help Marissa unharness Belle and take care of her while I measure this board and cut it. I have to take it to the barn to get power for my saw. But when I get back, you and I can nail it in place, okay?"

"Okay." Ryan hurried to follow his instructions.

Even with Ryan helping, the repair didn't take long, and soon the three of them headed for the house, where Becky was waiting with hot chocolate, Christmas cookies and peanut butter sandwiches cut on the diagonal and garnished with pretzel antlers, raisin eyes and candied cherry noses.

"Reindeer sandwiches!" Ryan took one on his plate, but couldn't seem to make himself eat it. "I'm gonna save it to show Granny when I visit her tomorrow."

Oliver laughed. "You can eat that one. I'm sure Becky has another one to take to your grandmother. Did you like the reindeer?"

Ryan happily filled him in on all the details, including the names of every animal on the farm. The kid had an amazing memory.

"Hey, Ryan." Chris rubbed his thumb and forefinger over his bearded chin. "If a triceratops has three horns, could we call a reindeer a biceratops? Tri means three, and bi means two."

Ryan shook his head. "No."

"Why not?"

"Marissa said reindeer don't have horns, they have antlers."

Oliver's deep booming laugh rang out. "He's got you there."

A sense of longing seeped into Marissa's heart as she watched Ryan and Chris laughing and talking with Becky and Oliver. If only Chris wasn't so stubborn, they could have had a son this age, born before the accident that left her unable to have children.

Chris said he wasn't father material, but look at him. That boy slurped up his attention like a strawberry milk shake.

Sometimes, when she was feeling discouraged, she wondered if she should have married Chris anyway, hoping someday he would recognize in himself those fatherly qualities she saw in him. But that wasn't how she did things. It would have been dishonest. And she made logical decisions based on the information at hand, not on some faint possibility. She wanted kids. Chris didn't. It was as simple as that. But as she watched him laugh at something Ryan said, and then reach over to wipe a hot chocolate mustache from the boy's face, it didn't seem so simple anymore.

They moved into the living room, where Oliver settled into his recliner. Tiger jumped onto his lap. Her uncle told Ryan stories of the foxes that lived near the creek that ran through the back of the farm, and about the eagles' nest high up on the bluff behind them. Ryan crept closer to stroke the cat as he listened, fascinated.

The artificial tree Marissa and Becky had put up twinkled in front of the window. Chris turned to Becky. "Is there anything I can do for you while I'm here?"

"I think you've done enough, repairing that front step. Thank you."

"Actually," Oliver interjected, "I have a little chore for you and Ryan, if you have time."

Chris checked his watch. "Sure. We don't need to go for another two hours or so. What can we do for you?"

"Take Marissa and go cut us a real tree. It's something I've done ever since we bought this farm, but I'm not up to it this year. That plastic tree just doesn't do it."

"Oh, come on," Marissa said, defending the tree they'd spent half a day setting up and decorating. It was an old-fashioned one with color-coded branches that fit into matching holes on the trunk, except most of the color had worn off. Becky had picked it up at a garage sale years ago, thinking it would be useful at parties, until she discovered how long it took to set up. "It looks nice, fuller than the native spruces. The branches on them are at least a foot apart."

"Looks aren't everything. It doesn't smell like a real tree. Besides, cutting a tree is our tradition. You're not going to get lazy just because I can't come, are you?" The lines around Oliver's eyes fanned out as he teased her.

Becky reached across to pat her husband's arm. "You've got to respect tradition."

Marissa couldn't deny him. "Okay, fine." She looked over at Chris. "Are you guys up for it?"

Ryan jumped to his feet. "I never cut a Christmas tree before. Can I use the ax?"

Oliver laughed. "I usually use a bow saw, and I'm sure Chris will give you a turn. Now go find us a good one." The three of them bundled up. Lack of snow didn't mean temperatures were any warmer than normal. Marissa passed out flashlights, and gathered a rope, a saw and a tarp. She led them toward the trees on the rise behind the house. Cutting the Christmas tree was something she and Oliver had done together beginning the first year she lived here. Becky always stayed behind to get out the stand and ornaments, letting it be their special outing.

It felt bittersweet, remembering the way Oliver would pull her along on a plastic sled the first few years. They'd discuss the relative merits of at least a dozen trees before they chose the perfect one. Would Oliver ever be well enough to cut another tree? Or see another Christmas?

Ryan ran ahead, dashing toward the nearest tree, a thirty-footer. "This one's pretty."

Chris laughed. "Remember, it has to fit inside the house."

"Okay. I'll find a shorter one." He darted farther into the forest.

Chris looked at Marissa and pressed his gloved hand at a spot below her shoulder blades. "You okay?"

She nodded. "I'm just remembering."

"Good memories, I'll bet."

"The best."

He smiled and rubbed his hand in a circle over her back. "Maybe the transplant will come through. Becky told me a little about the situation while I worked on the step. She's hopeful."

"So am I, but it's hard, waiting." Tears stung her eyes, but she blinked them back. Crying in front of Chris and Ryan would not only be embarrassing, but in this weather, might freeze her eyelashes together.

"I can only imagine how hard it must be." Chris wrapped his arms around her and pulled her into a hug. "I'm glad you're here with them, now."

There was something so comforting about being in his arms. Somehow, when he held her, she believed everything would work out. She laid her head against his shoulder.

"So am I. Not with the circumstances that brought me here, but I'm glad I came."

"Chris. Marissa." Ryan waved his arms. "Come look. I found one. Hurry."

As if the tree was going anywhere… Marissa lifted her head and smiled at Chris. He released her and they went to inspect Ryan's find. He was getting closer; this one was maybe ten or eleven feet tall. Marissa had Chris stand beside it and pointed out that the ceiling in the farmhouse was less than two feet taller than Chris. The tree, on the other hand, was at least four feet taller.

Ryan's third choice was the one. At about seven feet, it was reasonably symmetrical, with only one big gap down low where a branch had broken off. Marissa assured Ryan that side could go toward the wall under the window.

Even letting Ryan take a turn, Chris was able to saw through the tree in a few minutes. They bundled it onto the tarp and dragged it back to the house, where the artificial tree now resided in a corner of the front porch. Oliver's smile when Chris secured the spruce in the stand made it all worthwhile. "Now it smells like Christmas."

Becky produced a pot of clam chowder. Chris and Ryan each gobbled down a bowlful, and then helped Marissa enrobe the tree in strands of white lights. When Marissa plugged them in, Ryan's mouth dropped open. "It's so pretty."

"It is." Chris looked at his watch. "I'd like to stay and help decorate, but I promised to have Ryan home by seven."

"Is it that late? Goodness." Becky came to give them each a warm hug. "Thank you both for everything. Goodbye, Ryan. Come again."

"Can I?" Ryan looked at Chris.

"I don't see why not. Good night, everyone."

Marissa gave Ryan a hug and turned to Chris. *Better not.* Her feelings toward him were confused enough. Instead, she rested her hand on his coat sleeve. "Good night, Chris. Thank you."

She stayed at the window, watching his truck bump its way up the lane. She'd convinced herself that underneath that surface layer of nice guy, Chris was basically selfish. But he'd gone out of his way to make a lot of people happy today, and there didn't seem to be anything in it for him. Becky had told her he was refusing to accept payment for the parties, too. Had he changed? He'd had ten years to mature. Or maybe she was the

one who had matured. Maybe she was starting to see Chris as he really was, not as the
villain in her own personal drama, but as a
man. A good man.

CHAPTER SIX

Fifteen days till Christmas

THANK YOU FOR APPLYING, *and we will keep your résumé on file.* Marissa rolled her eyes. Sure they would. She was eminently qualified for this job, heading up a team to study habitat impact of a proposed golf development in Arkansas, but they hadn't even offered her an interview. At least they'd taken the trouble to turn her down. Most didn't. They just hired somebody and left everyone else dangling. But if any of the three dozen places she'd applied to had wanted her, they would have contacted her by now. They hadn't.

Not a single request for an interview, and she'd heard nothing from Derrick Matheson, the headhunter who'd assured her he had some positions in mind for her. The job market for wildlife biologists was tight, but not that tight. Something was up, and she was afraid she knew what it was.

It took another hour and a half before Derrick returned her call and confirmed her suspicions. "I'm sorry, Marissa. With all the flak about the Ponzi scheme on the news, you're too hot to handle. I've done my best, but when the word *embezzle* and your name are mentioned in the same sentence, your résumé goes into the shredder."

"I had nothing to do with any of it."

"Hey, I believe you. But until they catch up with your boyfriend—"

"My ex-boyfriend."

"Whatever. It would help if they didn't keep running that picture of the two of you accepting the giant check at that fund-raiser two weeks before he absconded with the money. A lot of people think you know where he's hiding."

She hated that photo. Jason with his million-dollar smile, shaking hands with the chairman of a local service organization. Her holding the other end of the check, beaming into the camera like a plastic mannequin. That money, raised through spaghetti dinners and bake sales, was supposed to go toward a habitat improvement project on the banks of the river they were studying. Instead, it had disappeared along with Jason.

"Believe me, if I had any idea where to find him, I'd have turned him in. Prison is too good for him." Marissa thought about telling Derrick that she and Oliver had lost money with Jason, too, but it wouldn't make any difference. The people he had hurt needed somebody to blame, and Jason was unavailable, so she was the target. "Look, I really need a job, as soon after Christmas as possible. My uncle has some health issues, and with medical bills and all—"

"I understand, but I can't force them to hire you. I'll keep my ear to the ground. Maybe we can find something."

"Thanks. I appreciate your efforts."

"Hope they catch him soon."

"You and me both." She ended the call. Now what? It was bad enough that she couldn't get a job in her field, but it sounded like she was more or less blackballed from working for anyone. At least anyone with a television. Maybe she should apply for jobs with the Amish or something.

She opened her laptop. Stick with the plan. Somewhere out there was a job with a decent paycheck and an employer who was willing to give her a chance. She just had to find it.

FRIDAY AFTERNOON, Chris was carrying his Santa suit to his truck when Ryan showed up. Good thing he had it in a bag. He'd hate to have to explain it to Ryan.

"Hi. What's new?"

The boy dragged his foot along the ground. "I gave my Granny the reindeer sandwich."

"Uh-huh?" Chris hung the bag on the hook in his truck and slammed the door. "What did she say?"

"She thought it was funny." But Ryan didn't seem happy about it. "She forgot my name."

"Your granny did?"

"Yeah. She called me Patrick. That's my dad's name."

"Your granny is your dad's mother?"

Ryan nodded. "It was weird."

"Sometimes people misspeak. Where's your dad now?"

"He died a long time ago."

"And your mom?"

"I never had a mom. Just Granny."

"Oh. Was your granny happy to see you?"

"Yeah. She hugged me when she called me Patrick."

"Sometimes my sister calls me Kimmik." He said it as a joke, but he hoped it would make Ryan smile.

It did. He giggled in fact. "She does not."

"The other day, I left my coat on the couch, and Kimmik left his toys all over the living room. Dana told Kimmik to hang up his jacket. Since he doesn't have hands, I think she meant me."

"You're a grown-up. You're not supposed to make a mess."

"So Dana tells me. Did you enjoy the farm yesterday?"

"It was fun. I told Granny about it. She used to have chickens when she was a little girl, but she never got to feed a reindeer like me. Hey, Chris? Did you ever notice that Oliver looks kinda like Santa Claus?"

Chris grinned. "Yeah, I have."

Ryan seemed to be working something over in his mind. "I don't believe in Santa."

"No?"

"Don't tell April, okay? She's just a baby, and she believes. Sandy said I should write a letter saying what me and April want for Christmas, so I did. I didn't tell her I knew Santa wasn't real."

"Are you sure, though?"

"Yeah." But Ryan didn't sound convinced. He studied Chris's face as if searching for a clue. "Oliver does look like Santa, though."

"Uh-huh."

"And he has reindeer."

"True."

"But this isn't the North Pole."

"Nope."

"But maybe Santa pretends he lives at the North Pole, but really he hides, you know, like a secret identity."

"You think so?"

"No." Ryan shook his head, but then he peered up at Chris. "Do you?"

"Hard to say." He ruffled the boy's hair. "Listen, I have to go to work now, but Dana's inside. She'll let you in to play with Kimmik. I'll see you later."

"Okay. Bye, Chris." Ryan bounded up the stairs to the front door, obviously happier.

Poor kid. After losing his father and his grandmother, it wasn't surprising he had a hard time believing in anything nice, like Santa. On his way up the street, Chris spotted Brent raking up some broken twigs off his brown lawn. He stopped and rolled down the window. "Hey, Brent. Ryan's with Dana, in case he forgot to tell you."

Brent crossed the lawn to lean against the window. "Yeah, he told me. We took him to see his grandmother today."

"He told me she called him by the wrong name. Dementia?"

Brent shrugged. "Maybe. They don't share medical details. The nurse said something about getting her medicine dialed in. Or maybe she's just old."

"So no chance of her moving home with Ryan?"

Brent shook his head, sadly.

Chris drove on to the party venue, where Marissa was unloading one of the reindeer in the parking lot. He'd learned to do his own beard by now, so he just waved to her and Becky on the way inside to get in costume. When he came out, Marissa was setting up Santa's throne. He hurried over. "I'll take care of that."

"It's done now." She smiled at him. "Thanks for what you did yesterday."

"It was nothing."

"It wasn't nothing. Oliver and Becky really appreciate your help." He noticed she didn't include herself in the gratitude, but her shining eyes told a different story.

This evening's party, hosted by a local real estate firm, was mostly adults, with a dozen or so kids in attendance. It took place in the same community center they'd used for one of the daytime children's parties, but the room looked entirely different. Silver streamers floated above red-and-white flower arrangements on black tablecloths. A bar in the corner was doing a brisk business with partygoers in dark suits and sparkly dresses. The reindeer team was scheduled only for the first part of the evening. Presumably, the DJ setting up on the other side of the room would entertain during the second half.

Chris gave each child all the time they wanted with him, but since they'd been promised a reindeer ride after seeing Santa, most weren't eager to prolong the conversation beyond delivering their Christmas lists. He was just about to suggest to Marissa they head outside to help with the reindeer when a woman approached. Chris knew the type—shortest dress and highest heels in the room. By the wobble in her step, he figured she was three drinks in already. She stumbled, almost knocking over the fake tree in the process, and he upgraded that estimate. A couple friends drifted after her, laughing.

"I wanna sit in Santa's lap." She thrust out her lower lip in a pretty pout that had probably gotten her exactly what she wanted for most of her twentysomething years. Personally, Chris wasn't a big fan of pouters.

Marissa's eyes narrowed, but then, as she looked over at Chris, a little smirk tugged at the corners of her mouth. "I'm sure Santa would be happy to take care of you."

Chris raised his eyebrows. Marissa gave him a bland smile. "Right this way," he said.

Of course the woman couldn't make the step without stumbling, so Chris had to stand and catch her elbow. Why did party girls insist on wearing stilettos? She giggled. Chris sat on the big chair. "Why don't you stand here, and your friends can take your picture."

"No, I wanna sit in your lap."

Chris offered a knee, hoping she'd perch on the edge of it, but she slipped her hands around his neck and draped her legs over the arm of the chair. He wasn't quite sure how she managed it without flashing her underwear. Or maybe she did; he tried not to look. She leaned closer and asked in a husky whisper, "Aren't you going to ask if I've been a good girl?"

Chris shook his head. "No need."

She batted her eyelashes. "Oh, have you been watching me, Santa?"

He glanced around the room, where several people had stopped talking to stare in their direction. A young man with his arms crossed over his chest stood apart from the crowd, scowling. One of her friends was snapping photos on her phone. "Everyone's watching you. Why don't you smile and wave, and then move along? I need to get back to the kids."

The pout returned. "But I haven't told you what I want for Christmas."

"Fine. What do you want?"

She whispered something in his ear. Fortunately, he couldn't understand much of it, because what he did hear wasn't suitable for a family Christmas party. He set her back on her feet and helped her down the step. "All right then. Your boyfriend is waiting for you. Merry Christmas."

As soon as she moved away, Chris shot Marissa a glare, but she just smiled sweetly and encouraged the other young women gathered around to pose with him for photos. At least they didn't insist on sitting in his lap. By this time, several others had wandered over and decided they needed a photo with Santa, too. It was another half hour before Chris and Marissa were finally able to escape.

On the way out the door, he leaned close to her ear. "Thanks a lot. Did you throw Oliver to the wolves like that when you used to do this in high school?"

She smirked. "Surprisingly, it seldom came up. But I know you like posing with pretty girls, judging by all those pictures of you on the internet."

"You looked for me on social media?"

The smile died and her cheeks grew pinker

before she turned away. Busted. "I stumbled across a few pictures."

Chris didn't spend much time online, but he had a suspicion she would have had to go looking to find photos of him. He'd assumed that once Marissa made up her mind to dump him and move away, she'd never given him a second thought. Maybe he'd been wrong about that.

MONDAY MORNING, CHRIS stood in his office, sorting through his file cabinet, desperate to find something productive to fill his time. Through the window into the warehouse, he could see the plow trucks with their hoods gaping open like hungry baby birds. He had Kenny checking all the belts and hoses, even though he knew they were fine.

The phone rang. "Hey. It's Squid."

"Hey, man. How's it going?" Chris sank into his desk chair. Squid was a fellow crew member from last summer's fishing boat and self-proclaimed ski bum.

"Good. Getting a poker game together. You interested?"

"Maybe. Depends on when it is."

"Before Christmas, anyway. I'll text you once I know. So, you told me to call if I heard of any good boats for sale. You know Mike Wommet? He's talking about selling."

"Yeah, I know Mike. He's got a nice setup. Is he selling the permit, too?"

"I think so."

"Okay, thanks. I'll give him a call."

"Sure. Later, dude."

It turned out Mike was indeed looking to sell, so after a two-and-a-half-hour drive, Chris parked his truck at the Seward harbor. He'd seen snow lying on the pass, and the mountains jutting from the water across the bay sported white peaks, but Seward was as snow-free as Anchorage. A cold breeze swept in from the water, and he tugged his wool cap down over his ears.

Chris located the slip number Mike had given him. The purse seiner *New Beginnings* bumped gently against the rubber tires of the dock as she rocked on the waves. She looked to be in decent shape, her crisp white hull accented with stripes of royal blue and red-brown. Chris walked around, inspecting her from all angles, counting two picking boom winches and three topping winches, as well as the deck winch. Far above, the crow's nest perched at the top of the heavy mast. He wondered what the hold capacity would be, maybe thirty or thirty-five thousand pounds in the main?

Mike came hurrying along the dock. "Sorry, I got tied up on a phone call. So, you want to see her?"

"I do." Chris followed him on board.

"She's got aluminum five-seventy-five diesel tanks and…" With as much pride as a new father, Mike rattled off all the technical details from memory as they went over the boat from bow to stern. He had good reason to be proud. While the *New Beginnings* was showing her age in a few areas, she was a fine boat and well cared for.

"What do you think?"

Chris traced his finger along the smooth raised rail enclosing the galley table. The wood gleamed under layers of varnish. "She's a beauty."

Mike beamed. "Let's take her out."

Her 460 horsepower engine rumbled smoothly in the test drive around the bay. The price, while high, was fair for a seiner this size. But it would take basically every cent Chris had to buy her. He'd have to sell off the trucks and plows in order to put together enough capital for fuel and equipment for the season. And it meant he'd have to let his last two employees go.

That wasn't the plan. He'd always intended the fishing boat to be an addition to the plow business, not a replacement. First of all, fishing, like snow plowing, was unpredictable, which was exactly why he'd saved all these years rather than take out a loan to buy a boat. Two seasonal businesses would give his income more stability. And then there were the guys. Brad and Kenny, both road construction workers in the summer, relied on him for winter income. They'd been with him since his second winter. Kenny was only sixteen then, shoveling walks while Brad and Chris plowed driveways, before Chris switched to commercial plowing.

"Why are you selling, anyway?" Chris asked. Mike was only about ten years older than him, not old enough to retire.

He shrugged. "Wife says she's had enough Alaska winters. She's down in Florida now. I figure I can sell the boat and hire on with somebody down there."

"How long have you been in Alaska?"

"All my life. Never thought I'd leave it but, you know. The things we do for love, right?"

"Sure." Not that Chris had made any great sacrifices. He'd been prepared to follow Marissa to her first job, in theory, but only because he'd assumed she'd be taking the first opportunity to return to her family in Alaska. That was ten years ago, and she'd never come home until now. If they were married, would he be satisfied following her around wherever her job led her, like a family pet? Not that it mattered now. He ran his hand over the smooth wood of the wheelhouse instrument panel. "She's a fine craft."

"That she is." Mike picked up a cloth and rubbed at a dull spot on the wood.

It was right after the breakup that Chris started saving for a boat. He'd never finished college, but that didn't mean he couldn't be successful. Captain Chris Allen. That was his ten-year goal. And he was going to get there, but not today. Not until he was completely sure of his game plan. Marissa's planning tendencies had rubbed off on him when it came to business decisions. "I'll sleep on it and let you know what I decide."

"Okay, but don't take too long. I've got some other people looking at her tomorrow. I can't hold her for you."

"I understand. Thanks, Mike."

They shook hands and Chris returned to his truck, but before he climbed in, he took a moment to look across the blue water toward the snow-capped peaks. An eagle soared overhead. The breeze carried the scent of seaweed and salt.

The town of Seward clung to the narrow

strip of land between the ocean and the peaks behind it, parallel to the mountain range across the bay. Old-fashioned stores with false fronts lined the main street downtown, ending at the modern Sea Life Center at the bay. In the summer, the town would be teeming with tourists, but this time of year many of the businesses and restaurants closed for the season, and Seward reverted to a tiny fishing village, scraping a living from its relationship with the sea.

Here in the harbor, the ocean seemed almost docile, but Chris knew better. She might be part of the "peaceful" Pacific, but she was peaceful only when she chose to be. He'd experienced all her moods, even her wildest, when waves tossed his boat like a loose shopping bag caught in a dust devil. And he loved her in spite of, or maybe because of, her unpredictability.

The *New Beginnings* was a fine boat. If he bought her, he wouldn't change the name. It would be a new beginning for him, the first time his main source of revenue would be from his own boat, not just his share of the crew catch.

He wanted that boat. But he hated to give up his snowplow business. It was his first taste of ownership, and he'd been successful, growing from one truck to six. Of course, this snowless winter was kicking his butt, but winter was far from over. It could still work out. If the next few months turned snowy, he might make enough to cover the rest of the cost of the boat and still leave a nest egg for expenses. And he'd finally have everything he'd been working for.

CHAPTER SEVEN

Seven days till Christmas

A FEW SNOWFLAKES hovered toward the end of the seven-day forecast. A spark of hope flared, but Chris was well aware that forecasts could and did change, especially this far out. All the same, the possibility dangled before him like a carrot on a string. Mike had said nobody else had made an offer, so the *New Beginnings* was still available. The dream was alive.

No snow today, though, and Chris had managed about as much file organization as he could tolerate in one sitting. He shut down his computer and opened the office door. "Hey, Kenny."

The wiry redhead looked up from his push broom, Chris's latest make-work project for him. "Yeah?"

"Go home. You can finish tomorrow."

"Okay, thanks." Kenny took him at his

word, tossing the broom into the closet and trotting toward the coat rack. "See you."

Chris was only five minutes behind him. A yellow school bus pulled out of the neighborhood as he turned in. It must have dropped Ryan at the bus stop, because when Chris approached their street, he saw the boy plodding along, backpack half-zipped and hanging over one shoulder. He'd almost reached his house when Chris stopped and rolled down the window.

"Hi. If you don't have anything going later, why don't you come over and we'll work on that dinosaur. Once you've done your homework and everything."

Ryan's eyes opened wide. "Okay."

"Good. See you later."

Chris continued to the house, where Kimmik greeted him and accompanied him to the living room. Three deep red stockings now hung over the fireplace. Chris's name appeared in sparkling gold script across the cuff of the one on the left. He smiled. They might have been short on family celebrations during their childhood, but now Dana was making up for lost time. She embraced every Christmas tradition out there, in spite of the full class load she carried. She was probably fattening a Christmas goose somewhere.

Sam had presumably arrived back from his two-week rotation on the North Slope this morning, as scheduled. The unlit Christmas tree indicated he and Dana were out, most likely Christmas shopping. Chris had done all his shopping online right after Thanksgiving, although he did need to get the presents wrapped and under the pretty noble fir he'd carried upstairs and set up according to Dana's orders. She'd draped it in multicolored lights, but hadn't hung any decorations yet.

He did want to get something fun for Ryan. He'd seen a huge stuffed dinosaur in a store a few days ago, but there was no use getting Ryan a gift so big he couldn't take it with him when he moved to his next foster home. The idea of the boy moving on left an uneasy feeling in the pit of Chris's stomach. He pushed the thought away and wandered into the kitchen to snitch a cookie.

In the living room, Kimmik was rooting around in his toy basket. Chris's cell rang. Squid again. Chris answered. "Hi, man. Thanks for the tip on the boat."

"You buy it?"

"Not yet, but I'm thinking about it."

"Cool. Hey, you up for some skiing?"

Chris laughed. He'd seen the bare mountain at Girdwood on the way in. Only the tip of the peak held snow. "Waterskiing?"

"No, heli-skiing. They've got deep powder over at Valdez."

"That's nice, but I'm buying a boat. I don't have the cash for heli-skiing."

"That's what I'm telling you. I know a guy who did one of those eight-person packages, but two of his friends bailed. So, free powder, dude. You in?"

Skiing. That rush of adrenaline, carving his way down the hill. One of the best things about living in Alaska. "When?"

"Now. We can drive over and crash tonight, wake up to skiing in the morning and for the next three days."

Chris considered. No snow in the immediate forecast, so he wouldn't be working. He could give Kenny the week off. He glanced over at Kimmik, who was holding a ball in his mouth and looking hopeful. Ryan had spoiled that dog.

Ryan. He was coming over later to work on his dinosaur. Chris couldn't disappoint the boy, not with all the other disappointments in his life. Besides, Chris realized, to his surprise, he'd rather build dinosaurs with Ryan than crash with a bunch of extreme skiers, even with the bonus of virgin powder.

"I can't. Thanks for the offer, but I have plans tonight."

"Oh, come on. Break 'em. We're talking deep powder, man."

"Sorry, but no."

"Last chance. If you don't go, I'll have to call Carl, and you know how he is. He'll probably drone on about his passive-aggressive girlfriend all the way to Valdez until I fall asleep at the wheel and kill us both, and it'll be all your fault."

Chris laughed. "I'm willing to take that chance. Have fun."

A couple of hours later, Dana popped through the kitchen door, carrying two boxes of pizza. Sam followed, loaded down like a pack mule with bags and boxes. He dumped his load on the kitchen island. "I'll fetch the rest while you get the plates out."

"Thank you." Dana beamed at him. He leaned over for a kiss before heading back into the garage.

Chris shook his head. "You two make a mockery of marriage. Don't you know newlyweds are supposed to fight over who cleaned the bathroom last? It's not natural to be lovey-dovey all the time."

Dana laughed and reached into a cupboard.

"I wasn't aware of the rules. You want some pizza?"

"Sure. Say, Ryan's coming over later to build a dinosaur model. Why don't I give Sandy a call and see if he can have pizza, too?"

"Fine with me." Dana grabbed another plate and carried the pile to the table. "In fact, Sam and I got a bunch of stuff to decorate the tree. If he wants, Ryan can help."

"Good idea. He'll like that."

Dana stopped setting the table to look up at Chris. "You're spending a lot of time with Ryan."

"He's a good kid. And I gather things are a little tense at Brent and Sandy's because the baby's teething."

"Poor April. I'll have to ask Sandy about that." Dana placed forks and napkins beside each plate. "Have they decided to keep Ryan after Christmas?"

"Not that I know of."

"I was hoping they would. I hate the idea of the little guy getting bounced around. I'm sure most of the foster homes are good people like Brent and Sandy, but you hear stories."

"I know."

She sighed. "Anyway, I think it's great that you're spending time with him. Especially since he's always lived with his grandmother. He's probably starved for a male role model. You're good for him."

"I don't know about that. I'm not that good at relating to kids."

"Are you kidding?" Sam stumbled in, balancing another heap of packages. "You're perfect. You're basically an overgrown kid yourself."

Chris raised an eyebrow. "I'm not sure that's a compliment."

Sam dumped his load and grinned. "It wasn't meant to be. Now hang up your jacket, wash your hands and help your sister get dinner on the table."

Chris saluted. "Yes, sir."

WEDNESDAY WAS THE annual Christmas party at an assisted living home. Oliver and Becky had started volunteering years ago, but this year Chris and Marissa offered to take their places so that Becky could stay home with Oliver.

One of the staff took Chris to a room where he could get into costume. When he was finished, she led him to the gathering place, where a flocked tree with shiny blue balls reached for the ceiling in one corner. White poinsettias graced the tabletops. Across one wall, a cardboard sleigh and a row of reindeer galloped toward the sky.

The residents came by foot, by walker and by wheelchair, crowding into the communal area. Marissa and some other volunteers greeted them as they arrived and presented each person with a stack of song sheets and a shiny jingle bell. Chris circulated around the room, shaking hands and talking with the seniors, who seemed as excited to see him as the kids were.

One of the women rested her hand on his elbow. "My goodness, Santa. You're looking younger. Have you discovered the fountain of youth?"

Chris grinned. It had been a long time since he was considered a youngster, but he supposed compared to this group, and Oliver, he was. He leaned closer and whispered, "The secret is cookies."

Once the residents had all arrived, a woman sat down at the upright piano in the corner and launched into a rollicking version of "Jingle Bells." Another lady, who might have once been an opera singer, judging by her physique, stood to lead the crowd. Counting her impressive mound of jet-black hair, she barely measured five foot two, but her voice was powerful enough for three women.

She shook her jingle bells and encouraged the rest of the group to sing and ring along with the bells Marissa had given them.

The residents ranged from enthusiastic singers, dancing in their chairs, to those who sat and looked on mutely. One man, presumably hard of hearing, sang at the top of his lungs two beats behind the rest of the group, but no one seemed to mind. Women outnumbered men at least three to one.

Chris sang along, circulating around the room and encouraging everyone to join in before he settled in an empty chair beside a tiny woman with a few white streaks in her brownish hair. She wasn't singing, but smiled serenely. She looked to be in her sixties, about Becky's age, but there was something fragile about her, like a slender bird. Maybe a dove.

"Suggestions?"

The residents shouted song titles to the former opera singer and she jumped into "Frosty the Snowman." When they switched to "Oh, Little Town of Bethlehem," the woman beside Chris suddenly joined in, her voice thin but clear. He noticed she wasn't using the song sheets, but singing all the verses from memory.

After the carol ended, she turned to Chris. "Are you Santa Claus?"

"Yes, I am."

"I thought so. I remember." She flashed him another smile and joined in the singing of "Oh, Holy Night." Chris wasn't sure exactly what she meant. Did she think he was Oliver from last year, or was she just speaking generally? Whichever it was, she seemed happy he was there.

A group of girls about Ryan's age, dressed in identical uniforms, followed their leader into the room like so many brown ducklings. They turned out to be a local Brownie troop, who lined up in front of the room and performed a couple of cute songs about snow, while the women oohed and ahhed over them. One of the girls kept waving at a lady in the front row whose tight halo of curls glowed an unlikely shade of fluorescent red. Presumably, the two were acquainted.

After about ten minutes, the Brownies mingled with the crowd, and the singer led them all in more carols. The woman beside Chris squirmed in her seat, leaning forward so she could watch the girls.

Between songs, Chris nodded toward the closest Brownie. "Cute, aren't they?"

The woman scanned the room. "Is my grandson here?"

"I didn't see any boys. What's your grand-son's name?"

She started to answer, but the piano drowned her out, playing "Santa Claus Is Coming to Town." His cue. He excused him-self and worked his way to the front of the room, where Marissa was waiting beside a pile of packages.

"Ho, ho, ho. Merry Christmas! Who's been good this year?" His question generated a sprinkling of laughter and a few raised hands. "Aw, come on now. Look at all these presents. Elf Marissa, have you checked the list?"

"I did, Santa, and I believe they've all been good." She shook her finger at one man. "Ex-cept you, Fred. Making fun of my lovely elf shoes. It's lucky for you everyone else was extra nice to make up for it." She waved the top package. "This one is for Ruby M."

"Ah, Ruby, a precious jewel." Chris took the parcel. "Ruby, where are you?"

The red-haired woman in the front row with a Brownie on her lap waved a hand. "That's me!" Chris bent to kiss her cheek and handed her the package.

She tittered. "Thank you, Santa."

"You're welcome." He winked at the wide-eyed little girl in her lap and turned to Ma-rissa. "Who's next?"

"Iris P."

A woman in the back waved her arms. "Bingo!" From everyone's amused laughter, Chris got the idea this was a running joke.

"You're a winner, Iris. Here you are." When he went to give her the package, she dimpled and presented her cheek for his kiss. Oops, he seemed to have set a precedent.

Marissa read the next tag. "Martin W.?" She handed the package to Chris, but the big man in the wheelchair chortled.

"I want my kiss from the pretty elf."

Chris laughed. "I don't blame you, Martin, but I'm fairly certain that would violate EEOC rules. And the elf union would have my hide." He handed over the package.

Martin accepted the present and grinned. "Huh, you probably just want the kisses for yourself."

"Is she your girlfriend?" one of the ladies asked.

"They do make a cute couple."

"I'll bet they're married."

"She's not wearing a ring."

"Neither is he."

Chris wasn't sure if the seniors were hard of hearing or simply didn't care that he and Marissa could hear them discuss their relationship. He looked to her with raised eyebrows. She shrugged and laughed.

One of the Brownies ran up to Chris and stamped her foot. "Santa Claus is married to Mrs. Claus, not an elf."

"Of course you're right, honey." The woman who'd led the singing stood and patted the girl on the shoulder while giving the rest of the room the stink eye. "They were just teasing."

"Mrs. Claus stayed home to feed the reindeer today," Chris assured the girl. "She sent Elf Marissa along to help me. They're good friends." He considered the young kid for a moment. "Maybe you can help, too. Can you deliver this gift to Mary M.?"

The residents behaved themselves for the rest of the gift distribution, but as soon as the Brownies left, the teasing began anew.

"Are you telling me you and that handsome Santa aren't an item?" A lady dressed in a purple-and-green caftan clucked her tongue. "What's wrong with you, girl?"

Marissa gave an exaggerated sigh. "You know what they say about dating the boss. It only leads to trouble."

"Ain't it the truth? I dated my boss. Then I married him, and next thing you know I had three babies in diapers, an eighteen-month-old girl and twin boys. Don't think I slept for a year."

Marissa laughed and continued to chat with the ladies.

"Refreshments are ready. Sugar-free on that table." The song leader apparently also served as town crier. The residents surged toward the cookies and eggnog one of the volunteers had set out.

After a while, Martin beckoned Chris closer. He nodded toward the buffet table where Marissa was standing. "That one reminds me of my Rosie. A real pip. Is she married?"

Chris looked over at Marissa, who was smiling at someone's remarks while she ladled punch into cups. "No, she's not."

"Are you?"

"No."

"Then what are you waiting for? Ask her out."

Chris laughed. "I did. A long time ago."

"Shot you down, huh?"

"You could say that."

Martin nodded sagely. "So that's what you're doing here. I wondered why somebody as young as you would be wasting his time with a bunch of old fogies. Trying to impress the girl, huh?"

"Not exactly."

"Men nowadays have no stamina. It takes persistence to win a woman over. I had to ask my Rosie six times before she agreed to marry me."

"Really? Six times?"

"The first time was on our second date. She didn't think I was serious, but I knew right away she was the one for me. Took a little longer to convince her I was the one for her."

"But she finally said yes?"

"She did, and I made sure we got hitched before she could change her mind back. We were married for fifty-eight years."

"Fifty-eight years."

"And every day I tried to make sure she never regretted her decision. The love of my life. Lost her eight years ago, and still miss her every single day."

It was hard to argue with success. When Chris looked up, Marissa had moved away from the punch bowl, but he located her on the other side of the room, talking to the dove lady Chris had sat beside earlier. Her name was Winnie, and when they'd handed out her gift earlier, she'd widened her eyes and clutched her hand to her chest as though surprised there was something for her. Now she was hugging Marissa and gracing her with that same beatific smile Chris had seen earlier. Marissa always seemed to bring out the best in people. Except maybe him.

Martin followed his gaze. "Well? Are you going to do it?"

Chris shrugged his shoulders. "Marissa and I were engaged once, but it didn't work out. We're just friends now."

Martin eyed him. "Um-hmm. That's what Rosie said to proposal number five. 'Let's just be friends.'"

"Is that so?"

"Persistence. That's the ticket."

"If you say so."

"I do." Martin tapped his finger against his wedding ring. "Fifty-eight years with the most beautiful girl in the world. I know what I'm talking about."

CHAPTER EIGHT

Four days till Christmas

MARISSA SWEPT THE wooden floor of the living room where Oliver sat in his recliner, watching the daily news. As she bent to sweep the dust into the pan, the stock market report ended and Marissa thought she heard Jason's name mentioned. She dropped the broom and spun around to stare at the television.

"...possibly spotted in Cuba. Police neither confirm nor deny the rumor that the alleged architect of a complex Ponzi scheme is hiding there."

The camera cut away from the reporter to a police spokesperson at a podium studded with microphones. "We are actively investigating all avenues to find and prosecute Jason Kort, and recover the stolen funds. Anyone with knowledge as to Mr. Kort's whereabouts, please contact us immediately. Thank you."

The scene flashed a close-up of Jason with his trust-me smile, perfect teeth glow-ing white against his tanned face. If this were a movie, he would be the falsely accused hero framed by some evil genius to take the fall, but in the end, he'd prove his innocence and ride off into the sunset with the woman who loved him. But this wasn't a movie and Marissa didn't love him. He'd stolen from her family without any visible prick of conscience. Did he worry even a little about the people he'd hurt, or was he tanning on a beach somewhere, laughing at all the stupid people who trusted him? Could he really be in Cuba?

Oliver clicked the TV off and smiled at her. "They'll catch up with him eventually. They always do."

Not always. But Marissa knew Oliver was trying to make her feel better, so she smiled back. "I know. I just wish I had some idea where he might be."

"He never mentioned anyplace he was looking to visit?"

"Not that I remember."

Oliver patted her hand. "It'll all work out."

She wished she had his faith. Jason wasn't stupid. He'd managed to siphon off a huge amount of money without anyone catching on for years. If he could pull that off, he probably had a pretty good plan for hiding out.

She just hoped the people chasing him knew more than they were saying.

The hope was extinguished that afternoon. Marissa was outside feeding the reindeer when she saw an official-looking dark sedan bumping along the drive. She dusted the hay from her jacket and hurried to the farmhouse, arriving as a man in a suit and topcoat climbed from the car. "Marissa Gray?"

"Yes."

He flashed a badge. "Detective Matt Simonton. May I have a few minutes of your time?"

"We can talk inside."

Marissa led him into the living room and introduced him to Oliver, who eyed him skeptically. "I hope you're here to tell us you've caught up with that rat and you need Marissa to testify."

The detective nodded politely. "Not yet, I'm afraid. I'm hoping Miss Gray can give us some information that will help in the search."

"If she knew where he was, she would have told you."

"Yes, well." He turned to Marissa. "Is there somewhere we can talk alone?"

Oliver struggled out of his chair, panting.

What little color was in his face drained away. "Does she need a lawyer?"

Marissa rushed to his side. "Uncle Oliver, please sit. It's fine. I have nothing to hide. Maybe something he asks will help jog my memory."

Oliver sat down, but raised his chin. "All right, but call me if you need me."

"I will." Marissa led the detective into the kitchen with a wry smile. "My uncle. He's a little overprotective."

"He doesn't look so good. Is he okay?"

"No." Marissa didn't elaborate as she pulled off her down jacket and hung it on a hook. "Have a seat. Coffee?"

"Thank you." He settled into one of the rush-seated chairs, pulled out a notebook and pen, and unbuttoned his coat. "Br-r-r, it's cold out there."

"This is Alaska." She measured coffee into the filter. "So, is there any truth to the rumor someone's spotted Jason in Cuba?"

He shrugged. "Hard to say. Have you ever been to Cuba?"

"No." She pushed the brew button and turned, leaning against the countertop. "Have you?"

"No." His mouth quirked in an almost

smile. "Have you ever heard Jason Kort mention Cuba?"

"Not that I recall." She pulled two mugs from a cabinet. "I've had this conversation with another detective. I don't remember Jason ever mentioning any place he might run away to, even as a joke."

"Have you received any letters from overseas?"

"No."

"Phone calls? Emails?"

"No."

"Do you use a phone other than the landline in this house and cell phone number you reported earlier?"

Marissa looked at him sharply. "You're tapping my phone?"

"Please answer the question."

What difference did it make if they were? She wasn't covering for Jason. "No, I only have the one cell phone, and it usually can't get a signal out here."

"Have you been in contact with Jason Kort at any time since…" the detective consulted his notebook "…November 16?"

"No." She poured two cups of coffee and set one in front of him. "Cream or sugar?"

"Black is fine, thanks. Do you have any sort of signal or communication whereby

Jason Kort might contact you indirectly?" Simonton held up his hand as she started to shake her head. "Think before you answer. Some person you both know who might get a message to you. An online forum you both read?"

She considered. "We worked together. Of course there are people we both know. But none of them have contacted me since the police closed the research center down. As for forums, I haven't looked at the center's website since then. If it's still up, there is a comments section. Have you checked it?"

He didn't answer. "Do you have a computer here?"

"Of course." She pulled her laptop from the messenger bag hanging by the back door and opened it on the table so that they could both read the screen. "I'll pull the website up."

It was still there. A photo of a red-winged blackbird darting across the river adorned the home page. A fresh surge of anger flared inside her. She'd taken that picture. She and the other scientists had put so much work into their research, and now it was all for nothing. The research was locked away in an evidence locker somewhere until it became clear to whom it belonged. The River Foundation was closed. And Jason was gone.

She clicked over to the blog page. Of course, it hadn't been updated since the center shut down, but the comments section was open. Hundreds of new posts filled the column, mostly lamenting the loss of the River Foundation and the research center. Many of them included veiled and not-so-veiled threats against Jason. More than a few were directed at her.

She skimmed down the columns. More of the same. Then she saw it. "Look at this one."

A real shame, losing this jewel. All that valuable research on rufous hummingbirds. I hope they get the documents back within three months or so.

"What about it?"

"We didn't study rufous hummingbirds. We noted seeing a few migrate, but they're primarily a West Coast bird ranging from California to Alaska."

"So?"

"I don't know. I just think it's strange that someone would be so specific and get it wrong."

"Hmm. Does the term *jewel* mean anything to you?"

"Jewel..." Something niggled at the back of her mind. "Yes. Right after I started working there, Jason was going through a divorce. One of the researchers joked that he must have decided his wife wasn't such a jewel, after all. I guess Jewel was his nickname for her." Maybe it meant something. "Have you found her?"

"Who was the researcher who mentioned it?"

"Bob Duffy." She lifted her chin. "Now why won't you answer my questions?"

Simonton looked up from his notepad. "No, we haven't found her. Are you familiar with a man named Leo Markesan?"

"The name sounds familiar."

"Perhaps you were introduced at a fundraiser?"

"Leo, yes." He'd sat at their table at the last charity dinner. An average-looking man who had a way of raising his head and peering at people through his glasses as though he knew something disreputable about them. "He worked for Jason in the investment firm. He was head of a department."

"Finance."

"Yes, I met him. Why?"

"He called in sick on November 14 and hasn't been heard from since."

Marissa raised her eyebrows. "You don't seem to be having much luck keeping track of your suspects."

The detective had the grace to look embarrassed. "We're working on it. That's why I'm here. So about Markesan's disappearance..."

"The fourteenth," Marissa said slowly. "And the last time anyone saw Jason was when he dropped in to the center on the sixteenth to say he might be going out of town for a few days. Interesting."

"Mr. Kort gave no indication as to where he was going that day?"

"None."

He narrowed his eyes. "You were his girlfriend. Didn't that strike you as odd?"

"Not really. He was in a hurry and I was in the middle of checking some river samples. I assumed Jason would call me later to fill me in."

"So nothing about his behavior seemed unusual?"

Had it? There was that expression as he was leaving; she might even classify the look as one of regret, but it was hard to say if it was really there or she'd imagined it. "Like I said, he was in a hurry, distracted. He apologized for breaking our dinner date, said something came up and he might have to travel."

"That's it?"

"That's it."

Simonton stood and handed her a business card. "If you think of anything else…"

"I will call you." She jerked her head toward the living room. "My uncle in there? He needs a heart transplant. He invested most of his savings with Jason, as did I. I can't get another job because prospective employers think I was involved in this. Believe me, nobody wants Jason caught more than I do."

At first the detective said nothing, simply studied her face. She met his gaze without blinking. After a moment, he nodded. "Thank you for your time."

"You're welcome. I hope you find him. Soon."

Marissa stood on the porch and watched Simonton drive away. Becky squeezed her truck past him on the narrow drive, home from running errands. Marissa followed her to the garage to help unload the groceries.

"Who was in that car?" Her aunt handed her a canvas tote and a milk jug.

"A detective, looking for Jason."

"They came all the way up here to talk with you again? You told them everything you knew." Becky grabbed another grocery tote and a stack of mail.

Marissa followed her into the kitchen. "This guy asked a lot of questions about whether he'd contacted me. I guess they think I've been covering for him and are hoping I've changed my mind."

"How can they think that, after what he's done? He's a horrible man." Becky set some cans in the pantry and slammed the door. "I never trusted him."

Marissa looked up from unpacking her bag. "You didn't? Why not?"

"He was too ingratiating, talking with us, asking all those questions. People like him don't treat regular people that way unless they want something. Oliver assumed it was because he was smitten with you and wanted to make a good impression, but it was more than that."

"So why did you invest?"

"Oliver. He always thinks the best of people. Jason was your boyfriend and Oliver wanted to help him out any way he could. You know your uncle."

She did. Every kid in the area selling candy or magazines or raffle tickets knew Oliver was a soft touch. He may have been the only victim who was more interested in Jason's personal success than in the outstanding rate of return quoted. And this was how Jason had repaid him.

Marissa picked up the mail. An envelope

with a return address from a mortgage company lay on top. She held it up and caught Becky's eye. "You mortgaged the farm?"

Becky shrugged. "Medical bills."

For Becky's sake, Marissa bit back the word she'd been about to say and threw the mail on the table. After a moment, she turned back to her aunt. "I'm so sorry. It's all my fault."

"It's not. Oliver and I don't blame you."

"I do." Marissa grabbed her coat from the hook.

"Where are you going?"

"I don't know."

Becky rested her hands on her hips and studied Marissa. "Well, if you're feeling the need to break something, you could always saw some logs. I'd tell you to split wood, but I wouldn't trust you with a maul right now."

In spite of everything, Marissa laughed. "Good advice."

Becky wouldn't let her leave without a hug. "We love you. Don't ever forget that."

With everything going on in their lives, they were worried about her. Marissa blinked back a tear. "I love you, too."

Marissa took Becky's advice and went to work sawing birch limbs into usable lengths for the fireplace. As the pile grew, her anger cooled to the point where she could stop thinking about Jason and concentrate on where to go from here.

It all came down to money, something she'd never much worried about in the past. She wasn't into designer clothes or fancy cars. She'd selected jobs based on interest and opportunities, never on how much they paid. But thanks to Jason and his seemingly insatiable desire for money, her family was hurting. They might lose everything.

Marissa needed money. She had to pay off that mortgage and Oliver's medical bills. She needed money to get the farm spruced up enough to sell, so Becky and Oliver could retire. Bottom line: she needed a job. Soon.

CHAPTER NINE

Still four days till Christmas

CHRIS HELPED BECKY tote out equipment after another small party, while Marissa loaded up the reindeer. A clipboard lay on the seat of the car, with their monthly schedule on top. Chris checked for the next booking.

Friday evening was marked as a reindeer/ no Santa event. It wasn't on the list Becky had given him. He turned to her. "Does no Santa mean you need me out of costume or not at all?"

"You get the day off. Marissa and I can handle that one alone. It's a cabin wedding. The plan was for the couple to leave the wedding in a reindeer-drawn sleigh, but without the snow we'll have to use the cart instead. It's not as pretty, but we're dressing it up."

"I didn't realize you did weddings. I thought weddings were usually in the spring."

"I've always been partial to winter weddings. After all, Christmas is the most romantic time of the year." Becky smiled, plumping out her rosy cheeks. "Oliver and I were married at Christmastime, on the same date as this wedding, actually. The church was full of poinsettias. My bridesmaids wore red and I carried a bouquet of white lilies and red roses."

He could picture it, a young Becky, her skin smooth and dewy, her eyes lit up with excitement. Her hair would have been dark then, under her wedding veil. "I'm sure you were a beautiful bride. You'll have to show me a picture sometime. Which anniversary is this for you?"

"Our fortieth."

"That's wonderful, Becky. What are you doing to celebrate?"

"Oh, nothing much. We'll probably have a nice meal after the wedding."

"I see. Well, congratulations to both of you."

Chris rubbed his chin. He was no expert, but didn't people usually do more than have a nice meal for a fortieth anniversary? Like throwing a party or going on a cruise? Maybe they were keeping things low-key because of Oliver's health. But surely they deserved something special.

When Becky went inside, he sidled up to

Marissa. "Becky mentioned it's their fortieth anniversary this Saturday."

"I know. Isn't that great?"

"But she said she's working a wedding. Why aren't they having a party or small get-together?"

Marissa didn't meet his eyes. "I wish they could but…" She trailed off and fiddled with the latch on the trailer.

"But what? Is it Oliver's health?"

"Partly. And partly, well, there's a problem with money."

Medical bills, Chris assumed. But still. "And you didn't want to throw them a party yourself?"

"I, uh, don't have any money, either." She took a step away, but suddenly turned back and lifted her chin defiantly. "I lost all my money in a scam. Oliver invested, too. We're basically broke." Marissa didn't flinch, but Chris could tell it cost her to admit they were in trouble, even if her flushed face hadn't given her away.

"I'm sorry to hear that."

"So you see, we don't have the money for things like parties right now."

"What kind of scam?"

"Uh, a Ponzi scheme that involved the place where I worked."

Ponzi scheme... Research center. The news had been full of it for a while, until some political scandal knocked it off the front page. Chris hadn't paid much attention at the time. "You were involved in that whole mess they've been talking about? Where the guy and his girlfriend stole all that money from investors and that research foundation and then ran away to Cuba?"

"Yes. But no."

"What?"

"Yes, that was how we lost the money. No, he didn't run away with his girlfriend."

"And you know this because...?"

"Because I'm not in Cuba. I'm here, trying to pick up the pieces."

"You're the girlfriend?" How could the Marissa he knew ever have gotten involved with a low-life con man like that? She'd never been the type to be overly impressed with wealth or flash.

She tossed her head. "Not anymore, obviously. Anyway, the point is I can't afford to give Becky and Oliver a party or send them on a trip."

Chris was still trying to wrap his head around the idea that Marissa had been involved with a swindler, but he pushed that aside to concentrate on Oliver and Becky. "Is your uncle well enough to spend the night away from home?"

"I believe so. He travels to the doctor. You mean like a hotel?"

"Actually, I was thinking of a bed-and-breakfast inn. Do you remember Ursula?"

"Sam's auntie?"

"Uh, yeah. She's running an inn now, down on the Kenai Peninsula. Really pretty place. They could spend the weekend there."

"Hmm." She was clearly tempted. "How much would it cost?"

"It's on me. An anniversary present."

Marissa pressed her knuckle against her lip, the way she used to when he was trying to tempt her into deviating from her plans. "They'll insist on paying their own way. You know how proud they are."

He considered. "Then I think they'll have to win it. You can say you entered a sweepstakes for a winter wonderland weekend. Ursula will go along with it."

"If it's just a B and B, they'll need to go out for other meals. I'm not sure Oliver's up to that."

"I'll clear it with Ursula, but I'm sure she'll take care of all the meals. She's a great cook, and I don't think she's getting a lot of business this winter with no snow."

She hesitated. "I'd really like for them to do something special for their anniversary."

"I'll check it out with Ursula." Chris walked over to his truck to make the call, in case Becky returned. Five minutes later, he gave Marissa a thumbs-up. "It's all set. Ursula's excited about it. She's looking up some sort of ruby anniversary cake recipe as we speak. She's going to call your cell phone in a few minutes and announce that you're the winner."

"Just like that."

"Yep."

Marissa stepped closer to him. "I really appreciate this, Chris. I'll pay you back."

"No, you won't. Ursula's charging me her promotional rate, which is a bargain. I want to do this."

She looked up at him, smiling, and for a moment it felt like old times. He knew he'd probably regret it, but he couldn't resist bending down to kiss her. Just before their lips touched, her cell phone rang and she jumped back and checked the screen. "Forget-me-not Inn."

He sighed. "Ursula." The woman had horrible timing, but it was probably for the best.

Becky came outside. "All set." She noticed Marissa was on the phone. "Oh, sorry."

Marissa smiled at her and held up a finger. "Yes, she's right here." She handed over the phone. "For you."

"Who is it?" Becky pressed the cell to her ear. "Hello...?" Her eyes grew wide. "Yes... She did?" She continued to listen, occasionally interjecting a word or two until she ended the call and handed Marissa the phone. "I can't believe it."

"What?" Chris did his best impression of innocence.

Becky turned to him, a dazed expression on her face. "Marissa entered Oliver and me in a drawing for a romantic weekend at a B and B, and she won!"

"That's amazing."

"I know. The innkeeper sounds so nice. She says Marissa told her it was our fortieth anniversary Saturday, so we can go tomorrow and spend the weekend." Becky smiled. "She even asked about our favorite foods. Apparently, the romantic getaway package includes all meals. This is going to be so much fun. Wait until I tell Oliver." She opened the door to the truck, but stopped suddenly and turned to Marissa. "Oh, but the wedding is Saturday."

"I can handle it by myself."

"I don't know. Five reindeer and the cart to decorate and everything."

"I'll help." Chris stepped forward. "Marissa and I can do the wedding while you and Oliver celebrate your anniversary."

"Are you sure you don't have other plans? You weren't scheduled."

"I'm sure. Now go home and start packing. And have a wonderful anniversary."

Chris grinned as Becky climbed into the cab, chattering away to Marissa about running the farm while she was gone. The older woman, usually so down-to-earth, was all but fluttering. He only hoped Oliver would be as thrilled.

In the meantime, he'd better call Squid and the guys and let them know he wouldn't be making that poker game, because he had to help Marissa at a wedding. There was a certain irony in that.

THE WEDDING TURNED out to be much grander than Chris had anticipated. The cabin Becky mentioned was a three-story log home overlooking the frozen lake. Ice luminarias lined the front walkway, with twinkling white lights woven into the bare birch trees around the house. A caterer's truck was parked half in and half out of the driveway, blocking a florist who was trying to leave. Marissa stopped Oliver's truck in the road, waiting for the drivers to resolve their differences. Chris checked his mirror and saw another white van coming down the hill behind them.

"Why don't we head on down to the boat ramp and park in the lot there? We can walk the reindeer up, can't we?"

"How far is it?"

"Maybe a quarter mile? I don't remember exactly, but I think it's at the end of this road."

She took one last glance at the men standing in the driveway arguing. "I'll have to back up to go around." She started to reverse, but stopped almost immediately and cut her tires the other direction. "Ugh, I hate backing trailers. They always go the wrong way."

The driver of the van behind them had seen what Marissa was trying to do and had stopped farther up the road, waiting for them to get out of the way. Chris opened his door. "Why don't I park the trailer and you go inside and figure out where and when they want us?"

Marissa shot him a grateful look. "Thanks."

She slipped out of the truck and waved to the people in the driveway on the way to the cabin. Chris maneuvered the trailer around the caterer's vehicle and down the hill to the parking lot. By the time he had the truck and trailer parked, Marissa had walked there. "They want us up at the cabin when the guests start arriving, in about an hour. Can you help me unload the cart?"

They rolled it out of the trailer. The cart was a simple thing with two narrow seats and four medium-size spoke wheels. The front and sides flowed into a curving shape to resemble a sleigh on wheels instead of runners. Chris chocked the wheels to make sure the cart didn't roll into the lake. "I like this. It's an interesting design. Where did it come from?"

"Oliver made it years ago to drive in the Independence Day parade. He used a horse cart, but lowered it and added the enclosure. We never thought we'd be using it at Christmas."

"Good thing you had it. Why do you use wagons instead of this cart with the children?"

"This one takes five reindeer, but you have to know how to drive them. It's safer with the kids to have one reindeer per sled or wagon, and lead them. And the teenagers can do that."

"You know how to drive a team?"

"Of course I do. I grew up driving reindeer.

Just not backing trailers. Becky or Oliver always did that."

"Aha. Did Becky and Oliver make it to the inn yesterday?"

"They did. They called last night and said the place is beautiful and Ursula is treating them like royalty. There were two other couples there last night but nobody except them scheduled for today, and she's making prime rib, Oliver's favorite dinner. They're having a blast."

"I'm glad."

"That was a nice thing you did, arranging for them to celebrate at the inn. In fact, you've been doing all kinds of nice things lately. What's gotten into you?" Her tone was teasing, but she waited for an answer as if she was genuinely curious.

Hey, he was basically a good guy. He carried bags of dog food at the grocery store for seniors and donated to every fund-raiser he encountered. Why was Marissa so surprised he would help out her family? He shrugged. "No snow. Nothing better to do. So should we unload the reindeer now?"

"No, we need to decorate the cart first. We'll wait until closer to the wedding to harness up."

She pulled out some sort of soft velvety

blanket in deep red with gold fringe, which they draped over the sides of the cart like the caparison on a medieval warhorse. Marissa tied it with gold cord, and finished up with bunches of white netting formed into the shape of roses. She draped a white furry blanket on the backseat.

Chris stood back to examine the transformation. "This looks fantastic."

Marissa nodded. "Becky pulled a Scarlett O'Hara. She found some old curtains at a thrift shop and made them into this cover. It will fit the sleigh, too, so it's a good investment. Or at least it will be if they still have the farm next winter."

Building carts, sewing covers, training reindeer—Becky and Oliver were talented people. It was a shame they were getting older and couldn't maintain things the way they used to. He supposed they would eventually sell their property to someone younger, but odds were it would no longer be a reindeer farm.

Marissa must have been thinking the same thing. She unloaded the first reindeer and tied her halter to a ring on the trailer, and then paused to pat her neck. "I'll hate to see them go. Remember when Snowflake here was born?"

"I could never forget." Watching that baby reindeer come into the world was one of the most memorable events of his life. She'd emerged a sticky mess, but her mother went to work and soon she was clean and dry, covered with pale brown fuzz, all except for the white spot on her forehead. Marissa had instantly dubbed her Snowflake. It took her no time to wobble to her feet and find her mother's milk for her first meal.

Chris stroked the old girl's face. "Are Oliver and Becky definitely selling?"

"We haven't discussed it, but I think they'll have to. You've seen the farm. They can't keep up with it anymore."

Chris couldn't argue with that, so he unpacked a harness and helped Marissa fit it onto Snowflake's body, bells jingling as they worked. "I have trouble picturing Oliver and Becky living anywhere except the farm."

"Me, too. My parents and I visited them in their house in Anchorage a couple of times when I was little, but I hardly remember it. They seem to belong at the farm." Marissa disappeared into the trailer and brought out another reindeer. "But they'll adapt. They always rise to the occasion." She sighed as she tied the second reindeer to the trailer, but after a moment, she gave Chris a little smile.

"So, what do you do the rest of the year? Still fishing summers?"

Chris nodded. "Actually, I'm considering buying my own boat. I was in Seward a few days ago looking at one."

"Did you like it?" Marissa pulled a brush from her pocket and smoothed the reindeer's coat before letting Chris set the harness in place.

"A lot. It's a great boat, in good shape and well equipped. Comes with a permit, too."

"Are you going to buy it?"

"Not right now."

She flashed him a look he couldn't quite decipher. "Was the price too high?"

"I think it was fair."

"So, it's just what you want, in good condition, at a fair price, but you're not buying?"

"Not yet."

She shook her head and laughed. "Still won't make a commitment, huh?"

That stung. "There are good reasons to wait."

"There always are, and you'll always find them." She raised her chin. "You won't commit to a boat because it would tie you down. The same way you wouldn't commit to me."

"Hey, as I recall, I was the one who proposed."

"But as soon as I said yes, you started backpedaling."

"Not true."

She crossed her arms over her chest. "That's how I remember it."

"Well, the way I remember it, I was sticking to the commitment. You were the one who called it off, because I wasn't willing to have kids. I suppose I should have realized reproduction would be crucial to a wildlife biologist."

"That wasn't the only reason I called off our engagement."

"Oh, really? Then why?"

"You were different, withdrawn. You wanted out, I could tell."

"I didn't want out. Maybe I was nervous. I grew up in a house with a bad marriage. I've seen how miserable that can be. But for you, I was willing to take the risk. I loved you, Marissa. I wanted to marry you. I didn't realize you only wanted me for breeding stock."

She stared at him. "What did you say?"

"You heard me."

Without another word, she turned and disappeared into the trailer. After five minutes or so, she led another reindeer outside and handed Chris the lead rope without meeting his eyes. "Can you harness Peppermint while I get Starlight out? We need to get moving."

So Marissa had decreed the discussion over. Well, what did he expect, an apology? "Fine. Come on, Peppermint."

They got the reindeer hitched to the sleigh-cart. Marissa changed from her work jeans and down jacket into black pants under a long black coat with a little cape sewn to the collar, a black top hat and gloves, and a red muffler. She climbed into the cart and picked up the reins. "Coming?"

"Let me get the chocks from behind the wheels, and I'll be right there." He climbed in beside her. The narrow seats forced him to press his thigh against hers, but she showed no reaction as she flicked the reins and sent the reindeer and wagon up the hill.

Marissa was all business for the rest of the night, but once or twice he caught her looking at him with a shadow of pain in her eyes. Whether it was for herself, or him, or what might have been, he didn't ask.

The wedding itself went very well, and the reindeer behaved beautifully for all the people who wanted to pose with them and Marissa. Chris took dozens of pictures with guests' cell phones when they wandered in and out of the reception. Finally, it was time to transport the newly married couple up the hill.

They stepped from the house. The groom, already wearing an overcoat, draped a white fur cloak over the bride's shoulders and kissed her lightly before bustling her to the cart, while the assembled guests threw birdseed. Chris held Peppermint's halter as Marissa helped the couple into the cart, draped the blanket across their laps and climbed into the driver's seat. She nodded at him to let go, and flicked the reins.

By the light of the moon, Chris watched them pull away, the couple kissing in the backseat while Marissa sat up front and drove the five reindeer up the hill. A perfect scene, right out of a fairy tale. Chris never even met the couple, but he hoped they would have a long and happy marriage. Somebody's dreams should come true.

CHAPTER TEN

Three days till Christmas

MARISSA SHOVELED REINDEER manure onto the compost pile. Just for fun, she tried to count all the types of manure she'd dealt with in her years on the farm and as a wildlife biologist, either cleaning or tracking. She was up to forty-four when her phone signaled a new email.

She peeled off her glove and checked the screen. Her headhunter, asking her to call. Finally. It was odd for him to contact her on a Saturday, though. She went to the house to use the kitchen phone. "Hello, Derrick. It's Marissa."

"Hi. I have news."

"A job, I hope."

"Nothing permanent yet, but a marine research center in California needs someone to fill in for two weeks. I know it's not much, but it never hurts to have a potential employer owe you. They even hinted that they might have something long-term coming up soon, and if they like you, you'd be first in line. Besides, they're a prestigious organization, so if they're willing to take a chance on you, that could influence others."

"Sounds promising." Maybe this was it—the chance to repair her career after Jason wrecked it.

"And they're paying twice your former daily rate to get someone on so little notice."

Even better. "How soon do they need me?" Only three days and two parties until Christmas, and then she could go.

"Monday."

"The day after tomorrow?"

"Yes. You can't afford to pick and choose. I think you should take it."

Marissa pressed her knuckle to her lip. Everything he said was true. She couldn't afford to turn anyone down. They certainly needed the money. Becky, Chris and the elves could probably manage the last two parties without her if necessary.

But they shouldn't have to. She should be here with her family, doing her share. And as much as she tried to avoid thinking about it, it might be Oliver's last Christmas. She couldn't miss spending it with him.

"So, what do you say? They're willing to spring for a round-trip plane ticket."

"I can't. Not until after Christmas."

"They can't wait that long. They need someone to be on-site over the holiday."

"Then I'll have to decline. I'm sorry, but I can't leave my family before Christmas."

"Are you sure? If you turn this down, I can't guarantee anything else will open up."

"I'm sure."

He paused. "I wish I could say sleep on it, but I have to move on to the next person."

"I understand. Thank you for the offer, Derrick, but I'm needed here."

"All right. Merry Christmas."

"Merry Christmas to you. Goodbye."

She picked up her shovel, glared at it for a moment and then threw it like a javelin over the compost pile. It bounced off the frozen ground with a clang. Not fair. It was bad enough that Jason's treachery should cost her her savings and her family's security. It shouldn't cost her her career, too. She'd worked so hard in her field, sacrificed so much. Her hand went to her abdomen. She couldn't feel them through her puffy coat, but she knew they were there, the jagged round scar from the bison's horn and the neat vertical line from the surgeon's scalpel.

Chris's accusation rang in her ears. *"...you only wanted me for breeding stock."* Exactly the way she'd felt when Robert dumped her. How self-absorbed she must be, not to have seen the parallel before. She'd never been a big believer in karma, but her history did seem to tie up in a neat little bow.

Chris's refusal to discuss the possibility of children, to give any ground, had convinced her he wanted out, that this was the excuse he was looking for. He wouldn't be the one to call it quits, so he'd forced her into it. But maybe she was wrong. Maybe she'd truly hurt him when she'd called off the engagement.

She knew she had a tendency to be single-minded about achieving her goals. Maybe this fiasco with Jason was her punishment for being so focused on her own plans that she'd glossed over other people's needs and wants. She wanted kids, so she'd assumed Chris wanted kids. She wanted the River Foundation to thrive, so she'd assumed that was Jason's goal, also. Maybe if she'd paid more attention, she would have realized that he was on a different track. But if this was karma, how did Oliver and Becky get caught up in it? They'd done nothing but good their whole lives. Did karma allow for collateral damage?

Why was she even spending time thinking about this? She had a U-Haul–size load of regrets, but second-guessing all the decisions that brought her here wouldn't solve her current problems. She and Chris were over ten years ago. She needed to concentrate on now.

CHRIS LOOKED IN the mirror and straightened his fur-trimmed hat. This would be his last time in the red suit. A Christmas Eve open house at a private home. Instead of asking children what they wanted for Christmas, his job today was to hang around with Marissa and the reindeer and chat with the kids about how busy he'd be tonight. Meanwhile, Becky and the elves would be giving reindeer rides at another party across town.

It was also quite possibly his last time to see Marissa, and that bothered him. What's more, it bothered him that it bothered him. She exasperated him to no end, and yet he'd find himself arriving early for every party so he'd have more time to spend working alongside her. He stayed late to help load and laugh about some of the funny things the kids said. And in between parties, he missed her.

But why should that surprise him? He'd been missing her for the past ten years. He thought of her whenever he made a subtle joke and his date du jour would miss it entirely or giggle vaguely. Marissa always got his jokes and usually topped them. Every time he floated the Kenai, he'd remember those incredible eyes of hers, the same rich turquoise color as the river. Every time he saw the northern lights, he remembered the time they went night skiing. He'd held Marissa in his arms as they watched the green fire dance across the heavens. They'd even seen some flashes of red and violet in the sky that night.

None of that would change. She would go back to her work with wildlife somewhere far away. Maybe this time, she'd find a good man and have those kids she wanted so much before her biological clock ran out. Meanwhile, Chris would lie in his bunk at night on his new fishing boat and try not to wonder about what might have been.

It was better this way. He could hold on to the perfect days they'd had together, without having to face the reality that a marriage between them never stood a chance. They were too different, and neither of them was willing to bend. If they had married, those sterling memories would be tarnished with bitter resentments and failures.

He straightened his shoulders. Today was Christmas Eve, and he was Santa Claus. Time to jolly up.

"Chris, your ride is here," Dana called down the stairs.

"Be right there." He tucked his cell phone and wallet into his red jacket.

His sister was already outside, standing beside the open driver's window and talking with Marissa. Or to be more accurate, interrogating her. "How old were you when you moved to Alaska?"

"Nine."

"So you grew up on the reindeer farm. That must have been amazing. Do your aunt and uncle have all kinds of stories?"

"Oh, yes, Oliver loves to tell stories. They actually went to Norway to choose the reindeer and arranged to import them."

"Is the farm open to visitors?"

"In the summer. Tourists are their main source of revenue."

"I'll have to go visit this summer. I imagine after the busy Christmas season you've had, you'll be glad for a little break. Would you like to go out for coffee sometime after Christmas?"

"I don't know how much longer I'll be here—"

Chris slid into the passenger seat, slammed the stubborn door shut and waved to his sister. "We have to go. Bye, Dana."

"Bye. Marissa. Chris has my number. Give me a call if you want to get together sometime."

"I will. Thanks. Nice to meet you, Dana." Marissa smiled and rolled up the window. She waited until they were going over the speed bump halfway down the block to comment. "So, that's your sister."

"Yep."

"You don't look much alike."

"No. She looks like her mother."

"She seems…friendly."

"It's okay. You can say pushy." Chris laughed. "Actually, she's usually pretty mellow, but she's been wanting to meet you ever since I went to work for you."

"Why?"

Chris shrugged. "I think she's curious about our history."

"What did you tell her?"

"I didn't tell her anything. Sam probably filled her in."

"In that case, I'm surprised she wasn't throwing rocks at me."

"Why would you say that? Sam always liked you."

"I saw him once not long after we broke up. Let's just say he was not happy with me."

"That was a long time ago. Sam's mellowed, too. Especially since Dana showed up."

Marissa shook her head. "It's so weird to think Sam is married. To your sister. Who I didn't know existed."

"If it makes you feel any better, Sam didn't know either until this past summer. They got married in September."

"Love at first sight?"

"It must have been pretty close. I was out fishing so I didn't see it all happen, but it didn't take them long. I wasn't thrilled with the idea initially, but I came around. I guess some people just know when it's right." Like the way he felt the first day he met Marissa. It just felt right. But that was before it all went wrong. So maybe he didn't know what he was talking about. Time to change the subject. "Where exactly is this party?"

"In Stuckagain Heights. Do you mind driving once we reach the foothills? I'm not terribly confident of my trailering skills on winding roads, even without snow."

"No problem." Ten years of working with plows and other snow equipment meant Chris was used to driving most anything, in all kinds of weather.

Once they arrived, Marissa sent him to check in with the party hosts. He made his way past several bird feeders to the front door of the three-story log home. Chickadees and nuthatches ignored him as they bickered over sunflower seeds. In the two-story glass entryway, a tree at least twelve feet high glowed with thousands of tiny lights. Birdhouses, nests and imitation birds of all shapes and sizes decorated the tree.

He pushed the bell, but instead of a ringing sound, he heard the honk of a Canada goose. The hostess answered the door, wearing a Christmas sweater featuring a raven with a red bow tied around its neck. She looked a little like a bird herself, with a cap of glossy black hair and bright eyes. "Merry Christmas, Santa. I gather the reindeer are here."

He gestured toward the yard, where Marissa was unloading the two animals. "Yes, ma'am. Do you have any special instructions for us?"

"Just keep the kids entertained. They should be arriving soon. And try not to let the reindeer tear up the bird feeders. We're always having trouble with moose. I wouldn't mind so much if they just ate the seed, but no, they have to pull the feeders down and stomp on them."

"We'll keep them far enough away. Merry Christmas."

By the time he returned, three girls and a boy had gathered. Marissa handed him Peppermint's lead rope and led Dazzle a few steps away. The trio of girls tagged after her. The boy hanging around Chris seemed to be more interested in petting the reindeer than talking, so Chris was able to eavesdrop on Marissa's conversation.

"Are you really an elf?" The smallest girl gazed up at her with wide eyes.

"Of course I am. You have to have the right qualifications to get onto Santa's team."

Another girl stroked Dazzle's head. "What do elves do in the summer?"

"We usually take a vacation, and work on our studies."

"You study?"

"Oh, yes. Elves have a lot to keep up with. I have an advanced degree in reindeerology from NPU."

The third girl tugged at Marissa's dress. "What's NPU?"

"North Pole University. That's where all the elves study. We have toy designers and sleighamotive engineers and behavioral specialists." She turned to the smallest girl, who was hanging back now, watching the others. "What do you want to be when you grow up?"

"I want to drive airplanes."

"Fantastic. A friend of mine does that."

"For Santa Claus?"

Marissa grinned. "No, she used to work for Santa but now she flies an air taxi out of Ketchikan…" Marissa and the girls drifted farther away so he could no longer hear them.

More kids arrived, and Chris was kept busy for the duration of the party. Mostly, he chatted with the children about their Christmas plans and made sure they didn't crowd too close to the reindeer. The big animals behaved well, but Chris did have to convince one boy to stop eating seed from the bird feeders and go inside for refreshments instead. Fortunately, as Santa Claus, his suggestion carried clout and the boy obeyed without argument.

At the end of their scheduled time, the home owner came outside and gestured to Marissa, who handed Peppermint's lead rope to Chris and followed her indoors. A gaggle of kids still hung around, petting the reindeer and peppering Chris with questions.

"Why don't these reindeer fly?"

"They haven't had their special flying food yet. Flying takes a lot of energy, so I don't give them the food until we have the sleigh all loaded and ready to go."

"How can you go to every house in one

night?" The boy who asked was maybe three or four years older than Ryan. He'd obviously been drilled not to spoil it for the younger kids, but he couldn't resist poking holes in the theory.

Chris winked at him. "It all has to do with the space-time continuum. There's some high-level science involved. Honestly, I don't understand it all, but an elf of mine is a theoretical physicist, and she's got it worked out."

One of the girls piped up. "That elf lady that was holding the reindeer?"

"No, Elf Marissa is an animal specialist. She knows how to keep the reindeer happy and healthy."

"I thought elves made toys."

"Yes, some of them do, but there's a lot more than just toy-making going on at Santa's workshop."

Marissa came out and gave him the nod. Chris waved in acknowledgment. "Well, kids, we have to go now. It's time to get these two home to the North Pole so we can head out tonight."

"Bye, Santa. I'll leave you a cookie."

"Thank you. I love cookies. Merry Christmas, everyone. Ho, ho, ho."

He followed Marissa into the back of the trailer, where they secured the reindeer. Chris shut the gate and waved a final goodbye to the kids. "You want me to drive down?"

"I'd appreciate it." Marissa climbed into the passenger seat.

Chris checked his mirrors to make sure all the kids were accounted for, and pulled out of the driveway. Marissa waved until they were out of sight.

"So, I guess that's it for this year." He shifted into a lower gear and the truck rumbled down the road.

"I guess so. The family was pleased. Gave us a big tip."

"Good. Any news about Oliver's transplant?"

"Nothing yet." She sounded discouraged. Chris wished he knew what to say to cheer her up, but other than offering his heart to Oliver, he couldn't think of anything.

He weaved his way down the steep road. As the sun set, twinkling Christmas lights appeared out of the gloom. The yard display in front of one of the houses lit up, almost blinding him with the sudden brilliance of a thousand colored lights. No vehicles were behind him, so he pulled over to gaze at the spectacle. Chaser lights traced every roofline, door and window of the house. More lights covered the roof of a life-size manger scene including a sheep, a cow and a camel. Snowmen, reindeer and a couple vaguely familiar cartoon characters joined the shepherds and wise men gathering around the holy family. An angel dangled from wire stretching between two trees. The whole thing was illuminated by green floodlights that changed to purple as they watched.

"This is..." Marissa shook her head.

"Bizarre? Tacky? A massive waste of electricity?"

A grin spread across her face. "Glorious. I love the way they've embraced the whole Christmas theme and tied it together in an explosion of joy. I wish Ryan were here to see it."

Chris laughed. "He'd love it."

She stole a glance at him. "Is he still moving to a different home after Christmas?"

"As far as I know, although not until just before school starts in January." Chris put the truck into gear and resumed their journey down the hill.

"You can bring him back to the farm again before he goes, if you want."

Chris glanced over at her. "He'd like that. Thanks."

"Becky did invite him."

"She did." He turned down his street and

parked the truck and trailer in the cul-de-sac in front of his house. "Will you be there, or do you have a job lined up?"

"Nothing yet, but I'm hopeful."

He turned toward her. "Well, good luck. I hope everything goes well for you."

"Thanks. For everything. I hope you get that boat you want."

"I will, eventually." He reached for the door handle.

"Chris?"

He turned back. "What?"

Marissa scooted across the seat and kissed his cheek just above the white beard. "Merry Christmas."

He watched her drive away. Once she was gone, he headed over to check the mail, but before he reached the box, he noticed Ryan under one of the streetlights, making his way up the block to play with Kimmik. Chris almost called a greeting before he realized he was still in costume.

Ryan looked up and his mouth dropped open. Chris waved and trotted down one of the trails that led into the forest and out of sight. He made his way along the trail that ran parallel to the neighborhood until he was able to pop out of the woods several blocks away.

Fortunately, friends of his lived in one of

the condos there. Chris rang the bell. Rob opened the door, a puzzled frown on his face. "I think you've got the wrong address."

"Rob, it's me, Chris."

Rob did a double take. Once he recognized Chris, he roared with laughter. "What are you doing in that getup?"

"Long story. Can I come in?"

"Sure. Angie?" Rob called into the kitchen. "Chris is here. You've got to see this."

Rob's wife hurried through the doorway. "Chris, is that you? You wouldn't even dress up for our Halloween party. Since when did you get this into Christmas?"

"I was filling in for a friend. Say, I know this sounds weird, but I need to use your shower and borrow some clothes."

"Oh, no. That doesn't sound weird at all." Rob turned to Angie with a smirk. "Santa Claus wants to use our shower."

"Okay, but what's wrong with your shower?"

"Nothing, except I can't get to it." He held up his hands. "Okay, here's the story. There's this kid on our street. He saw me dressed as Santa Claus, and I didn't want him to get close enough to know it was me, so I ducked into the woods. I need to wash this dye out of my beard and change my clothes before I go back out again."

"So you're doing all this so the kid won't realize you're not really Santa Claus."

"Exactly."

Angie snorted. "You know he probably doesn't believe in Santa anyway. Kids talk to each other."

"Maybe so, but just in case, I don't want to be the one to spoil it for him."

"Okay, you can shower here, but only if I get to take your picture first for blackmail purposes." Rob chuckled as he pulled out his phone and snapped a photo. He led Chris up the stairs through the bedroom and opened the door to the bathroom. "So what's your angle? Does the kid have a hot single mom or something?"

"No. He's just got a lot going on in his life right now and I don't want to make it worse." Chris pulled off his hat and wig.

"Right." Rob clearly didn't believe him, but handed him a towel and some sweats. "Here you go, Santa. I'll get a garbage bag for your suit. Have a nice shower."

Chris washed the dye from his beard and eyebrows and stepped from the shower. He dressed and stuffed his costume into the bag before borrowing Angie's blow-dryer to complete the transformation back to himself. Rob loaned him an old ski jacket. After thanking his friends again and enduring a few more good-natured insults, he wished them a Merry Christmas and hiked back the way he had come.

Ryan was in the yard, throwing sticks for Kimmik. Chris emerged from the woods and waved. Ryan ran to him. "Guess what? I saw Santa Claus."

"At the mall?"

"No. Here. In front of your house."

"What was he doing here?"

"I don't know. He went into the woods where you were. Did you see him?"

"Nope. He must have taken a different trail."

"Do you think it was the real Santa?"

"I don't know. I didn't see him. Did he look real?"

"Yeah." Ryan nodded slowly. "Maybe he was checking out the neighborhood to see where the kids were so he could leave presents."

Chris nodded in turn. "I'll bet that's exactly what he was doing. Tomorrow, if you're not too busy, you'll have to show me what he brought you."

"You think he'll bring me stuff?"

"You wrote a letter, right? And you've been good. Sandy told me you've been doing your chores and got all A's and B's on your report card."

"But how will he know I'm here instead of at my granny's house?"

Chris laid his hand on Ryan's shoulder. "Don't you worry. Santa knows about things like that."

"You're sure?"

"I'm absolutely sure."

CHAPTER ELEVEN

Christmas Day

THE SCENT OF BAKING crept into Chris's dreams. He woke, delighted to discover the aromas of coffee and cinnamon were real. Ursula's famous cinnamon rolls, no doubt. He was lucky he wasn't drooling on his pillow. Ursula had driven up from her B and B to spend Christmas with them. She and Dana were in full yuletide mode, towing Chris and Sam along in their wake.

Chris had to admit that Christmas Eve was a lot of fun with Dana in charge. Singing carols, going to midnight mass, even wearing the ridiculous red-and-green-striped sweater Dana insisted he unwrap early. He climbed out of bed, pulled on some jeans and the Christmas sweater, and made his way upstairs. Ursula stood at the kitchen island, frosting the rolls. Sam sprawled in a chair in the living room with Dana curled like a kitten in his lap and Kimmik lying at his feet.

Lights flickered on the Christmas tree and carols played in the background.

All they needed to complete the scene was snow. Chris glanced past the holly wreath hanging in the window to brown grass and bare pavement beneath the streetlight, but he noticed a lack of stars in the sky. Snow clouds, maybe?

"Merry Christmas. Coffee's made." Ursula smiled at him.

"Merry Christmas, Auntie." Chris kissed her cheek and dipped his finger in the frosting bowl. She swatted his hand. Ursula had been taking care of Sam since his mother left when he was twelve, and once he and Sam became friends, she'd taken Chris under her wing, as well.

He poured a cup of coffee after licking the cream cheese frosting from his finger. "Yum. Are those almost ready?"

"Earn your keep." She used a spatula to transfer two rolls to red plates. "Take these to Sam and Dana first, and then you can have one."

He delivered the rolls, managing to draw Sam and Dana's attention away from each other long enough to exchange Christmas greetings, and returned to sit at the island.

Ursula plunked a plate with a huge roll in

front of him. "I like your reindeer farmers. It's nice to see such a sweet couple celebrate their anniversary."

"I know. Oliver and Becky are good people."

"They have quite a story. Did you know they spent their honeymoon on the Alcan Highway?"

"No, I never heard that."

"They were engaged, living in Colorado, and wanted to see Alaska, so they both applied for summer jobs at a hotel in Denali. Becky got a job as cook, but they turned Oliver down, so Becky declined. They scheduled their wedding, and then the day before they were to say I do, the hotel offered them both summer work. So right after the reception, they piled into an old camper and drove up. At the end of the summer, they decided they didn't want to leave."

"And they never did," Chris murmured thoughtfully. "Thanks for hosting them. They're going through some stuff right now, so I'm glad they were able to get away for the weekend and celebrate their anniversary."

"He doesn't look well."

"He isn't. He needs a heart transplant, and they've gone through an unrelated financial setback, but Marissa says they had a great time at your place."

"This is the Marissa you almost married, right?"

"Um-hmm."

"Are you back together?"

"Definitely not."

She eyed him skeptically. "Then why are you buying her relatives anniversary get-aways?"

Chris shrugged. "As I said, they're having a hard time. And they're good people. It has nothing to do with Marissa."

Ursula didn't look as if she believed him, but she patted his arm. "Well, it was a nice thing to do."

After breakfast, they gathered around the tree and unwrapped their gifts. Chris chuckled to himself, picturing how excited Ryan must have been when he found that Santa left him presents. There was one from Chris under his tree, too, delivered to Sandy last week while Ryan was in school.

When all the presents had been opened, Sam pulled one from behind his chair. "Oops, one more for Ursula." He and Dana watched her intently as she unwrapped the box and opened the lid.

It looked like a photo album, but when Ursula turned it over, Grandma's Brag Book was printed on the front. She squealed. "Is this what I think it is?"

Sam laughed and reached for Dana's hand. "That's right. The baby's due in late June."

"Oh, my goodness, that's wonderful." Ursula jumped up to give Dana a hug.

Chris grinned. His little sister was having a baby. He hurried over to join in the congratulations. "That's great news."

Sam pounded him on the shoulder. "We're counting on lots of diaper changes from Uncle Chris."

Uncle Chris. He liked it. "I was thinking more along the lines of buying footballs. Or is it a girl?"

"We don't know. We want to be surprised." Dana's face glowed with happiness. "Besides, girls like footballs, too."

Chris hugged his little sister. Dana was going to be a great mother. She was already a great wife, as Sam attested at every opportunity. How she'd learned these skills was anyone's guess, but she had. Maybe it was instinctive, something built into her character that made her know how to take care of everyone.

Chris always felt he'd made the ethical choice when he decided never to have kids, even if it did cost him Marissa. All he'd learned from his own father was what not to do. Bungee parenting—long periods ignoring your children, only to drop in periodically to disrupt their lives. Bragging about your son's accomplishments to others, while never praising him directly. The hypocrisy of demanding total honesty while living a lie. Treating the mother of your children like an employee. Not a good foundation for a happy family.

And Dana had had it even worse. She'd spent most of her life struggling to please a father who barely remembered she existed. If Dana could overcome their upbringing, maybe he could have, too.

Dana pulled out her phone, and Ursula gushed over ultrasound pictures. Ursula looked at Sam. "Does your mother know?"

Sam nodded. "I told her yesterday when we talked on the phone."

"How's she doing?"

"She says rehab's going well. She likes the doctors there, and she's excited about becoming a grandmother."

"Getting to spend time with her grandchild will be a great motivation for her."

"I hope so." Sam hugged Dana from behind and rested his hands on her belly. "I feel like she might actually be able to stop drinking for good this time."

Look at that. Sam, after so many years of focusing solely on his career, was happily married, expecting a baby and was actually optimistic about the mother who'd deserted him when he was only a boy. It really was the season of miracles.

After a lunch of turkey and all the trimmings, Dana brought out something she called a Yule log for dessert. Chris eyed it doubtfully. It did look like a fallen log, with deeply grooved dark brown bark and even mushrooms growing out of it. However, when she cut into it, it turned out to be a rolled-up chocolate cake with raspberry filling and dark chocolate coating. The mushrooms were made of something sweet, almost like cotton candy.

"Impressive. How did you learn to do this?"

"I have my secrets." Dana laughed. "And the internet is a wonderful thing."

Sam volunteered himself and Chris to do the cleanup, which was only fair, considering the amazing meal Dana and Ursula had prepared. By the time they'd loaded the dishwasher and washed about a thousand pans, Chris was ready to relax in front of the fire and let his turkey digest.

He must have dozed off, because he woke to the sound of his name. "Is Chris here?"

At Dana's invitation, Ryan galloped up the stairs, his arms full. "Chris, you were right. Santa did come. Look."

Chris climbed out of his recliner and hurried over to admire Ryan's treasures. "Show me."

"See, I got this coat, and a dinosaur chaser car, and this archaeopteryx and two more dinosaurs, and paints. And socks and clothes and stuff. And these books. Sandy says they're from you and I'm supposed to tell you thank you. See, this one's about brachiosaurs, and this one is triceratops, and they're all about different dinosaurs. Can we read them?"

Chris grinned at his enthusiasm. "Sure. Let's sit on the couch." Sounded like the clerk at the bookstore had steered him right. She'd assured him her sons loved this series.

Ryan plunked down beside him, opened the first book and started reading aloud. Chris wasn't sure how well a seven-year-old was supposed to be able to read, but he was amazed at the few words Ryan needed help with. In fact, when it was Chris's turn to read, Ryan corrected him on the pronunciation of one of the dinosaurs.

They read three of the books before Ryan grew tired of sitting and took Kimmik outside to play with his new training dummy. Afterward, Dana and Ursula plied him with cookies and milk, and Sam admired his plastic dinosaur. Still nibbling on a cookie, Ryan finally wandered back over to the recliner. "Chris?" He seemed hesitant.

"What's on your mind, my man?"

"You know Oliver, out at the farm?" His voice was almost a whisper.

"Uh-huh."

"And how he kinda looks like Santa Claus?"

"Yeah."

"Well, I was thinking. Maybe that's how he knew where to find me. Maybe he really is Santa Claus."

"Could be."

"I painted him a picture this morning. To tell him thank you."

"That's cool. Are you going to mail it to him?"

"I wondered if you could take me to see him so I could give it to him. They said I could come back."

"Sure. Maybe one day this week."

Ryan dragged his toe across the carpet. "Can we go today?"

"Today? I don't know, Ryan. Today's

Christmas. Don't you need to get back to Sandy and Brent's house?"

"We already had dinner and April's asleep."

Chris leaned closer. "Oliver might be pretty tired, you know, Christmas Eve and all. He could be sleeping."

"Oh." Ryan nodded. "I didn't think about that." He looked so deflated Chris couldn't let him down.

"I'll tell you what. I'll give them a call, see if they're up for company. If they say it's okay, and Sandy says it's okay, I'll take you to the farm."

"Yay!"

WEARING HIS NEW red flannel shirt, Oliver lay back in his recliner. A broad smile split his face.

Marissa smiled back. "You look content."

"How could I not be? Celebrating my favorite day with my two favorite girls." He reached out to take Becky's hand with his left and Marissa's with his right.

Marissa squeezed his hand. It may have been her imagination, but he seemed to have a little more color in his cheeks today. It was a good day, a better Christmas than she'd experienced in a long time. Why hadn't she been coming home for Christmas? What was so important that kept her away? Sure, airfares were high, and she was busy, but so what? It was Christmas.

She would spend Christmas with them next year. No matter where she was or how little vacation she'd accrued, she was coming home for Christmas. Even if they sold the farm and moved to town in the meantime. She just prayed Oliver would still be here. It was impossible to imagine Becky without Oliver by her side.

Becky gazed toward the spruce Ryan and Chris had cut. "Do you remember that Christmas when you asked for a snare drum?"

"Pa rum pum pum pum." Marissa laughed. "I remember. I'll bet you and Oliver were about ready to throw me and the little drummer boy out in the snow before the day was over."

"We didn't mind," Oliver said. "You were having a good time. Christmas is all about seeing joy on a child's face. That's why we started the business, you know."

"I know." They loved children. Why such a loving couple never had any of their own, when there were so many bad parents out there, boggled her mind. But she was forever thankful they were there to raise her.

The phone rang. Becky jumped up. "Now

who could that be?" She disappeared into the kitchen, only to return a few minutes later grinning happily. "Guess what? Chris is bringing Ryan out to see us this afternoon. Apparently, Ryan has decided you just might be the real Santa Claus hiding out, and he has something to give you."

"Well, isn't that nice." Oliver beamed.

Marissa fidgeted with the cuff of her sweater. Chris inviting himself over on Christmas? She hoped he hadn't misconstrued that kiss on the cheek yesterday. It was supposed to be a thank-you for all he'd done to help out over the holidays, not any sort of signal that she wanted to start up with him again.

She almost said something, but looking at Oliver's happy face, she decided to hold her tongue. Besides, she'd said Chris could bring Ryan out again. Maybe this was exactly what he said it was, a chance for Ryan to see Oliver. There was no reason to believe Chris was using Ryan as an excuse to spend Christmas with her. Perversely, she felt a little let down at the thought.

Half an hour later, Marissa heard the truck drive up. She stepped out on the porch. Ryan jumped from the vehicle and flew up the steps. "Hi, Marissa. Is Oliver here?" He had a piece of paper clutched in one hand and a toy dinosaur in the other.

"Yes, he's inside." Marissa couldn't help but laugh as he tore into the house. She turned to Chris, who followed at a more conventional speed. "He's excited."

"I know. He was afraid Santa wouldn't be able to find him, but he did." He came closer and dropped his voice. "He's on the fence about whether he believes in Santa or not, but he wants to believe in something. That's part of the reason he loves the farm so much."

Marissa looked around, this time noticing the beauty of the sun shining through the groves of spruce and the elegance of the reindeer milling around their pen. Chickadees chirped and fluttered among the bare branches of the lilac bush beside the porch. In June, that bush would explode with fragrant purple plumes. The crabapple tree would bloom, too, and by the end of summer yield an abundance of golf ball–size apples for jelly, cider and reindeer treats. New calves would be born. It was winter now, but spring would come again to the farm. "It is a special place."

"It is."

Chris followed Marissa into the house, where Ryan was already ensconced between

Becky and Oliver, pointing out the parts of the picture he'd painted for them. "And here's the books Chris got for me, and the Legos, and this is the rabbit I gave April. It squeaks when you squeeze it, and she laughs."

"I'll bet she likes it best when you do it," Marissa said.

"Yeah." Ryan grinned. "She's funny."

"This is a wonderful picture, Ryan." Becky pointed at a square in the corner of the picture. "Who's this?"

"Santa Claus is outside, watching through the window. He was there yesterday."

"When he delivered the presents last night?"

"No, yesterday. I saw him, by Chris's house."

"You did?" Marissa's eyes crinkled as she looked at Chris. The corners of his mouth twitched, but he managed to hold in his laughter.

Ryan looked up at Oliver. "Where were you yesterday?"

"Me?" Oliver gave a sly smile. "Oh, you know. Here and there."

"Oh." Ryan nodded solemnly, as if he were agreeing to a pact.

"So, Ryan..." Marissa stood. "I need to

give all the animals their Christmas treats. Want to help?"

"Yeah!" He jumped up, but turned to Oliver. "I'll be back later."

"I'll be waiting for you."

Marissa gathered a bag of carrots, crab-apples and lettuce, while Becky made sure Ryan was properly bundled up in his coat, gloves and hat. This time, Chris tagged along, and Ryan proudly introduced him to each of the animals by name. Chris let Ryan instruct him on how to hold his hand to feed the goats. "Heidi likes apples best, but Rosa like carrots." Willa bulled her way forward between the goats and Ryan laughed. "Willa likes everything."

Chris grinned. "Well, she is a pig."

Next, Marissa let Ryan take the rabbits out of their hutches so they could run around the floor and eat the carrots and lettuce he'd brought them. Marissa stroked a big black-and-white-spotted rabbit. "Did you know some people think at midnight on Christmas Eve, animals can talk?"

Ryan looked up from the lop-eared bunny he was feeding. "Can they really?"

She smiled. "I've never heard them, but then, I've always been asleep at midnight on

Christmas Eve. What do you think the rabbits would say if they could talk?"

Ryan grinned at the bunny in his lap. "More lettuce, please."

In the chicken coop, Marissa tied bundles of lettuce leaves onto strings and hung them from hooks above the chickens' heads. The hens gathered under the lettuce piñatas, reaching up to peck at the bundles and send them swinging. Ryan giggled at their antics, but after a moment, he became concerned. "Sadie isn't getting any."

The little black bantam kept trying to reach, but before she could jump up and grab a bite, another hen would peck the bundle and send it in another direction.

"You're right. Here." Marissa handed him a lettuce leaf. "Why don't you give her some?"

Ryan crept closer and offered the leaf to Sadie. She grabbed a bite. One of the other hens ran over to share, but Ryan moved between her and Sadie so that Sadie could eat in peace. Marissa smiled. It was sweet the way he looked out for all the animals, making sure nobody missed out.

Chris rested a hand on her back and spoke in a low voice. "Thanks for doing this."

"I don't mind. He's a great kid."

"I know." Chris watched Ryan gently stroking Sadie's feathers. "After the start of the year, he'll be moving to a different foster home, and I'll probably never see him again."

Chris sounded so forlorn she turned to look at him. "That bothers you, doesn't it?"

Chris nodded. "I don't know what it is about him, but he's gotten under my skin."

"I know what you mean." Ryan looked up and she flashed him a smile. "Hey, are you ready to go give the reindeer their apples and carrots?"

"Okay." Ryan hopscotched toward them. "I'll bet they're real hungry after last night."

The boy made sure each of the reindeer got a special treat. By the time they left, the breeze had picked up. They closed the gate and started toward the house.

At a sudden gust, Marissa held up her hand to shield her face from what she thought were bits of hay blowing toward her, until she realized what those dancing white specks actually were.

Chris stopped in place, a big grin spreading across his face. "It's snowing."

CHAPTER TWELVE

SNOW—FINALLY. IT had been there in the forecast all along, but Chris hadn't believed it
until he saw it with his own eyes. It was really coming down now, huge flakes swirling
as though someone had broken open a thousand down pillows. After dropping Ryan off,
Chris went straight to his office and called
Brad and Kenny in to work. Tomorrow, when
the stores opened, their parking lots needed
to be clear.

Brad arrived within fifteen minutes of
Chris's call. "Looks like we're back in business." He rubbed his hands together.

"Looks like. Sorry to call you in on Christmas."

"No problem. We already opened presents
and ate turkey, and the kids are so into their
new video games they hardly looked up when
I left. Is Kenny coming?"

"I'm here." Kenny let the door slam behind
him. "I call dibs on the new Ford."

Chris laughed. "Fine, but that means you

get the biggest lots. According to the forecast, it may snow all night, so we'll probably have to do them all twice. I'm sorry, you guys. I know we need more people, but I couldn't afford to keep everybody on."

"My brother-in-law might be able to help out," Brad said. "The one with the Christmas light business. He'll work hourly."

"Has he ever driven a spreader?"

"I doubt it, but he drives a school bus."

"Good enough. Give him a call, see if he's available for tomorrow morning. We'll put down sand, starting about six."

Chris divided up the assignments, giving Brad South Anchorage and Kenny midtown. He took the east side, which had some of the trickiest lots. The snow kept coming down. As Chris reached the far end of a lot, snow was blanketing the area he'd already cleared. He and the team worked steadily through the night.

About four, the snow stopped, or at least paused. Almost a foot had fallen, a huge dump for Anchorage. Chris worked his way gingerly around an island that bisected the parking lot in front of one of his first commercial customers, a plant nursery. In the summer, the raised bed displayed a wild profusion of flowers, but it tended to hide under a heavy snow, and discovering it accidently wasn't good for the planter or the plow, which was why he liked to handle this lot himself.

At five thirty, he followed the city plows back to the warehouse to meet Brad's brother-in-law and get him set up with one of the sand and gravel spreaders. Chris had just gotten him out the door and was about to climb into the other spreader when his phone rang. Marissa.

"Good morning."

"Chris. Thank God I reached you. It's Oliver. They have a transplant available for him, in Seattle."

"That's great."

"Yeah, except we're snowed in. It's drifted up to four feet out here, and I can't get the truck through."

"I'm on my way. What flight is he on?"

"They're letting him piggyback on a corporate jet. They're holding it for him, but he needs to get there as soon as possible."

"Understood. I'm coming." Chris abandoned the spreader and hopped back into the plow truck. He took a few precious minutes to gas up and check in with his team before heading down the Glenn Highway.

The road was clear for the first few miles, but on the far side of Eagle River, he caught up with the plow and was forced to follow behind it for several more miles until he reached the turnoff and virgin snow. He called Marissa to let her know he was starting. The slow pace of plowing usually didn't bother him, but with Oliver's life hanging in the balance, it seemed to take forever to make his way down the long road. Thirty minutes in, he tried to call Marissa to update her on his progress, but he was too far from the highway to pick up a signal.

Finally, he spotted the top of the reindeer farm sign above the snow. He was almost to the drive. Another twenty minutes to clear it and he should be at the house. He looked to the left and laughed out loud. There, against the snow, he could clearly make out the shape of four reindeer pulling the sleigh. Smart girl.

He reached the entrance to the drive and focused on clearing enough space to turn the truck around while the reindeer closed the gap between them. Marissa brought the sleigh to a halt at the end of the lane. Chris pushed through the snow to take Oliver's arm around his shoulder, then half carried him to the truck, with Becky close behind.

Marissa grabbed a couple suitcases from the sleigh and slung them behind the seat. She hugged Oliver and Becky and helped them into the truck. She rubbed a mittened hand across her eyes and turned to Chris. "Thank you. I can't tell you how much—"

"Tell me later. I've got an important delivery to make."

She threw her arms around his neck, gave him a tight squeeze and let him go. "You're right. Get out of here."

Chris glanced over at Oliver as he drove. The older man was panting a little, but his reindeer adventure didn't seem to have done him any harm. Due to road conditions, they had to go slower than usual, but at least the roads were plowed. On the highway, they saw several cars and SUVs in the ditch.

Oliver shook his head. "You see it every year after the first snow. It's like people forget that snow is slippery."

"They may not have gotten around to putting their snow tires on," Chris said. The big tires of his plow truck hummed on the pavement.

"We really appreciate this, Chris," Becky said. "I know you must be busy, with all this snow."

"We got it done. My guys are sanding the lots right now. Don't worry, everyone will be able to get to the stores and exchange their Christmas gifts without any problem."

"Did you get any sleep last night?"

"Not yet, but once I drop you off I'll grab a few hours. I'll be fine."

Becky looked out the window at the all-white landscape. The sun wouldn't be up for hours, but now that they'd reached Anchorage, the streetlights bounced off the snow and illuminated the whole area. "Poor kids. The perfect snow day, and there was no school to miss."

Chris laughed. "Here's hoping they'll get lots of chances for snow days between now and breakup."

"More in the forecast," Oliver said.

"Good news for me." They were approaching the airport. "Which terminal?"

More quickly than Chris could have imagined, a wheelchair and a porter met the truck at the curb and whisked Oliver away. Becky lingered behind. "Chris, I hate to ask anything more of you—"

"I'll plow out your driveway and make sure Marissa and the farm are okay. You just concentrate on taking care of Oliver."

"Thank you." She hugged him and hurried after her husband.

Chris checked in with his crews. According to Brad, the lots were in good shape and the equipment locked up. "More snow in the forecast this afternoon, so we'll probably be plowing again tonight." Brad spoke with the relish of a kid anticipating a birthday party.

"Sounds good. I'll check on conditions later and text you."

Exhaustion finally hit as Chris pulled into his own driveway. He yawned, relieved to see that Sam had already run the snowblower and shoveled the walk. But he had one more call to make.

"Hi, Marissa. They're on their way to Seattle."

"Thank you so much."

"You're welcome. Listen, I'm going to grab some sleep, but I'll come out late this afternoon and plow your driveway. Will you be okay until then?"

"Of course, but you don't need to do that."

Oh, but he did. He'd promised Becky. "I'll see you later. Goodbye." He ended the call before she could argue more. Sometimes that girl was too independent for her own good. Or for his.

A FEW HOURS OF sleep made all the difference. Chris sipped coffee from his travel mug. Dana was right; brewed coffee was better than instant. The Glenn Highway had been plowed and sanded and cars in the ditch had all been towed, but new snowflakes were already drifting down.

He stopped to gather the mail from Oliver and Becky's mailbox and text Marissa that he was on his way before he lost the cell signal. As he was about to put his truck in gear, the phone rang. Mike Wommet.

"Hi, Mike."

"Chris. Say, are you still interested in the *New Beginnings*?"

"She's a fine boat, Mike, just a little out of my price range at the moment. If it keeps snowing and she's still for sale in the spring, I might be."

"What if I cut the price in half?"

"Including the permit?"

"Yeah. Limited time offer."

Chris paused. "Why would you do that?" The original price was fair.

Mike made a sound somewhere between a snort and a sob. "She left me, Chris."

"The *New Beginnings*?"

Mike's throaty laugh was forced. "My wife. Turns out, she's been shacking up with some guy in Florida for the past three months while I've been trying to wrap things up here. She wants a divorce."

"I'm sorry, Mike."

"Yeah."

"But if that's the case, why aren't you keeping the boat and staying here?"

"Oh, that's the best part. I have to sell. Her lawyer informs me she doesn't want half interest in a fishing boat I'm running. She wants cash. So why should I try to get a good price for the thing when she's just going to swoop in and grab the money, anyway?"

"Hey, I hear you, but don't cut off your nose to spite your face. Think about this first, Mike."

"I didn't call for your advice," he growled. "I called to make you an offer. You want the boat or not?"

"I don't think you've—"

"Whatever. Give me a call if you change your mind." The call ended.

Chris slid his phone into his pocket. Poor guy. Here he was, willing to sell his boat and work for somebody else in order to make his wife happy, and she'd already moved on, three months ago. She just hadn't bothered to tell him. What kind of person did that, especially to someone they'd vowed to love and honor all their lives? He shook his head. It was stories like this one that had Chris feeling lucky he'd never made it to the altar. He put the truck in gear and continued to the reindeer farm.

It didn't take too long to clear the driveway, piling up a berm along the edge. When he reached the house, Marissa stepped onto the porch and waved to him. He waved back and went to work clearing the barnyard. Snowshoe tracks led from the house to the barn, chicken coop and reindeer corral. Marissa must have already been out to take care of the animals. He pushed the snow between the house and outbuildings into a pile to the south of the barn, leaving room for more snow as the season progressed.

Then he circled around the back to the garage. Oliver's truck was stuck in a huge drift about twenty yards along the drive. Chris plowed around it as well as he could. He'd dig it out with a shovel later, and, if necessary, he had a tow chain in the plow truck.

As he recalled, Oliver had a small plow attachment for his lawn tractor, but he probably hadn't hitched it up and Marissa wouldn't know how. It wasn't up to handling this much snow, anyway. Maybe Chris could get it set up later so Marissa could plow before the snow got too deep in future, enough to get to the barn, at least, before he could get here after plowing out his commercial clients. He chuckled to himself. Funny how he'd mentally made the commitment to drive all the way out here past Eagle River to plow after every snow. Marissa would argue she didn't need his help, so he wouldn't tell her. He'd just show up.

Once he had the ground cleared, he parked and grabbed a shovel to clean the doorways and front steps. Marissa was already half finished, working with a wide shovel of her own.

Chris gave her a smile. "Hi. Have you heard from Becky yet?"

"They're in surgery. She's praying."

Chris nodded. "We all are."

Marissa blinked and he thought he caught the sheen of tears. "I was so scared this morning when the truck got stuck in the snow. I didn't know who to call."

"I'm glad you called me."

"So am I." Marissa gave him a tentative smile. "You've done so much for us. I'm sorry I treated you the way I did."

"What do you mean?"

"You know. Trying to keep Becky from hiring you. Accusing you of ulterior motives when you brought Ryan out here."

"I don't remember you saying that about Ryan."

"No, but I thought it."

He laughed. For a moment, he'd thought she was finally going to apologize for breaking their engagement, but maybe that was too much to ask. Or maybe she wasn't sorry. Anyway, she was trying.

"Apology accepted. Let's get these steps cleared and then we'll get the truck out. After that, I'm hoping for hot chocolate."

"You've got it."

It took them almost an hour working side by side before all the paths were clear and the truck was parked in the garage. Chris followed Marissa into the kitchen. He'd always loved this room. The butcher-block counters had been sanded down and refinished numerous times, but still had enough scars to give them character. Everything from eggs to roasting pans to baby reindeer had been washed in the big white farmhouse sink. A tiny live Christmas tree decorated with miniature candy canes sat in the middle of the pine table. When Chris brushed against it, the odor of rosemary filled the room.

Marissa opened the door to the refrigerator. "I have that hot chocolate, but how about a turkey sandwich first? We have Christmas leftovers."

"I'd kill for a turkey sandwich. Do you have any of Becky's cranberry-orange relish?"

"I do." Within a few minutes, Marissa had two turkey sandwiches on hearty whole-grain bread, pickles, and a basket of chips on the table. "Beer?"

"Better not. It's supposed to start snowing again soon, so I'll probably be plowing tonight. I'll get that plow installed on the garden tractor for you before I go."

"I'd appreciate that. I looked at it after you left this morning, but couldn't figure it out." Marissa glanced at the clock. Chris knew she was thinking about Oliver, but when she turned to him, she asked, "What did you decide about the boat?"

"Funny you should ask. Mike just called me about that. He lowered the price."

"Great. So are you going to buy it?"

Chris shook his head. "He dropped the price because his wife is divorcing him and he wants to get back at her by selling the boat for rock bottom to reduce her share."

"But if he does that, he'll get less, too."

"I know. I guess hurting her is more important to him than his own welfare."

"That's sad." She took another bite of sandwich and chewed for a moment. "Still, if he's determined to sell, it's a real opportunity for you."

"I know. It's tempting, but I can't take advantage of the guy's bad luck."

"Somebody will buy it."

"I know. But it won't be me."

She nodded. A lot of people he knew would call him crazy not to take advantage of the situation, but she understood. "So what else is new with you?"

"Big news, actually." He grinned. "I'm going to be an uncle."

"Really? Your sister and Sam?"

"Uh-huh. Due in June."

"Uncle Chris." She laughed.

"Sounds pretty good, doesn't it?"

"It does. I wish I had brothers or sisters and nieces and nephews."

"I know." She'd always wished for siblings, for more family. And he'd always thought she was being greedy, considering what a great family she had in Oliver and Becky. But now he saw her point. Someday Oliver and Becky would be gone, and she'd have no family left. "I wish you did, too."

She shrugged. "If wishes were horses…" She carried her empty plate to the sink.

Chris handed her his plate. "I'll go get that plow installed, and then I guess I should go." He picked up his coat from the hook by the door.

"Chris?" When he turned, she was looking at the clock again. "Do you think you could stay a little longer? Just until I hear from Becky that Oliver's all right?"

Chris did some mental calculations. If it was snowing in Anchorage, he needed to get back and round up his guys. Although, if it was only two or three inches, they'd wait until early morning to plow. Then he noted the rare hint of vulnerability in Marissa's eyes and it didn't matter. He'd make it work. "Of course. I'll take care of that plow and be right back."

It didn't take long to install the plow. When he returned, Marissa was lighting a fire in the living room. She closed the screen and turned to him. He handed her a bundle of letters. "I almost forgot. I picked up your mail."

"Thanks." She leafed through the envelopes and pulled out one with a yellow forwarding label. "Maybe it's about a job."

He frowned. Was she still determined to move away and leave Oliver and Becky alone after all this? But she did say she'd lost all her money. He understood the need to pay the bills.

Marissa opened the envelope and unfolded the letter. Her face froze and color drained away. She let the sheet of paper slip from her fingers, and walked over to stand in front of the fire.

"What's wrong? What was in the letter?"

She didn't turn. "Hate mail."

"What?" Chris picked up the paper from where it had fallen. The note was handwritten in bold lettering. Ugly, vindictive words filled the page, accusing her of plotting with her boyfriend to steal other people's money. It ended with a vague threat. *Someday you'll get what you deserve.*

"Marissa, don't let this get to you. You know it's not true."

"It is true." She turned and met his eyes. "Oh, not that I helped him steal money, but I was there at fund-raisers, assuring everyone that their contributions would improve the river and keep it healthy." She blew out a breath. "Oh, Chris, we were doing such good work. The river was healthy again. One species of fish we suspected might be completely wiped out had started to reestablish. The community was involved. Now the center is closed, and the people of the town may never trust again. It's bad enough that Jason fooled so many folks into making investments in his company, but inexcusable that I helped him gather donations to embezzle."

"It's not your fault. You didn't know."

"I should have known. I should never have agreed to help with the fund-raisers without checking the books. I shouldn't have invested my money without questioning how he got such high returns. I shouldn't have introduced him to Oliver and Becky."

"This guy conned a lot of people. You weren't alone."

"But I was there. I should have realized when he started dating me something was off. Why would a seemingly wealthy man want to go out with me, unless he was up to something shady? I'm so stupid."

"You're not stupid." Chris grasped her shoulders. "You had no reason to be suspicious. You're smart and beautiful and compassionate. Any man, including a legitimate billionaire, would consider himself lucky to be with you." He saw her eyes open wider for a split second before he covered her mouth with his own, and her eyes closed. His hands slid from her shoulders to her waist to pull her against him, and her body seemed to melt into his. She slipped her arms around his neck and tugged him closer as the kiss deepened.

It was still there, that same fire. Just the touch of her lips set his heart pounding, his blood racing, his thoughts shattering into a million shards of feeling. In the last ten years, he'd kissed a lot of women, but no one ever affected him the way Marissa did.

Suddenly, she stepped back. She stared up

at him, her eyes wide, her breath coming fast. "I…" She trailed off.

"You what?"

"I think—" The phone rang. Marissa blinked and looked toward it as if she didn't recognize the sound for a second. Then she ran and grabbed the receiver.

"Yes. Yes. Thank goodness." She sank into Oliver's chair. "I'm so glad. No, it's a shame, but at least something good came out of it…I will…No, I'm fine. Chris plowed me out and got the truck unstuck. Don't worry about things here…I love you, too. Bye."

She met Chris's eyes. "He's out of surgery. Everything went fine. Now it's a matter of recovery."

"I'm glad."

"I know." She stood, but didn't break her gaze from Chris's, and he couldn't seem to look away, either. They stared at each other, that kiss hanging over them like a cartoon anvil, threatening to crush them if they didn't move. And yet somehow, Chris couldn't.

Finally, Marissa broke the spell. "Well, I know you have work to do tonight."

"Yes, I should be going." Chris grabbed his jacket. "Let me know how Oliver progresses."

"I will. Thank you, Chris. I seem to be saying that a lot, lately."

"You're welcome. Goodbye." He slipped out the door, climbed into his truck and started the engine. But before he put it into gear, he closed his eyes and let his head fall backward against the seat.

He'd kissed her. And not just a friendly peck on the cheek; he'd gone all-in on that kiss and was still feeling the effects. He'd let Marissa get under his skin, once again. Had the past ten years taught him nothing?

CHAPTER THIRTEEN

CHRIS PULLED THE plow into the warehouse and hopped from the cab. The other plows and spreaders were already parked, and it looked like everyone had gone home. Another good night of plowing. Now he needed to get those invoices sent out and get paid. But first, coffee. He filled his electric kettle at the industrial sink in the warehouse, carried it into his office and plugged it in.

He jumped at the sound of the door buzzer. Brad and Kenny had keys. Who else would be stopping by at six in the morning? He crossed the warehouse to find Sam waiting outside. "Hi. What are you doing out so early?"

"On my way to the airport. My alternate got sick and I need to go up to the slope a couple of days early, but I wanted to talk to you before I leave. Got a minute?"

"Sure. Come on in." Chris led him back to the office, where the kettle had started to boil. He pulled out a mug and a jar of crystals. "Coffee?"

Sam grimaced. "Not that instant stuff, thanks."

Chris shrugged and prepared his own mug. Sure, it wasn't as good as the coffee Dana made, but it had caffeine and that was the main thing. He turned back toward Sam. "What's up?"

"I wanted to ask you to keep an eye on Dana."

"Of course, but why? Is something wrong?"

"No, she's fine. She'd kill me if she knew I was asking you, but I don't like leaving her alone when she's pregnant. I need you to fill in."

Chris sipped his coffee. "So, doing the math, if she's due in June, she's been pregnant for a while, right?"

"Yeah, but she didn't want to tell everybody until twelve weeks."

"So, why are you suddenly worried about leaving her?"

Sam gave a wry smile. "I've been worried all along, but seeing the ultrasound—all of a sudden the baby's real. I need you to take care of them both when I'm gone."

Chris eyed him with suspicion. "What exactly is it you want me to do?" He'd watch over Dana and make sure she wasn't lifting furniture or climbing ladders, but he wasn't planning on doing any Lamaze classes with her.

"I don't know. Be nice to her. Ask how she's feeling. Bring her flowers."

Chris raised an eyebrow. "Flowers?"

"Okay, maybe not flowers. Just…be there. All right?"

"We do live in the same house." He laughed at the helpless look on the face of his usually competent friend. "Hey, she's my little sister. I'll take good care of her. I promise when you get back in two weeks, she'll be fine."

"Good. Thanks." Sam picked up a paper clip from the tray on Chris's desk and bent it apart. "Also, I wanted to ask about Marissa."

Chris's hand jerked as he set down his cup. Coffee sloshed onto the papers on his desk. He reached for a napkin to mop it up. "What about Marissa?"

"Are the two of you back together?"

"Why would you ask that?"

"I know you were working for her family's business while you were waiting for snow, but you went out there on Christmas." He kept his eyes on the paper clip he was fiddling with, rounding out the two loops into the shape of a lopsided heart. "That's not exactly an employee-employer sort of thing."

"I took Ryan. He's convinced Oliver is the real Santa, and wanted to see him."

Sam smiled at the mention of Ryan's name. "That kid's something. I think it's great you're spending time with him. I'm just not so sure it's great that you're spending time with Marissa." Sam crushed the mangled paper clip and tossed it into the trash can. "Last time she dumped you, it took you months to recover."

Little did he know. It took months before Chris could act as though he didn't care. It took him years to recover. If he ever truly had. "I'm not with Marissa."

"Okay. Because you know she's not staying."

Chris didn't blink. "I said we're not together."

"Right. Okay then. I'd better be heading to the airport."

"Yeah, you do that. And I'll make sure Dana's okay. I promise."

"Thanks, Chris." Sam slapped him on the shoulder. "I owe you."

THE NEXT MORNING, Chris checked the balance of his checking account with satisfaction. It looked a lot better when money flowed in as well as out. After three days of plowing, next week's payroll wouldn't be a problem, either.

No snow tonight or tomorrow, though, so he'd paid the guys and sent them home early. Besides, it was New Year's Eve and his employees had plans. Chris's only plans involved a beer, a couch and an old movie.

He locked the office and the warehouse and drove home. Ryan and Sandy were in the front yard. Ryan seemed to be pushing snow into a pile. Chris stopped and rolled down the window. "Hi, guys."

Ryan waved. Sandy walked over to his truck to chat. Baby April slept in a pack on her chest, only her little pink cap visible. "Hi, Chris. Ryan wanted to build a snowman, but he can't get it to stick together."

Chris nodded. "It's too dry. You can't build a snowman from powder. April seems happier. No more teething?"

"No, she cut the tooth and she's herself again."

"Glad to hear it. You and Brent have plans tonight?"

She rolled her eyes. "We did. Some friends are having a party, but our babysitter backed out. I think she got a better offer." She sighed. "I guess if I'm going to be a mother, I need to get used to things like that."

"I suppose so." Chris watched Ryan give up on packing the snow and instead fall backward into the heap, wildly thrashing his arms and legs to create a snow angel. Chris laughed and turned back to Sandy. "I could sit if you want. I don't have plans."

"Could you?" Sandy looked excited, but then her smile faded. "But have you ever looked after a baby?"

"Uh, no. But there's always a first time, right?"

"Do you know how to change a diaper? Prepare a bottle?"

"I'm willing to be taught. In fact, I'd like to learn. I don't know if Dana told you, but she and Sam are expecting."

"That's exciting. So you're going to be an uncle. Congratulations." She eyed him thoughtfully. "You really want to try this?"

He chuckled. "Now that you're looking at me like that, I'm having second thoughts."

"It's not that bad. Brent didn't know how to do any of that baby stuff either, before we got April. The party's not far from here. We could be home in five minutes if anything goes wrong."

"Okay."

"I'll tell you what. Come at eight. I'll show you how to change a diaper, then give April her bottle and put her to bed. Hopefully, she'll sleep through the night and you won't even know she's there. Ryan's easy. He'll read those books you got him all evening long if you let him."

"Yeah, I can handle Ryan."

"Okay. See you at eight."

"I CAN'T BELIEVE you're going to spend New Year's Eve babysitting." Dana slipped a pair of sparkly shoes into a tote bag and slid her feet into snow boots.

"I gather you're going out."

"I'm getting together with a few of my fellow student teachers downtown. I was going to ask if you wanted to come along."

"Nah, I have a hot date with a six-month-old. I figure I'll get in a little practice before I'm officially an uncle." Chris reached past her to snag his coat from the closet.

"Good for you. Here." She picked up a square Christmas tin from the countertop and handed it to him. "Give them this fudge."

He hefted the box in his hand. "This is a lot of fudge."

"I know. I got a little carried away making Christmas treats. Tomorrow is January 1, and I need it out of the house, or I'm going to gain fifty pounds."

Chris laughed. "Why wasn't it a problem in December?"

"December calories don't count. January calories count double. It's a scientific fact." She reached for her own coat. "Don't tell Sandy."

"Are you sure you want it gone?" He waved the tin under her nose. "You're pregnant. Aren't you supposed to get fat?"

"No, I'm supposed to be pregnant. It's the baby that's supposed to grow, not me." She slipped her arms into her coat. "Are you sure you'll be okay?"

"I think so."

"Well, I'll keep my phone handy, so if you get in trouble, give me a call."

"Too bad Sam has to work over New Year's."

"I'm just thankful he was home for Christmas." She smiled. "It was a great Christmas, wasn't it?"

"It was." Far better than the sum of all the Christmases they experienced growing up. "Be careful driving. Sam would have my hide if anything happened to you."

She smiled. "I will. Seriously, call if you need me. I'd go with you except I don't want to miss this chance to see the people moving on after this semester."

"I'll be fine. I'm babysitting two kids for a few hours. Twelve-year-olds do it. What could go wrong?"

For some reason Dana's laugh as she walked into the garage reminded him a little of a supervillain's, but maybe he was imagining it.

He locked the house and shuffled up the street. Sandy opened the door, dressed in a glittery silver sweater over dark velvet pants. He handed her the tin. "From Dana. Fudge."

Ryan reached for the box. "Can I have some?" He'd sampled Dana's fudge before.

"One piece. Later." Sandy placed the box on the countertop and turned to Chris. "Thanks. Are you sure you want to do this?"

"No, but I'm here."

Sandy laughed and led him and Ryan into the nursery, where Brent was lifting April from her crib. She was making these cute gurgling noises at him. Little charmer.

"Hi, Chris. Sandy says you want to learn to take care of a baby."

Chris nodded. "Uncle training."

"Then we'll jump right in. Her diaper needs changing. I'll show you how."

He watched closely as Brent demonstrated. It didn't look too hard. Afterward, Sandy showed him how to hold April and give her a bottle. The baby seemed a lot happier than she had when she was teething, staring up at him with big blue eyes. Occasionally, she would reach for his face and pat his beard.

"She likes you." Sandy smiled.

"That's good."

Ryan stepped closer to watch, and without letting go of the nipple, April twisted her head to look at him.

"I think she likes Ryan, too," Chris said.

"She loves Ryan. She tried to crawl today, to get closer to him."

"She wants my Legos, but she can't have them. She might eat them," Ryan informed Chris. "So they have to stay in my room unless I'm playing with them."

"I see."

As the bottle emptied, April's eyelids seemed to grow heavier. Sandy laid a cloth over Chris's shoulder. "Now, you burp her."

"I didn't know burping was something you could do to somebody else. What's the towel for?"

"Just in case. Now hold her against your shoulder, like this." Sandy took April from his arms and arranged her against his shoulder. "Now rub her back."

Just in case, like the waterproof Santa trousers. Hopefully, he wouldn't be needing the towel, either. Chris rubbed his hand up and down the baby's back. She was dressed in something soft and fuzzy. She seemed to melt against his shoulder, giving off the scent of baby powder. Sweet little girl. Just then, she let out a surprisingly loud belch. Chris laughed.

"There you go. Now rock her until she's sleepy and we'll put her to bed. With any luck, that's the last you'll hear from her tonight."

It didn't take long before April's eyelids drifted shut. Sandy laid her in her crib, where she let out a miniature snore.

They tiptoed out and closed the door. In the living room, Brent pointed out the baby monitor. "If she wakes up, she probably just needs a diaper change or has another bubble she needs to burp up."

"I left an extra bottle in the refrigerator, but she shouldn't need it," Sandy said. "Ryan's had dinner. I told him he could stay up until ten tonight. Make sure he brushes his teeth." She turned to the boy. "You be good for Chris tonight."

"I will."

"Here's where we'll be, and our phone numbers. Call if you need us."

"Will do. Have fun."

Sandy gave one more anxious glance at Ryan and Chris as Brent tugged her toward the garage. Once they were gone, Chris turned to Ryan. "So, what do you want to do this evening?"

"Play dinosaurs."

The first hour was a piece of cake. Ryan dragged out all his dinosaur paraphernalia, including the balsa wood model they'd made together, and they set up a dinosaur colony on the living room floor. Then he brought out a tub of blocks and built walls for the dinosaurs to knock down. It was edging toward ten and Chris was thinking of starting cleanup when a cry sounded from the baby monitor.

Chris waited to see if April might just have cried out in her sleep, but a furious wail convinced him she meant business. "I'll get the baby. You'd better pick up these blocks and put them in the tub."

"Okay. Can I have a piece of fudge first?"

"Sandy said you could have one piece."

Chris went to get the baby. She stopped crying for a moment when he walked into the room, but when she saw his face, she wailed louder. He obviously wasn't the person she wanted.

"Shh, it's okay, April. What do you need, sweetheart? Do you need to burp?" He picked her up and held her against his shoulder. She continued to scream.

He settled into the rocking chair and rubbed her back as he had before. It seemed to have no effect. He shifted her into his lap and rocked her. Her face grew redder. That couldn't be healthy.

Chris positioned her against his shoulder again, bouncing her up and down as he'd seen Sandy do, and walked into the living room to check on Ryan. April downshifted from screaming to whimpering.

Ryan had put a few of the blocks in the bin, but seemed to have gotten sidetracked. He'd built a ramp against another bin and was marching his dinosaurs up the ramp and into their box. Traces of chocolate clung to the edges of his mouth. On the counter, the fudge tin lay open with the lid resting beside it.

"Hey, bud. It's after ten. You're supposed to be in bed. You need to get this cleaned up and brush your teeth."

"I am cleaning up." Ryan grabbed another plastic dinosaur and marched it slowly up the ramp.

"Okay, but hurry. I'll be right back." Chris took April into the nursery and checked her diaper. Ewww. Okay, he'd probably cry, too, if he'd messed his pants like that. What with the screaming and frantic kicking, it took him four times as long as it had taken Brent, but he finally managed to get her cleaned up and into a new diaper, albeit slightly askew. But when he picked her up, she seemed no happier.

Chris returned to the living room, where Ryan had made a little progress, and was now lying on the carpet rubbing his stomach. "Chris, I don't feel good."

Chris was pacing and jiggling April, which seemed to dial the crying down a decibel or so. He stopped and studied Ryan. "What's wrong? Your stomach hurt?"

"Yeah."

April protested, so Chris started walking again. Did they both have food poisoning? What did they have for dinner? But that made no sense. Sandy had told him April wasn't eating solid food yet, except a little cereal for breakfast.

Chris's eye fell on the open tin. "How much fudge did you eat?"

Ryan moaned. "Just one piece."

Chris walked over to the tin. One uncut slab of fudge covered the entire bottom of the tin. Another slab would have fit above it.

"Ryan, that was, like, a pound of fudge. No wonder you're sick."

Ryan responded by rolling onto his knees

and emptying the contents of his stomach all over the living room rug.

Chris shifted April farther up his shoulder and blew out a long stream of air. And he thought fish guts were messy. They were nothing, compared to kids'. He carefully set April into the portable crib in the living room. She screamed and kicked, but he needed to see about Ryan.

He wet a towel from the kitchen and mopped off the boy's face. "Does your stomach feel better?"

Ryan rubbed his hand over his abdomen. "Yeah."

Chris looked doubtfully at the dark brown puddle in the living room. "Do you know where Brent and Sandy keep the cleaning supplies?"

Between the two of them, they located what he needed, and Chris cleaned and scrubbed the rug, dumping the wet towels in the washing machine. All the while, April cried. By the time he finished, Ryan seemed to have recovered. Chris rescued the baby from the crib and walked with her while he talked Ryan through tidying up, brushing his teeth and climbing into bed. April's screams had stopped, but she whimpered and squirmed, obviously unsettled.

"Good night, Chris. I'm sorry I made a mess."

Chris ruffled his hair. "It's okay, bud. Just remember not to eat so much candy at once next time. Good night." He flipped off the lights and carried April into the living room. Suddenly, she let out a huge belch and Chris felt wetness spread over his shoulder. Right, the just-in-case towel.

He wiped her mouth, laid her in the portable crib again and removed his shirt, stuffing it into the washing machine with the towels. He added detergent and started the load. When he returned to the living room, April kicked her legs and gave him a huge, one-toothed grin. Instantly, he forgave her.

He picked her up and she cuddled against his chest, cooing at him. He carried her into the nursery and settled into the rocking chair. He didn't know any lullabies, so he sang a slow ballad as he rocked. He and Marissa had danced to that song once, a long time ago. He remembered the feel of holding her in his arms, wishing the song would never end. He almost laughed, thinking what Marissa would say if she could see him now, rocking a baby in a house that smelled of puke and carpet cleaning solution.

April finally shut her eyes, and he laid her

in her crib. Her mouth pursed in little sucking motions, but she didn't stir. He switched off the light. In the living room, he discovered a block that had escaped Ryan's notice. He picked it up and carried it to the boy's room.

The light streaming in from the hallway was enough to find the bin and to see Ryan's face, relaxed in sleep. A stuffed stegosaurus rested under his hand. He looked as though he hadn't a worry in the world. A small smear of chocolate stained the underside of his chin, but Chris resisted the urge to wipe it off and possibly wake him.

The wash cycle had ended, so Chris transferred the towels and his shirt from the washer to the dryer, put away all the cleaning supplies and collapsed into a living room chair. He picked up a magazine to pass the time.

The sound of the front door opening woke him. Sandy and Brent gaped at the wet spot on their rug, and then at him. Chris picked up the magazine from where it had fallen on the floor and stood, the draft from the door cool against his bare chest. "Hi. Did you have fun?"

"More than you, apparently. What happened?"

"First of all, everything's fine. The kids are both asleep. Second, I don't know how you do this day in and day out, but you have my utmost respect."

Sandy laughed. "Where's your shirt?"

"In the dryer. I forgot about the towel on the shoulder thing."

Brent stepped into the laundry room and fetched the shirt, while Chris gave Sandy an overview of the evening's events. "Anyway, once their stomachs felt better they were both fine. Sorry. I should have cut off a piece of fudge instead of leaving it up to Ryan."

"Don't worry about it. You can't be everywhere. We really appreciate you filling in."

"No problem." Chris buttoned his shirt and pulled on his jacket. "Good night."

"Happy New Year."

Chris looked at the clock. Almost one. He'd slept right through the fireworks. But at least he'd managed to keep two kids alive for a few hours. That was something. He waved as he headed out the door. "Happy New Year."

CHAPTER FOURTEEN

Marissa shifted the phone to her other ear. "That sounds great. When do you think you'll be able to come home?" She smiled as she listened to Oliver grumble about overcautious doctors. He was starting to sound like his old self. "You'd better do what they say. They've done this before and you haven't. Everything is fine here. Love you, too. Bye."

Maybe it was her imagination, but she thought Oliver's voice already sounded stronger. And why shouldn't it? With a healthy new heart pumping blood through his body, everything about him was getting better.

Her sympathy went out to the family that made this possible. There was no way of knowing for sure, but she'd read of the Christmas Day pileup on the freeway outside Seattle. Six people had lost their lives that day. To lose someone you loved on Christmas Day— she could only imagine the shock, and the incredible generosity of the family to offer their loved one's heart to a stranger, even in their grief. She wished they could meet Oliver, to know what a special person had received this incredible gift.

Now that she'd talked to Oliver and Becky, it was time for chores. The chill air hit her as soon as she stepped outside, and she zipped the collar of her down jacket all the way up her neck. An inch or so of snow had fallen yesterday evening, but overnight the sky had cleared and the temperature plummeted. The new snow was marked with fox tracks circling around the henhouse, the fox obviously hoping for an easy meal. Marissa checked all the openings to make sure they were securely latched.

The sun barely peeked over the horizon in the south, turning the sky an icy blue. Marissa forked hay into the reindeers' feeding rack. As she worked, her breath formed a cloud around her face, condensing into tiny icicles that clung to her eyebrows. Snowflake nuzzled her and Marissa slipped her the carrot she'd hidden in her pocket.

Once she'd finished with the reindeer, she headed toward the barn, but paused outside the reindeer pen. To the west, a white plume of smoke caught her eye, drifting toward the sky. The Eriksson's house, their nearest neighbor, was almost a mile away, but it sat lower, with a small rise in between the properties. She could make out the snow-covered roof and smoke rising from the river rock chimney. Odd. Jim and Karen taught school in one of the villages up above the Arctic Circle and normally they used the cabin only in the summer. They must have decided to spend Christmas vacation there.

Had they been there all along? Quite possibly. Most days, a slight wind would have dissipated the smoke, but today the air was cold and perfectly calm.

Marissa finished her chores and climbed into Oliver's truck to drive to the main road and pick up the mail, passing the turn-in to the neighbor's place on the way. Trees blocked her view of the house, but white vapor still rose from the chimney. Undisturbed snow covered the drive and surrounding area. Strange that they hadn't cleared the driveway, but if their school was on the same schedule as the Anchorage district, it didn't start up again for almost a week, so maybe they were simply enjoying their isolation.

Today's mail held no unexpected bills and no accusing letters from Jason's victims. Marissa's face grew hot thinking about the way she'd poured it all out to Chris, the way he'd kissed her. The way she'd kissed him back.

That should never have happened. The last thing she needed was more complications in her life, and that kiss felt complicated. It had also felt wonderful, which was a complication in itself.

Stick to the plan. Number one: find a job. She would go through her contacts today and send out feelers asking if anyone knew of positions coming open. And it wouldn't hurt to follow up on some of those earlier applications.

Number two: check with the farm family in Palmer that took care of the place when Oliver and Becky traveled, and make sure they were willing to cover for her when she did get a job. It would take a big chunk of her salary to pay them, but it was only until Becky was back in the saddle. Then Marissa could direct that money toward paying down the mortgage and fixing up the farm to get it ready to sell, so Oliver and Becky could retire comfortably.

Number three: until then, care for the farm. She didn't have the money for maintenance and repairs, but she could keep the animals healthy and happy, and look after the house. In fact, she should do a walk-through of that closed-off wing, to make sure the roof wasn't leaking and no wildlife had moved in.

Number four: avoid more complications. Especially kissing. Especially kissing Chris. Because that could only get in the way of numbers one through three.

She returned to the house and grabbed a can of soup for lunch. While it was in the microwave, she opened her laptop and started going through her contact list. By the time the soup bowl was empty, she'd sent out messages to ten former coworkers. That was enough networking for today.

Housework should be next, but the thought of that smoke from the neighbor's chimney bugged her. They were probably fine, but what if they weren't? The reindeer could use some exercise, too. She raided Becky's pantry for a few goodies to share.

Marissa dressed warmly and harnessed up four of the younger reindeer to pull the sleigh. Since they'd learned on the cart, this would be good practice for them. Once they were ready to go, she tugged a balaclava over her head and flicked the reins.

The reindeer started out a little jerky, but soon settled into a smooth rhythm, working together to pull the sleigh. She kept to the trails, traveling up and down the hills, and then turned the team to follow the cleared area beside the shared road. No cars came along to disturb them, but then why would they? The Erikssons' cabin and the farm were the only houses on this road. This summer, cars would be coming and going to the camp ten miles farther along, but it was closed up and deserted in the winter. Eventually, she reached the signpost marking the Erikssons' drive. She turned the reindeer and followed the path to the cabin.

A pile of firewood took up most of the front porch, piled randomly on the bench, the floor and the porch swing. It looked as though someone dumped a load from a truck and never bothered to stack it. The snow surrounding the cabin seemed pristine, other than a path shoveled to the old outhouse, left over from the days before the owners drilled a well. The well house appeared undisturbed, which meant they probably had no running water inside. Odd, because the porch light was on, so they had electricity. Maybe it wasn't worth the time and trouble to start up the pump and then have to winterize all over again, although Marissa wouldn't have chosen to spend her Christmas break without hot showers, much less traipsing to the outhouse when the temperature hovered around zero. Ah well, to each his own.

Odd that the Erikssons had come all the

way out here, only to stay holed up in that tiny cabin. In the summer, they spent most of their time hiking, fishing, in the garden or on the porch. On the other hand, it had been five years since she'd last visited, and that was just a long weekend. Maybe the Erikssons had sold the cabin. But no, Oliver and Becky mentioned chatting with them that summer. They would have known of a change in ownership.

Marissa tied the reindeer to a tree at the edge of the yard and struggled through the snow, postholing through the crust with every step until she reached the porch. Good thing she'd worn her knee-high felt pack boots. Inside, she could hear an announcer's voice. It sounded like a football game, although the audio was so distorted by static she couldn't be sure. She was surprised they could pick up a signal at all with the hills around them.

She pulled the balaclava off her head and knocked on the door. No answer, but the game sounds grew fainter. She knocked again, harder. "Karen? Jim? It's Marissa. I brought you some salmonberry jelly and rhubarb preserves."

Still no response. Strange. Maybe she should just leave the food and go. But what if something was wrong? "Hey, are you guys okay? If I've caught you at a bad time, just say so and I'll leave."

She tried to peer through the window, but the blinds didn't leave even a crack. After a moment's debate, she tried the front door, but the dead bolt was locked. Finally, she heard steps moving toward the door, but it didn't open. A whispery voice called, "I'm fine. Laryngitis. Very contagious." It sounded like a man, but she couldn't be sure.

"I'm so sorry you're sick. I see you haven't been out. Can I bring you anything? Soup? Medicine? Want me to call someone to plow the drive?"

"No. I don't need anything."

"Okay, then." Marissa hesitated. Where was Karen? Was Jim there all alone? She hated leaving someone sick without any backup. "Your phone's working, right?"

"I'm fine. Leave me alone."

Strange. Jim usually loved company, but maybe he was one of those people who turned into a bear when he was sick. Or could he and Karen have split up? Maybe he was here to spend time by himself and Marissa had intruded.

"Sorry to bother you. I'll leave these jars out here. Don't let them freeze, or they'll

break. And call me if you need me for anything. I'll be over at the reindeer farm."

"All right." The floor creaked and steps
moved away from the door.

She left the jars on the porch. At least he
didn't have to worry about wood for the stove.
There should be enough for another couple
months. She untied the reindeer and turned
them toward home, but the thought of Jim sick
and alone in the cabin nagged at her. Should
she call somebody? But who? Karen surely
knew where he was. And Marissa couldn't
exactly call 911 to report a neighbor with a
sore throat who didn't want to invite her in.

She shrugged. Jim was a sourdough. He'd
spent most of his life in the wilds of Alaska
and survived a lot worse than a bout of
laryngitis. He'd be fine.

"Look. A moose." Ryan pointed excitedly into
a clump of trees near the shoulder of the road.

Chris instinctively slowed until he could
be sure the moose wasn't considering an
ill-advised dash across the highway. Most
winters averaged over a hundred moose-
car altercations in Anchorage, and the re-
sults were never pretty for either side. But
this young bull seemed to be busy pushing
against a spruce tree.

"He's only got one antler." Ryan laughed.

Chris took another quick look. "You're right. I guess he shed the other one already. No wonder he's rubbing against the tree. It must feel awkward to have that much weight on one side of your head."

Ryan looked ahead. "Are we almost there?"

"This is our exit. Then we follow this road awhile before we get to the farm."

"Will Oliver be there?"

"No. Remember I told you Oliver and Becky are down in Seattle right now. That's why we're going out, to plow the driveway and see if Marissa needs our help."

"I like Marissa. She's nice."

"Yeah." She was nice. Yes, her single-minded adherence to "the plan" sometimes drove him insane, but at her core, she was a good person. She didn't deserve to be in this situation, and she certainly didn't deserve the kind of vitriol he'd read in that letter the other day. Seeing her hurting like that made him want to run out and slay a dragon, but since that wasn't an option, he did something even more dangerous. He kissed her.

Which was one of the reasons he was glad Ryan was available to ride along today. Having him there would make seeing Marissa again a little less awkward. Besides, school was starting next week, and Ryan wouldn't be getting many more chances to ride out to the farm before social services moved him to another placement.

Chris had pulled Brent aside earlier for an update. Ryan's social worker wanted to move Ryan before the new semester, but was having trouble placing him, so it looked as though he might stay with Brent and Sandy a little longer. When Chris mentioned he'd like to keep in touch even after Ryan moved, Brent suggested a mentor program. Once Chris passed the security screening and interview process, he should be able to become officially partnered with Ryan, although it could take some time. And it might depend on Ryan's next home and how the new foster parents felt about it.

"There it is!" Ryan had spotted the sign. Chris turned in, angled his plow and chugged slowly up the long driveway. He stopped in front of the house. Ryan ran to the front door and rang the doorbell.

It took a few minutes before Marissa appeared, but she seemed thrilled to see Ryan there. "Hi. I didn't know you were coming today."

"Chris says we need to plow your snow

and see if you need help. Do you want me to feed the goats?"

Chris stepped up behind him on the porch. "Sorry if we're disturbing you. I should have called."

"It's fine. I was in the south wing. Actually, I could use your opinion on something. Ryan, I already fed the animals, but we can go out in a little while and check on them. Come on in. Leave your coats on—there's no heat there."

Ryan and Chris left their boots in a tray by the door and followed Marissa along the hallway. The door at the end groaned when she opened it. Chris knew Oliver and Becky had partitioned off the part of the old house they didn't use, but he'd never been inside.

"The former owners modernized the main house but not this section." Marissa led them to a bedroom. Inside, faded sheets covered what Chris assumed were pieces of furniture. Ryan went to pull back the heavy curtains, releasing an avalanche of dust. He sneezed.

Marissa lifted one of the sheets, exposing a dark wood vanity with turned legs and an oval mirror dimly reflecting the room. "Isn't this pretty?"

"I like it." Chris could picture Marissa sitting on the needlepoint stool, brushing her shiny hair. For a modern woman, she'd always had a soft spot for old-fashioned things.

She ran her hand over the smooth wood. "Do you think it's worth anything?"

"I have no idea. Did you look on the web?"

"Not yet. I was just checking the rooms and found it. I was thinking some of this furniture might pay for a few of the repairs around here."

"We can check it out. What else did you find?"

They snapped a picture of the vanity before spreading the sheet back over it and inspecting the rest of the furniture. An iron headboard rose above a ruined mattress. The nightstand beside it was one of those gangly tables that appeared to stand on tiptoe, but it had a nicely grained wood finish. Another room contained an old washbasin and a couple dented trunks. The bathroom in between had a deep claw-footed tub and a stained sink.

"I love this bathtub." Marissa climbed inside. "Even you could soak up to your chin in here."

"It's nice. The porcelain is chipped, but it could be refinished."

"I think the original farm family had eight kids. That's a lot of baths."

Chris laughed. "They probably each bathed weekly. One bath a day and two on Saturday."

"Come see," Ryan called. They followed his voice upstairs to yet another good-size room tucked under the eaves, lit from a cobweb-covered dormer window. Two bunk beds built of peeled poles with slat frames hugged one wall. Ryan had climbed the ladder to the top bunk. "I like it up here."

Chris stepped over to make sure the bunks weren't too rickety, but they seemed sturdy. Marissa looked around the room. "I wonder why they used bunk beds when there's so much extra floor space."

"Probably had another bed in here that they took along. They just left the bunks because they were attached to the wall."

"You're probably right."

Chris opened the next door to reveal another small bathroom with a funny little wall-mounted shower. Curtain rings dangled from a round rack at the top. A pedestal sink and toilet with a wall-mounted tank completed the tiny room. "Here's where the rest of the kids cleaned up."

Marissa stepped closer to inspect the fixtures. "This room belongs in a museum."

"Maybe, but I suspect if the water were on

in this part of the house, it would all be perfectly functional."

Ryan played with the sink spigots. "Why are there two faucets?"

"One for hot and one for cold. You mixed the temperature you wanted in the sink."

"Why?"

"I have no idea," Chris confessed. "It seems like a lot of trouble, but I suppose compared to using outhouses and boiling water on the stove, it was a huge convenience."

They returned to the hallway. A small door built into the wall in the alcove beside the stairs caught Chris's eye. He twisted the wooden catch and pulled on the tiny crystal knob. Inside, he found a wooden box. He took it out and blew off the dust to find a tarnished silver latch holding it closed. Chris carried it into the bedroom by the window in order to see how to unfasten the tiny hook.

It was empty, except for a single cardboard folder. Chris handed it to Marissa, who opened it to reveal a black-and-white photograph of a family. The mother and father stood in the center, a baby in the woman's arms. Seven stair-step children ranging from young teens to toddlers surrounded them.

"That's a lot of kids," Chris said. "With

that many mouths to feed, I doubt they had many extras."

"It must have been a hard life."

Chris studied the woman's face. That was probably her vanity in the other bedroom, where she'd sat and brushed her hair before pinning it up in the bun she wore in the picture. Her features weren't too clear in the grainy photograph, but she reminded him a little of Marissa. Something about the determined set of her jaw, coupled with a sweet smile. "She looks happy, though."

"She has her family." After a moment, Marissa looked up at him, and he thought he detected a hint of moisture in her eyes. Before he could be sure, she glanced out the window. "It will be dark soon. If we're going to see about the animals, we'd better go. Ready, Ryan?"

He jumped down from the top bunk, where he'd been playing while they looked at the photo. "Did you make sure Sadie got to eat?"

Marissa put a hand on his head and smoothed a lock of hair as they started for the stairs. "I put out enough for all the hens, but I'm sure Sadie will appreciate some special attention from her favorite boy. Come on, Chris."

They visited the goats. Ryan gave Petunia a treat and turned to Marissa. "Are Petunia and Daisy so little because they don't get enough to eat?"

Marissa crouched down so she was at Ryan's level and scratched the goat's chin. "No. Remember I told you they're Nigerian dwarf goats. They're bred to stay small."

"What does that mean?"

Marissa didn't brush him off with an easy answer. She patiently explained genetics and DNA in terms Ryan could understand, and let him spend as much time as he wanted with each of the animals, even though she'd already taken care of them that morning. She seemed to enjoy every minute with him. She would be a great mother.

A long-delayed twinge of guilt poked at Chris's conscience. It wasn't fair of him to ask her to give up her chance at motherhood. She'd been right to dump him and find another man who would give her the children she should have. But she never did. Why not?

The sky was darkening by the time Ryan had said goodbye to each of the reindeer and checked on the chickens. A sudden gust swirled snow around them as they walked toward the house. Chris realized Ryan's ears were exposed.

"Where's your hat?"

The boy patted his head and his pockets. "I must have dropped it in the chicken coop. I'll go get it."

"We'll wait here." They watched him run to the coop. Chris looked at Marissa. She licked her lip and glanced away. He should probably say something about that kiss. On the other hand, he could just let it lie and make small talk. Yeah, that sounded safer. "How was your day?"

Her face relaxed a little. "Good. Talked to Oliver. He sounds better every day. And I took some of the younger reindeer for a sleigh ride for practice. They did well. Strange thing happened, though."

"What's that?"

"Our neighbors, the Erikssons? They're usually only here in the summer, but I saw smoke from their chimney. I went by to see if they were okay—"

"Marissa! The chickens!" Ryan screeched. A cacophony of squawking accompanied his cry. Chris and Marissa dashed to the henhouse, in time to see a bushy tail disappear down a hole in the corner amid a shower of feathers.

Adele, the Chantecler hen, held her wing away from her body and shook. Drops of red stained her white feathers. Ryan was stroking her and talking softly. He looked up with tears in his eyes. "The fox hurt her."

The other chickens had stopped squawking and some were crowding toward Adele. Chris shooed them away while Marissa knelt beside Ryan and examined the hen. "It's not too bad. We'll take Adele in the kitchen to clean her up and let her heal. If we leave her out here, the other hens will peck at her."

"Why?"

"I don't know, but chickens do that." She smiled at him. "You were very brave, running off that fox. He's been after a chicken dinner for a long time. I thought we had the edges sealed off, but he must have found a gap and dug a hole. I guess heat from the chicken coop was enough to keep the ground against the building from freezing up."

"You two take care of the hen, and I'll find some rocks to fill the hole," Chris said. "I'll make sure Mr. Fox can't find his way back inside again. Good job, Ryan."

Ryan pushed back his shoulders and stood up straight, hugging the now calmer hen to his chest. She clucked softly as Marissa held the door for him. Marissa caught Chris's eye and smiled, sharing in his pride at Ryan's protectiveness. Chris smiled back.

Once they were gone, he wedged a few big

rocks in the outside hole and filled the remaining spaces with gravel. He topped the opening with a cinder block, and just in case, covered the tunnel inside the coop with a board, weighted down by another large rock. Using his flashlight, he inspected the perimeter of the chicken coop.

Oliver had sunk welded wire into the ground all around the edge, but the fox had managed to locate the one corner with a small gap. Persistent fellow. It must have driven him crazy, smelling those fat, juicy chickens right there for the taking, and not being able to find a way in. And when he finally did, a boy was there to run him out and protect the flock. Chris almost felt sorry for the fox.

Ryan's hat still lay on the floor. Chris picked it up, dusted the straw and feathers away and stepped outside, latching the door behind him. Across the way, the lights in the windows of the old farmhouse glowed. Behind the lace curtains, two shapes moved around the kitchen. Marissa and Ryan, working together to care for the traumatized hen. They were two of a kind.

Before long, Ryan would be moving to a new family, and Marissa would be moving to a new job. Maybe, if this mentor thing worked out, Chris would be able to continue to bring

Ryan out to the farm to visit Becky, Oliver and the animals. But it wouldn't be the same for Ryan or for Chris. Not without Marissa.

CHAPTER FIFTEEN

WHY DO YOU want to be a mentor? Good question. How did Chris get to the point of filling out this application to try to stay in Ryan's life? Until he met the boy, he'd never deliberately chosen to spend time with anyone below the age of eighteen since, well, probably since he was eighteen himself. Except for Dana, of course.

It wasn't that he avoided children. He'd exchanged a few words with most of the kids in the neighborhood. Occasionally, one of his friends would drag a kid or two along on a camping trip, and he never minded. But Ryan was the first kid he'd actually gotten to know. The first kid who needed him.

Maybe he was fooling himself that it really mattered whether he spent his spare time with Ryan or not. An occasional bowling night or trip to the farm wouldn't make much difference in the grand scheme of Ryan's life. What he really needed was a family. Someone who would care if he did his homework and make sure he was wearing warm clothes. Someone to attend his school events and tell him to eat his vegetables. Someone Ryan could come to when he messed up, knowing whoever it was would help him pick up the pieces. Somebody to love him.

His grandmother loved him; that was clear. From the things Ryan said about her, she'd been an excellent parent, but she couldn't do it anymore. Someone needed to step in and become Ryan's permanent, full-time family. Because Ryan deserved that.

Could it be Chris? He'd told Marissa he never wanted kids, and his reasons were sound. People learned by example, and his examples were lousy. He read stories all the time of people charged with neglect or abuse, who in turn had been neglected and abused as children. The cycle continued. Not that Chris was ever abused, or truly neglected. Just not loved. Could a person love a child the way he or she deserved without ever having received that sort of parental love?

Dana thought so. She was jumping into motherhood with both feet, and Chris had no doubts she would be a wonderful mom. If she could do it, why couldn't he?

Of course, looked at objectively, he was a poor candidate for fatherhood. He lived in someone else's house. He didn't have a full-time, year-round job. He did own a business, but it was entirely dependent on the weather. He planned to buy his own boat soon. That should demonstrate his dependability, except that he'd be out fishing for months at a time, even more than he had in the past, working as a crewman. Who would take care of Ryan while he fished?

Dana would, if he asked. She loved kids in general and Ryan in particular. But she was working so hard to finish up her college credits so she could teach, and this summer she would have a newborn. It wouldn't be fair to dump another kid in her lap for months on end.

Besides, if Chris were to do this, he'd want to be a real dad, not the sort of man who pawned off his kids, like his own father, who might engage him and his sister in an awkward conversation every few months and ignore them the rest of the time. He'd want to be the kind of father who read bedtime stories, and checked homework, and built tree houses. Chris chuckled to himself. And yes, cleaned up puke and nursed injured chickens.

So no, adoption wasn't in the cards. But he would fill out his application, get fingerprinted and do the interviews so he could become Ryan's mentor. And he would get Sandy to introduce him to Ryan's caseworker. Because he cared about that kid.

ANOTHER JASON SIGHTING, this one in the Bahamas. A call to Detective Simonton didn't yield a lot of information, except to say that the US did have an extradition treaty with the Bahamas and that it was irrelevant in this case. Marissa interpreted that to mean it wasn't Jason in the blurry cell phone photo the news channels had been flashing around. She wasn't surprised. It didn't look that much like him.

Marissa persisted. "So you have no idea where Jason might have gone? Don't you have some sort of passport record of where he went first?"

"He hasn't used his passport."

"Oh." With all the media speculation, Marissa had had the impression the police thought he was out of the country. "Does that mean he's still in the United States? Or did he use a fake identity?"

"We're investigating all the possibilities. I've already told you more than I should have. Do you have any more information for me?" Clearly, he wanted to end the conversation.

"Sorry, no. Thanks for your time, Detective. Goodbye."

She was getting used to rejection. She'd received another form letter thanking her for applying for the position, and two polite emails from former colleagues wishing her luck, but with no leads on jobs. She needed a paycheck. They hadn't received any medical bills for the transplant yet, but every day Oliver spent in the hospital had to be costing a fortune. Fortunately, a friend of Becky's from Seattle was wintering in Florida and insisted Becky stay in her town house while she was gone, so at least they saved on hotel bills.

Marissa had checked online to see if any of the old furniture was valuable, but judging by similar pieces listed for sale, she'd be lucky to get a few hundred dollars for the lot, excluding the cost to ship from Alaska. Apparently the furniture was neither rare nor expensive, which of course would have been why it was left behind in the first place. It was a shame, because that vanity was quite lovely, even if the oval mirror had lost much of its silvering and the veneer on the drawers was cracking. One more dead end in her quest for income.

Adele clucked from her box in the corner of the kitchen. Marissa smiled, remembering Ryan carefully making a bed for her with newspapers while Marissa cleaned her injuries. He couldn't understand why

Marissa didn't use bandages, but she'd explained Adele would just eat them. The hens were lucky Ryan was there when the fox broke in. He probably wouldn't have stopped with Adele. Fresh footprints showed he'd been back, sniffing around the chicken coop, but he'd made no progress shifting the cinder block Chris had placed over the hole, so for the moment, the chickens were safe.

And so was Jason, apparently. Was he lying on a beach somewhere, paying off the locals to pretend he wasn't there? Maybe he was on some private island, living in a thatch-roofed hut with his ex-wife. Or hiding out in some isolated house in the country. She filled a kettle with water and lit the burner to make tea. How would someone decide where to run after a crime? Would you go somewhere familiar or someplace you'd never been? If you were trying to disappear, it would make sense to go where nobody knew you. But how would you choose? Internet searches could be traced. You'd almost have to throw a dart, or base the decision on random conversations.

She paused. Kind of like the conversation Jason had had with Oliver. Jason had been extraordinarily interested in the isolation of the farm. Oliver had mentioned their closest neighbor's house was used only in summer. She considered the possibility. Could it be?

The kettle whistled, and Marissa poured the water over a teabag. No. It was wishful thinking to imagine Jason might be within her grasp. Jason loved sunshine and warm weather, and he had a bazillion dollars of other people's money to take him wherever he wanted to go. A tiny cabin in Alaska in the winter was the last place he would consider.

But he wasn't stupid. He was aware the investigators would talk to people who knew him. They would find out he loved water-skiing and hated snow skiing. That he found every excuse to play golf on Maui and tried to avoid traveling to see clients in Michigan except in the summer. The only reason anyone would look for him in Alaska was because Marissa was there. And if she'd been able to find another job after the center closed, she would be somewhere else.

Then there was that cryptic message about the rufous hummingbird. Leo Markesan, one of Jason's top financial people, had disappeared a couple of days before Jason. Suppose his departure caught Jason by surprise. Maybe Jason hadn't planned to go into hiding yet, hadn't gotten all his arrangements in order. Maybe he didn't yet have a fake passport.

What if Jason was supposed to meet his ex-wife, Julianna, a.k.a. Jewel, somewhere out of the country? After all, she'd sold her home in Malibu a year ago and gone overseas, but nobody seemed to know exactly where. If he couldn't join her yet, maybe Jason would try to get word to her that he was hiding out in a certain place until things quieted down or he figured out his next move. He might mention on a public website a certain hummingbird that migrated between California and Alaska.

Oh, but this all sounded crazy. Marissa could hardly call Detective Simonton and say, *I've been thinking about it, and it turns out that guy I swore I had no contact with might possibly be living next door.* Yeah, that would go over well. Especially when it turned out to be a cranky Swede with a sore throat instead.

Or she could call the troopers. *I think my reclusive neighbor with laryngitis is actually a wanted fugitive.*

Based on what, ma'am?

He was too rude to open the door when I dropped by.

They probably got calls all the time from people with cabin fever and too much imagination. They'd laugh in her face.

She'd seen the smoke this morning, so the cabin was still occupied. But what could she do? She'd already dropped by. She could try spying from a distance, but from the tracks, it didn't look like the person in the cabin was going any farther than the porch and the outhouse. If he saw her watching it would probably just spook him into running. If it was Jason. Which it wasn't. Right?

What were the possibilities? Most likely, Jim Eriksson was spending the break in his cabin and for some reason his wife hadn't come. None of Marissa's business.

Second most likely, Jim and Karen had given permission to a friend or relative to use the cabin and he wanted privacy. Maybe he was writing a book or something. Again, none of her business.

The third possibility was that some stranger was using the cabin without their knowledge or permission. She could check on that.

She found a phone number for Jim and Karen in Becky's address book, but it just connected to the village school, with the invitation to leave a message and someone would return the call after winter break. So she had no excuse to call the troopers about a possible intruder.

It was a complete and utter long shot that Jason was in that cabin. And yet, the more she thought about it, the more likely it seemed.

She'd even joked once that Alaska was a great place for criminals and runaway spouses to hide out. But how could she find out for sure? She needed a plan.

Marissa went into Becky and Oliver's room, to the large walk-in closet the former owners had converted from a bedroom. There, against the back wall, was Oliver's safe. She found the key in its hiding place in a cigar box in the bottom drawer of Oliver's nightstand and opened the heavy door. On the top shelf rested the .44 Magnum her uncle took along when salmon fishing in bear country. Beside it was a box of ammo.

Marissa knew how to use the pistol, thanks to hours of patient tutoring from Oliver. It kicked like a mule and it took all her strength to keep the heavy gun steady, but he made sure if she ever found herself in the position to have to shoot a bear, she'd be able to bring it down. Those target skills were sure handy in her career. When it came to shooting tranquilizer darts, she had a reputation for accuracy. She'd killed only once, a deer that had been hit by a car and was suffering, but she knew how.

If it was Jason in that cabin, would he be armed? Not likely. In spite of having founded the River Foundation, he didn't like to spend time outdoors. He preferred his nature tamed and controlled, like a golf course. On the other hand, a golf club could be a perfectly functional weapon, and desperate people did desperate things. She knew Jason well enough to know he wouldn't let sentiment stand in the way of his freedom. Better to be prepared.

Trouble was, Jason knew her, too, and regardless of all the wrongdoing, he was a human being. She wouldn't shoot him if he tried to run, and if she threatened to, he'd call her bluff. She needed muscle—someone she could trust.

She dialed the number. The call went straight to voice mail. "Hi, Chris. Could you stop by sometime today? Don't bring Ryan this time. I need to talk with you alone."

CHRIS PARKED HIS truck across the end of the drive beside the tall post with a carved sign that read Eriksson hanging from a crossbeam. The clock on the console read three fifteen, exactly the time Marissa wanted to start this…whatever it was. Only reindeer tracks and the parallel lines from the sleigh runners disturbed the snow on the path to the cabin. Smoke rose above the trees.

He looked at Marissa. He could tell by the

determined set of her jaw his suggestion was doomed to failure, but he made it anyway. "I think you should wait here. I've seen his picture. I can handle this."

She shook her head. "He's probably changed his appearance. I know his voice and his mannerisms. We'll stick to the plan." Her expression hardened. "Besides, I want to see his face when I bring him down."

"If it is him."

"If not, we apologize and leave. No harm done."

Chris agreed. Once Marissa made up her mind, it was useless to argue. "All right. We go with the plan." He pulled out two pairs of snowshoes and they strapped them on. Marissa shrugged into a backpack. He pointed to the holster on her hip. "Locked and loaded?"

"Check."

They made their way up the long path. Mentally, Chris reviewed Marissa's strategy one last time, looking for flaws, but he couldn't find any. Trees blocked their view of the cabin until they were almost upon it. At Marissa's nod, they stayed in the woods and circled around the north, windowless side of the cabin to the detached garage. Inside, they found an old beater truck with a Louisiana license plate and an even older snow machine. That fit. Cash down and no questions asked, although it was a wonder the old truck hadn't rattled to pieces on the trip up the Alaska Highway.

A few minutes with a screwdriver, and Chris ensured neither of the vehicles was going anywhere right away. He circled back to the main path, while Marissa took up a spot near the edge of the porch, just out of sight of the front door. Chris moved straight from the path to the porch as though he'd come from the road. They both removed their snowshoes. Chris stepped on the porch and knocked on the door.

No answer. He knocked again and called, "Hey, anybody home? Listen, I'm sorry, but I took out your sign up at the road. Patch of ice. I just want to apologize and pay to replace the post."

After a pause, a man's voice called through the door. "Don't worry about it." Chris looked toward Marissa, his eyebrows raised. She nodded, her face grim.

"Listen, I take responsibility for my mistakes. I'm not leaving until you let me pay you for the post."

"It's just a post."

"Yeah, but you're going to have to have

somebody dig it out and set up the new one. Would fifty cover it?"

"Fine, whatever." The door opened. Jason Kort had indeed changed his appearance from the pictures Chris had seen. He'd buzzed off most of his hair, and what remained he'd bleached a dirty blond, but he'd forgotten to do his eyebrows, still dark above deep-set eyes. His face looked haggard, hunted. He was a couple inches shorter than Chris, and thinner than he looked in the pictures. Chris probably had thirty pounds on him.

Jason held out his hand. "Give it to me and go."

"No problem." Chris took a step back and pretended to be searching for his wallet. "I know it's here somewhere. Ah, here it is." Chris took out a fifty and held it so Jason would have to step outside to reach it. He did.

"Hold it right there." Marissa stepped from the edge of the cabin, her hand gripping the gun in the holster.

"Marissa?" For a moment Jason froze, but before either Chris or Marissa could react, he jumped inside and slammed the heavy door, locking the dead bolt behind him. By the time they'd floundered through the heavy snow to the back, Jason had disappeared inside the garage. At Marissa's nod, Chris took up a position on one side of the door and Marissa on the other.

The cough of an engine failing to catch was followed by a string of colorful language. Chris had to hand it to him; this guy could outcurse most of the sailors he knew, although he had to deduct some points for lack of originality. They waited. A few minutes later, Jason trudged out, shivering in his jeans and sweatshirt. He looked at Chris and then turned his attention toward Marissa, his expression that of outraged innocence. "What's going on? You have a gun? You can get in big trouble for that, you know."

"You don't know big trouble, but you will. Let's go inside." Marissa's voice was eerily calm. If Chris were Jason, he'd be covering vital body parts about now.

Chris gripped Jason's arm. "You heard the lady."

Jason stumbled as Chris dragged him toward the cabin. "I don't know who you are, but unless you have a warrant, this is kidnapping."

"I believe it's called a citizen's arrest." Chris pushed Jason through the back door into the kitchen.

"You can't arrest me. I've done nothing

wrong. I could sue you for false imprisonment, take everything you own."

"I suppose you know all about taking what doesn't belong to you." Chris twisted Jason's arm behind his back. Marissa pulled a length of rope from her pack, and they tied his wrists together. Chris pushed him onto a kitchen chair, and Marissa used another length of rope to secure his legs to it.

She stood back and looked him in the eye. "I trusted you. Everyone trusted you. How could you do this?"

"You've got it all wrong, babe. It wasn't me. It was Leo. I'm just staying out of sight until I can prove my innocence."

Marissa didn't flinch. "Tell it to the judge." She picked up the phone on the kitchen wall and frowned. "No dial tone. They must cancel service when they're not here."

Chris pulled out his cell. "No bars, of course. I'll stay with him." He pulled the keys from his pocket and handed them to her. "You take the truck and call the troopers."

Marissa shook her head without taking her gaze from Jason. "I'll stay."

"I don't think that's a good idea. What if—"

She gave him a tight smile. "Don't worry,

Chris. I can handle him. I have a few things I'd like to say to Jason before they lock him up."

Chris hesitated. Every instinct told him not to leave her alone with a dangerous criminal. Actually, his instincts told him not to leave the criminal alone with the dangerous woman, but he knew from the set of her shoulders Marissa wasn't budging. He nodded. "I'll be right back."

"We'll be here."

JASON WAITED UNTIL the front door slammed before giving her that famous smile, familiar in spite of the blond hair. His brown eyes all but dripped with sincerity, just as they always had. "Marissa." He said her name almost as a caress.

She didn't look at him. Instead, she removed her coat, hung it on the back of a chair and swept her gaze around the little cabin. Cans of stew, spaghetti and Spam occupied part of a shelf in the kitchen next to some dusty-looking packages of pilot bread. Gallon water jugs, mostly empty, lined the wall along with a half-dozen empty wine bottles. A cheap radio perched on the windowsill near the table.

In the living area, an ancient brown love seat faced the woodstove. A milk crate full of assorted paperbacks served as an end table. One of them, a thriller from the eighties, judging by its cover, lay facedown on the seat. She raised an eyebrow. "No television. No Wi-Fi. No indoor plumbing. A little more primitive than you're used to, isn't it? Must have been torture, listening to nothing but your own thoughts for the past few weeks."

He shrugged. "Guess I should have checked the Forbes star rating first."

"Well, don't worry. Soon you'll be in a cozy cell, with lots of nice prisoners to talk to."

He looked up at her, his eyes brimming with sadness. "We had some good times together, Marissa. Why are you so angry with me?"

She glared at him. "You wrecked the foundation, stole money from hundreds of people and left me behind to take the blame. Why do you think I'm angry?"

"I'm sorry, Marissa. I didn't mean for that to happen." Once again, he managed to sound sincere. Of course, he was the master. *Look people in the eye. Smile. Use their names. It makes them like you, and if they like you, they'll be more likely to donate.* Good grief, he'd all but told her he was a con artist, and she still hadn't caught on.

She turned her back and walked into the

kitchen area. A stew pot for melting snow sat atop the propane stove. Two empty canning jars and a saucepan lay in the drainer beside the sink. Jason must have gobbled up the rhubarb preserves and salmonberry jelly in one sitting. If she'd known it was him, Marissa wouldn't have wasted Becky's talents.

Curious, Marissa opened the lid of the ice chest to find a half jar of gourmet mustard and an almost empty jar of pesto packed in snow. He must have run out of sandwich fixings and pasta a while ago and been subsisting on the Erikssons' cache of canned foods, a far cry from the restaurant fare he was used to. The thought brought a momentary smile to her face. She gazed out the window toward the driveway. A raven resting in the top of a dead tree squawked and flew away. How long until Chris came back?

"So, is that your boyfriend who's calling the cops?"

She didn't bother to turn around. "Just an old friend."

"Really? You called him Chris. Wasn't that the name of the man you used to be engaged to?"

"Yes."

"Sure didn't take you long to get over me

and fall back into the arms of your former fiancé, did it?"

She glanced at him over her shoulder. "Not that I owe you any explanation, but we're friends."

"Good, because a woman as intelligent and attractive as you can do a lot better than some Alaska backwoodsman."

Marissa snorted. "He's worth a hundred of you." She returned the saucepan in the drainer to its spot on the shelves beside the stove.

"I should have realized you would be the one to figure it out." This time Jason's voice held a hint of amusement. "You're smarter than the cops."

She spun around to face him. "Don't flatter me, Jason. If I were smart, I never would have gotten involved with you, much less let you take advantage of my family."

Jason leaned forward. "I never meant to hurt you. I didn't solicit investments from your family. Your uncle practically shoved the money at me. It would have looked suspicious if I didn't take it. I fully intended to return it before shutting down, but Leo forced my hand before I was ready. Something spooked him and he ran, so I had to run."

"Oh, well, that makes it all right then. It's

fine that you cheated people out of their retirement savings and their home down payments. It's okay that you took the money people gave to the River Foundation, because you didn't intend to take Oliver's money. Except you did."

He shook his head. "It wasn't supposed to happen this way. I started out legitimate. But the market took a swoon, and I promised more than I could deliver. I had to use new funds to pay off the old investors or the whole thing was going to cave in. I intended to pay it all back, but the debt just kept growing. After a while, I realized I could never get it straightened out, so I started planning an exit strategy." His eyes pleaded with her to understand.

"Was this before or after you established the River Foundation?"

He looked away. "Before."

"Because donations were even easier to manipulate than investments. You only had to spend enough to make it look good while you siphoned the rest into your own accounts. And you used me to bilk people out of more donations."

"We did some good, you and I. The team generated valuable research, and with the erosion control measures we put into place, the river has never been healthier."

"Don't. Don't even try to pretend you cared about the river. You don't care about anyone but yourself."

"I cared about you."

"Right. That's why you left me to take the heat while you ran. Nobody wants to hire a suspected embezzler. That's why you've almost bankrupted my family. My uncle just had a heart transplant—did you know that? He's been struggling through the last few months, unable to work, and the cushion they worked so hard to accumulate is gone. Now they'll be buried under medical bills for the rest of their lives. And it's your greed that did this."

Jason paused for a moment and then jerked his head toward the side of the house. "Take a look under the bed."

She eyed him with suspicion. "Why?"

"Just look." He glanced down at his tied feet. "I'm not going anywhere."

She checked the knots on his wrists before stepping into the bedroom. Under the log bed, she found a suitcase. It was heavy when she tugged on it, maybe forty or fifty pounds. She pulled it out and carried it to the kitchen. "Is this what you were talking about?"

Jason nodded. "Open it. The combination is three fourteen. Your birthday."

She opened the suitcase to reveal stacks of hundred dollar bills. A shudder of revulsion passed through her that he'd dirtied her date of birth, using it this way.

Jason didn't seem to notice. "There's over two million dollars in there. Take whatever I owe you and enough to pay Oliver's medical bills, and leave me the rest."

Slowly, she turned to look at him, but didn't speak.

He jerked his head. "Come on, Marissa. We don't have that much time. You can say I worked the knots loose and overpowered you."

"And where would you go? The snow machine is disabled."

"Don't worry about it. I'll head out on foot. Once I'm away from here, I can manage something. Cash can go a long way. I just have to hide out until Jewel can figure out how to get me the documents I need."

So his ex *was* in on this. Marissa looked again at the neat stacks of hundreds and pressed her knuckle to her lip. The temptation was there. She could undo the damage Jason had inflicted on her family. Replace all the money Oliver had lost, and the money she'd lost. She wouldn't take extra for medical bills, just what Jason owed them.

It wasn't as though Jason could actually get away. He had no mechanical skills, so he wouldn't be able to get the vehicles running. If he went in the opposite direction from where Chris would be bringing the troopers, Jason would have to wade through deep snow for ten miles and cross a river before he reached any sign of civilization. They'd track him down and catch him within hours. If they didn't, he'd die of exposure. Plenty of people would say it served him right.

She sighed. It was a nice fantasy, but she couldn't take the money. She and Oliver were only two of the hundreds of people he'd stolen from. The cash in this suitcase, along with whatever else they might be able to recover, belonged to all of them.

She looked out the window. "I could let you go. Let you and your stolen money go wandering off through the snow. It's almost sundown now, and it's supposed to fall to ten below zero tonight." She closed the lid of the suitcase and locked it. "They say it's not a bad way to die. At first you're shivering and miserable, but by the time you're dangerously hypothermic you're too disoriented to suffer. Most people just lie down and go to sleep. A few take off their clothes first. For some reason, just before you die, you feel hot." She turned to Jason. "Would you like that better than jail?"

His eyes went wide. "I, uh—"

She didn't blink. "It doesn't matter what you want, because it's not going to happen. You're going to have to face up to what you've done. Sit in a courtroom and let all those people whose lives you ruined look you in the eye and testify about what a worthless piece of trash you are."

"I am sorry, Marissa." He looked away and then turned back to her. "Take it anyway, what I owe you and Oliver. I won't tell."

"No." She raised her chin a fraction. "That money doesn't belong to us. That may not make any difference to you, but it matters to me."

CHAPTER SIXTEEN

MARISSA WATCHED DETECTIVE SIMONTON write something in his ever-present notebook. She wasn't sure why, since there was a camera in the corner of the room and a voice recorder on the table between them.

It should be all over. Jason was locked up now, awaiting trial. The cash he'd been carrying, along with some bearer bonds they'd found hidden inside his coat lining, had been confiscated as evidence. But Marissa wasn't off the hook yet.

"At what point did you first suspect Jason Kort was occupying the cabin owned by Jim Eriksson?"

She'd already given her statement to the troopers, but patiently went over it all again. She told him about noticing the smoke from the chimney, the unplowed driveway and what drove her to investigate.

"Once you'd formed this suspicion, why didn't you contact the authorities immediately?"

"Honestly, I was afraid of embarrassing myself. Most likely it was a false alarm and I'd have wasted everyone's time and looked like an idiot."

"So you and Mr.——" he checked his notes "——Allen decided to confront a dangerous suspect on your own."

"He wasn't dangerous. Not physically, anyway. And I was armed."

The detective nodded. "I see that in the report. Do you have a concealed carry permit?"

"It wasn't concealed, and no. I don't believe a permit is required in Alaska." In fact, the troopers had assured her of it when they came to arrest Jason.

Detective Simonton fixed her with his gaze. "Did you conspire with Jason Kort to conceal his whereabouts from authorities at any time?"

"I did not. I turned him in as soon as I knew he was here." Did he believe her? She'd never helped Jason, so they couldn't prove she did. But sometimes unproven suspicions were the worst. If the talking heads decided she'd helped him hide, she might never get another decent job.

The detective nodded and asked her several other questions, often the same ones she'd already answered in different words. Finally, he closed his notebook. For the first time, genuine emotion appeared on his face. "How's your uncle?"

Marissa smiled. "Much better. He's recovering from a heart transplant, and the doctors say he's doing well."

"I'm glad to hear that. I can tell you that Mr. Kort also states you had no knowledge of his decision to relocate to Alaska. He expresses regret and has turned over access to certain offshore accounts. This is going to take a lot of forensic accounting, but off the record, I think most of the investors will have at least part of their initial investments returned when it's all said and done. I hope that helps your uncle."

"It will. Thank you."

CHRIS PRINTED OUT payroll checks. Another snow yesterday evening meant next week's cash flow was looking up. This time he'd actually managed to move a little money into his boat fund instead of out of it. Mike's half-price offer on the *New Beginnings* still hung out there. Was he a fool for refusing to take advantage of Mike's need to make his wife suffer? If Chris didn't buy it, somebody would. But he couldn't see himself building a career off someone else's misery. Another boat would come along, something smaller he could afford.

His phone rang. Becky. Chris smiled and answered. "Hi. How are you?"

"Great. Oliver's doing so well he doesn't need as much monitoring, so they moved him to a different room this morning. If all goes according to plan, we might be able to come home before the month is out."

"That's excellent news."

"I've been meaning to call to thank you for the ride to the airport, and for helping Marissa."

"It was nothing."

"If you hadn't got us to the plane, Oliver would have missed his chance. You may have given me another ten or twenty years with the man I love. Let me say thank you."

"You're welcome."

"I heard your name on television yesterday."

"Oh?" Marissa had warned him she wasn't telling Becky and Oliver the whole story, only that Kort had been captured. She was hoping they'd be too busy to watch the news.

Becky laughed. "Good thing Oliver has a new heart. I'm not sure his old one would have taken the shock of hearing his little girl was out apprehending criminals. I'm glad you were with her."

"It wasn't nearly as dramatic as they made it seem."

"Don't worry. I'll let Marissa think she's protecting us. I'm just glad that man is behind bars where he can't do more damage. How's Ryan?"

"Good. He's back in school. Still with my neighbors for the time being. He's been out to the farm a couple of times since you've been gone."

"I'm glad. He has a real bond with animals. Well, I'll let you go, but thank you for keeping an eye on Marissa and the farm. She says everything's all right, but we worry."

"You don't need to. She's strong and determined. She'll be fine. Goodbye, Becky. Give Oliver my best."

They worried. With everything going on in their own lives—Oliver recovering from major surgery, the lack of money, the maintenance needed on the farm—they worried about Marissa. That's what real families did. They supported each other, helped when they could, and yes, they worried. Marissa wasn't even their child, and she'd been an adult and living her own life for a long time, but they never stopped worrying.

Catching the man who had wronged her was a huge accomplishment for Marissa, but it didn't solve everything. She'd confided to Chris how Kort had tried to bribe her and how tempted she was to take the bribe. Who could blame her, with no paycheck coming in and Oliver's medical bills hanging over them? But she did the right thing.

Marissa would get through this, mostly because she was too strong not to. She'd keep right on making plans and forging ahead until she'd put things right for her family. After she dumped him, Chris had managed to convince himself that Marissa was selfish and rigid, but that wasn't so. She was a lot like her aunt Becky. Family first.

He could have been part of that family, but he blew it. He'd been so arrogant, acting as though his refusal to have children was some sort of altruistic decision. He assumed because he had a poor father, he'd be a poor father. He'd never bothered to educate himself about parenting or spend time around kids to see if he could relate to them. No, he'd drawn a line and stubbornly refused to cross it. And it cost him the love of his life.

Now, after spending so much time with Ryan, he finally understood the strength of Marissa's need to have children, because he felt it, too. He wanted to be a dad. He wanted to be Ryan's dad. But how could he? He'd blown his chance to marry the only woman he ever loved. It would be tough to be a single dad. He was a fisherman, gone for months at a time. Ryan deserved a good family and a father who was there for him. Period.

Regrets—Chris was full of them. When Marissa broke their engagement, he should have fought harder to keep her. Just like he should have found a way to keep in touch with Dana after he'd left home. He'd allowed a disagreement with his father to separate him from his sister. For nineteen years. And it was only because Dana came looking for him after their father died that they were together now.

He'd never really considered how upset Dana must have been when he disappeared without a word. Poor kid. Only sixteen, and nobody to tell her where he was or why he'd left. Chris couldn't change the past, but maybe it was time he did something about it.

Maybe Sam had the right idea. On the way home, Chris swung by the florist. "I need an apology bouquet."

The middle-aged woman at the desk grinned. "How bad was it?"

"Pretty bad."

She led him to the cooler, slid open the door and pulled out a medium-size bunch of daisies in a basket. "How's this?"

"Worse than that."

She pointed to an enormous arrangement in a tall vase. "Nothing more romantic than red roses."

Chris shook his head. "It's for my sister."

"Oh. Well, that's different. What's her favorite color?"

What was Dana's favorite color? He should know this. Chris tried to think of the clothes she wore most often. "Pink?"

"Okay. Give me a few minutes." The florist walked over to another cooler and began choosing flowers from the various bunches in shades of purple, pink and white. He watched as she placed them in a pink teapot with white polka-dots. Once they were arranged to her liking, she pulled two balloons on long stems from a bin near the door. Each had a message printed on it.

"Which one?"

Chris considered. "Can we do both?"

"Why not?" She tucked the balloons among the flowers.

Chris pulled out his wallet. "Thanks. I think she'll love these."

"Of course she will. She's your sister. Sisters love it when you grovel."

As soon as Chris stepped through the front door, the aroma of beef stew set his mouth watering. Dana sat tapping on her computer, textbooks scattered across the kitchen table. She didn't look up. "Hi. Dinner will be ready in about fifteen minutes."

"Okay." Chris plucked one of the balloons from the arrangement and put it aside before setting the flowers on the table in front of her.

She gazed at the floral arrangement and then looked up at him, wide-eyed. "What's all this?"

"Flowers. For you."

A smile bloomed on her face. "They're gorgeous. I love the colors." She reached out to touch the teapot. "But I don't understand. Why does it say I'm Sorry on the balloon?"

"Because I am."

"What about?"

"The day I left home." Chris slid into the chair beside her. "I've been thinking about that day. How you must have felt when I drove away without talking to you. Yes, after what happened with Dad, I had to go, but I should have found a way to keep in touch with you. You were only a teenager. I should have made sure you were okay."

Her lip trembled. "I missed you so much."

"I missed you, too. I told myself it was better if I didn't drag you into the middle of the thing with Dad. That I should just stay out of your life. But I was wrong."

She studied his face for a moment, those big brown eyes blinking back tears. "It was really hard without you to talk to."

"I know. That whole situation was a mess. I shouldn't have left it all to fall into your lap. That wasn't fair." He smiled. "Although to be honest, you handled it much better than I ever could have."

She smiled back. "That may well be, but it doesn't excuse you for disappearing for nineteen years."

"No, it doesn't. I'm not making excuses, just asking for your forgiveness."

She didn't hesitate. "You're forgiven. But I expect payback in the form of babysitting. Sandy tells me you're quite the expert."

"Absolutely. I could teach classes. Just ask April."

Dana reached over to give him a hug. "I'm glad we're together now."

"Me, too. That's why I got this." He reached past her and tucked the World's Most Fabulous Sister balloon into the bouquet.

She laughed. "About time you figured out what an awesome sister you have."

Chris smiled. "I've always known."

THE NEXT EVENING, Marissa stirred the meat-and-tomato sauce and turned the burner down low to let it simmer. A skiff of snow had fallen overnight, not enough that she would have bothered with it, but Chris had called and said he was coming to plow, and bringing Ryan, and frankly, she was getting a little tired of eating alone.

Funny, because she'd been living by herself for years, and never really minded eating with only the television for company. But the farmhouse seemed too quiet with Oliver and Becky gone.

The rumble of Chris's truck had her grabbing her coat and hurrying to the front porch to meet them and invite them to stay for dinner.

Chris seemed pleased at the invitation. He called to clear it with Ryan's foster mother before accepting. Ryan came inside to check on Adele, while Chris finished the plowing and Marissa cooked the pasta.

Chris came to the back door, toeing off his boots in the mudroom before he stepped inside. "Something smells good."

"Spaghetti. You and Ryan go wash up and I'll get it on the table." Marissa smiled to herself. Even as she said it, she could almost hear the echo of her aunt's voice, saying the exact same words to her and Oliver. Maybe that's why she felt lonely, because this kitchen was accustomed to family meals, conversation and laughter.

The phone rang as she was putting the food on the table. She almost ignored it, but Oliver and Becky didn't have caller ID, so it could be one of them trying to reach her. "Hello?"

"Marissa Gray? I'm Sarah Ames from Channel Five." A reporter.

Darn it, she'd thought they'd moved on by now. One of the local television news crews wanted her to do an interview about capturing Jason. She just wanted to forget the whole sorry episode. She was finishing the call when Chris and Ryan returned. "No. Thank you for the opportunity, but I really don't have anything to say. Yes, I'll call you if I change my mind. Goodbye."

Chris sat down at the table. "More reporters?"

Marissa nodded and spooned spaghetti onto Ryan's plate. "Local. They want an interview. I said no."

Chris nodded and added salad to Ryan's

plate before putting some on his own. "I don't blame you." He passed Ryan the garlic bread. "Although it might not be such a bad idea."

"Why do you say that?"

"You were telling me yesterday you were afraid some people suspected you were helping Kort hide. This would be your chance to get the truth out there."

He had a point. Employers still weren't breaking down the doors to hire her. "What about you?"

"What about me?"

"You were there. Will you talk to them?"

"They're not interested in me. I only called the cops."

"But if they want to talk to you, will you?"

"I'll do whatever you want."

Marissa laughed. "Ryan, you're a witness. He said he'll do whatever I want."

The boy giggled. "What are you going to make him do? Eat bugs?"

"Nah, he rides a mountain bike. I'm sure he's already eaten plenty of bugs. I'll think about it until I come up with something really good."

"You could make him eat dirt," Ryan suggested.

Chris ruffled the boy's hair. "Hey, stop

helping her. She can come up with plenty of ideas all on her own."

Ryan laughed, looking up at Chris. Marissa smiled, but inwardly gave a little sigh. Why was it taking Chris so long to see what a great father he would be? She'd tried to tell him so ten years ago, but no, he had to be stubborn. If people would just follow the plan, life would be so much simpler. But they never did.

FIVE DAYS LATER, Marissa paced the living room, waiting for the Wednesday morning talk show to start. Why had she let Chris convince her to do that interview? She'd thought they would stick to Jason's capture, but somehow before they were through, she'd given them the whole story, about the River Foundation and why she felt fortunate to work there, how Jason had talked her into helping raise money, and the shock of finding out about the Ponzi scheme. Chris had been there with her, supporting her from behind the scenes. Maybe that's why she'd felt confident enough to bare her soul.

The doorbell rang and the front door opened. Chris, of course. "Okay if I come in?"

She raised her hands palms up. "Why not? The whole state is going to see what an idiot

I was. You might as well join in." She turned away from him, toward the screen.

He rested his hands on her shoulders. "You were passionate about what you were doing and a clever man took advantage of that passion. That doesn't make you an idiot."

Marissa blew out a breath. "At least they're only using five minutes of the interview. Maybe they'll edit out the really embarrassing stuff."

It started off worse than she thought, with background on the Ponzi scheme and that awful photo of her and Jason accepting a check for the River Foundation. Then they cut to her, and let her babble on about how much she'd loved the river. They even included a shot of her wiping a tear from her eye as she explained the river's Cinderella story and how it had come back from a chemical spill to the healthy ecosystem it was today.

But the reporter then went on to describe how she'd discovered Jason's whereabouts and brought him to justice. At the end of the clip was a shot of Chris, standing outside his warehouse. The reporter thrust a microphone in his face.

"I understand you assisted Marissa Gray in the capture of Jason Kort. There's been speculation that Miss Gray may have helped Mr.

Kort to evade capture, before she decided to turn him in. What can you tell us about that?"

"None of that is true. As soon as Marissa Gray had the slightest idea Jason Kort might have been hiding out in that cabin, she enlisted my help to bring him to justice. She's one of the bravest, most honorable people I've ever met, and I'm proud to know her." The show cut to a commercial.

Marissa turned to Chris. "You didn't tell me they'd talked to you."

"I didn't want to make you nervous."

"That was a nice thing you said."

"You are brave. And honorable."

"I'm not sure that's true."

"I am." He gave her that crooked smile that always made her smile, too. Even after their history, he stood up for her, in public. He was there for her family when they needed help. And whether it was comforting her when she was upset or going along with her plan to capture fugitives, he'd been a hundred percent supportive.

She cocked her head. "You remember the other night when you said you'd do whatever I asked?"

The corners of his eyes crinkled. "I'm afraid so. Are you ready to collect?"

"I am."

"What do you want me to do? It's not bug season."

She smiled and took a step closer. "Kiss me."

He raised an eyebrow. "That's it?"

"That's what I want."

He laughed. Ran a finger down the side of her face to brush her hair back behind her shoulder. And then he gathered her into his arms and pulled her tight against his chest. Her heart beat faster, and he hadn't even touched her lips yet. He lowered his head and brushed his mouth against hers like a whisper. She parted her lips to draw in a breath, and he captured her mouth. Her arms tightened around his neck, pulling him closer.

How she'd missed this. The way they fit together. His lips pressed to hers, exploring, caressing. His arms around her, holding her safe against his broad chest, his heart beating in time with hers. It was like the last piece of a jigsaw puzzle that snapped into the empty spot and brought the whole picture into focus. It had never been this way with anyone else. She wanted to stay in his arms forever.

Forever.

That's when she came to her senses. She didn't have forever. As soon as she found a job, she was out of here. She shouldn't be starting something she couldn't finish. He'd hurt her once, and she'd hurt him, too. It wasn't fair for either of them to have to go through that again. She pulled back.

"What's wrong?" Chris stroked his fingers along her cheek down to her chin.

"I—I didn't think this through."

He chuckled. "You don't have to plan out every detail of your life."

"It works better when I do."

He didn't answer. Instead he pushed his hand into her hair and cradled the back of her head, his fingers moving in slow circles as his eyes gazed into hers, hypnotically. She should pull away, but she couldn't seem to work up the will. Finally, he smiled.

"Let's make plans, then. I'll be back at six and I'll bring dinner." He bent forward to kiss her forehead, and then he was gone.

She stood, staring at the closed door behind him. The television blathered on, the hosts commenting on her interview, but she didn't hear them. What was going on here? She was acting on impulse and Chris was making plans.

Maybe later, she should check to see if Willa might be sprouting wings.

CHAPTER SEVENTEEN

THE PHONE RANG as Marissa stepped out of the shower. She wrapped a towel around herself and hurried to the extension in her bedroom, catching it on the fourth ring. "Hello?"

"Oh, sweetheart, we saw you on television." Becky's voice overflowed with enthusiasm. "You were wonderful."

"How? It was on a local channel." And not even a highly rated one.

"The Seattle news picked it up and ran part of the clip, about how important the River Foundation was to you and why you wanted Jason caught. The nurses are all talking about it."

"Really?" Was that good or bad? Hard to be sure. She decided to change the subject. "How's Oliver today?"

"Better than ever now that Jason is behind bars."

They talked for another ten minutes before Marissa hung up the phone and glanced at the clock. Chris would be here soon. She pulled on yoga pants and a soft hoodie and ran to the bathroom to dry her hair. When she turned off the blow-dryer, she could hear his truck bouncing up the lane, so she added a little mascara and lip gloss and hurried downstairs to meet him at the door.

Heavenly smells of garlic, tomato and basil emanated from the bag he was carrying. Marissa's mouth watered. "From Roman's?" Her favorite restaurant on the continent and she hadn't made it there since she got back.

He nodded. "Lasagna, eggplant parmesan and tiramisu."

"Yum, I like your plan so far."

"I thought you might." Chris followed her to the kitchen, where she wasted no time setting the table. "Where's Adele?"

"Back in the chicken coop. She's much better, and I think our fox friend has given up after you sealed off his hole. I haven't seen his tracks around the last two days."

Tiger rubbed against Chris's ankle and he reached down to stroke the cat before he pulled out a bottle of Chianti and his Swiss army knife to open it. "I think we're supposed to let this breathe."

Marissa unloaded the containers from the sack he'd brought. "It can yodel if it wants, but I'm not waiting on it. I skipped lunch and this lasagna is pleading with me to eat it now."

Chris laughed and pulled out a chair for her. "It would be wrong to let it suffer."

They stole bites off each other's plate and talked about everything and nothing, like they used to. "Sam's back from the slope, thank goodness. He seems convinced if he's not there to guard Dana every minute, some eagle is going to swoop down and carry her and the baby away."

Marissa felt that familiar little stab in her heart. She'd never be pregnant. Never have a man make a fool of himself, worrying about her and a baby. But just because it wouldn't happen to her didn't mean she couldn't be happy for other people. Sam and Dana were nice, even if Sam didn't approve of her. She smiled. "If he's that nervous already, imagine what a basket case he'll be in the delivery room."

"Tell me about it."

Eventually, Chris did pour the wine. Marissa held up her glass in a toast. "To old friends."

A look she couldn't quite interpret passed over his face before Chris raised his glass. "Old friends. And new beginnings."

New beginnings. She couldn't argue with

that. Now that Jason was in jail, maybe she could start again. She clinked her glass against his and drank.

Once he'd plied her with dessert and helped her load the dishwasher, he led her to the living room and sat beside her on the sofa, in front of the fireplace. His fingers scraped through his hair, releasing a tangle of curls. "I wanted to talk with you about something."

"All right."

He cleared his throat. "I, uh, well, I was wrong."

"No." She feigned shock. "What about?"

"Ten years ago. You wanted kids. I didn't. I was wrong."

"Chris—"

"I never intended to get married. In the house where I grew up, marriage looked like a bad idea. But then I met you, and the thought of losing you scared me more than the thought of marriage. So I proposed."

"Yes, I was there."

"But getting engaged didn't take away the fear. I wanted you as my wife, but part of me was terrified that once you really knew me, you'd grow to hate me. You say I withdrew. Maybe I did. Maybe I was trying to put some distance between us so it would be easier when you left me." A wry smile crossed his face. "For the record, it wasn't."

"I'm sorry I hurt you."

He shook his head. "No, it was my fault. I was stubborn, and stupid. You tried to tell me I could do it, that you'd give me time to grow into the idea of kids, but I wouldn't listen. And I wasn't strong enough to end it. I forced you to do that. And then I blamed you."

"And I blamed you."

"You should. I'm five years older than you, but I hadn't grown up. I didn't want kids, because I was convinced I was destined to be my father. But that's ridiculous. I'm not like him in the way I work, in the friends I choose or in what I find important. Why would I suddenly revert into my father when it came to children?"

Her eyes burned. Why now? Why would he come to this decision now, ten years too late? She tried to blink away the tears, but one overflowed and ran down her cheek. Chris reached to wipe it with his thumb, but he kept on talking, unaware that he was ripping her heart out.

"Now that I've spent time with Ryan, I know I can be a father. I want to adopt him. I'm giving up fishing. I'll find a new career, something where I can be around every day for him. I love that kid. And I love you, Bo. I always have. I'm ten years late, but I want to marry you. I want us to make a family for Ryan, and to give him little brothers or sisters. You'll be an awesome mom."

A sob from deep inside jerked its way past the lump in her throat, opening the spillway and releasing all the tears she'd been holding inside. Damn him. Why couldn't he have loved her the way he was supposed to ten years ago? They'd have that family. A little girl with his auburn curls and her greenish-blue eyes. A boy who followed his father around as he did chores, wanting to be just like his daddy. And Ryan, too. There was a special spot for Ryan in her fantasy. They would embrace him into their family. But it was too late for that.

Chris gathered her into his arms and pulled her close, letting her tears soak into the shoulder of his shirt. "What is it, Bo?" His hand rubbed up and down her back and she felt rather than heard a long sigh escape him. "I took too long. You don't love me anymore."

She shook her head, but couldn't seem to form words through the sobbing. He stopped talking and just held her, murmuring little comforting sounds as he stroked her back and rocked her, much as a mother would soothe a baby. How did he know how to do that?

Finally, the tears ran dry. She pulled away from him and ran into the bathroom, where she blew her nose and washed the black smears of mascara from her face. She was a mess, red-rimmed eyes, tangled hair. She ran a comb through the rat's nest and returned to the living room, where Chris watched her mutely.

She managed a weak smile. "Sorry about that."

He stretched out his hand "Did I ruin everything?"

"No." She sat beside him and took both his hands in hers. "You weren't wrong to tell me the truth, that you didn't want children. Children were important to me, and it would have been dishonest to let me go on believing you wanted kids when you didn't."

"I didn't know my own mind."

"I think you did, at the time. And now you realize you do want children. I get that. I know how strong the feeling can be. After all, I gave up the man I loved for the possibility of becoming a mother." She squeezed his hands. "I can't marry you. I love you, but I can't give you what you need."

"You love me?"

"I do."

"Then why can't we try again? You're only thirty-four. We have time."

"No, we don't." Marissa released his hands. She pushed her yoga pants lower and pulled up her sweatshirt, exposing her stomach.

Chris flinched at the sight of the lumpy red marks marring her smooth skin. He touched the tip of his finger to the big round scar and drew his hand back, as though afraid he would hurt her. "What happened?"

"An accident." She rearranged her clothes to cover the scars. "We were taking blood samples from wild bison. We'd herded them into a corral and ran them, one at a time, through a squeeze chute, where we'd take the sample and let them go. It was a portable setup, and we'd been working at it all morning. Apparently the guy who set it up hadn't tightened the bolts properly, and they worked loose. Anyway, when I climbed up to take the sample from the bull, he charged and the fence gave way. Everything happened fast after that and I don't remember all the details, but I ended up gored through the belly, and had to have an emergency hysterectomy."

"When was this?"

"About four years ago. I was engaged at

the time, but he wanted children, so…" She shrugged.

Chris laid his hand gently over her abdomen. "Bo, this doesn't matter. I love you, not your organs."

"But you want kids."

"Ryan's already born."

She shook her head. "What about those little brothers and sisters you were talking about?"

"Not as important as you." He looked as though he meant it, and at the moment, he probably did. Marissa wanted desperately to believe him, but she knew better. "Besides, we could adopt other kids."

"No, in the long run it can't work. I know. When you refused to have children, I did blame you. I despised you for taking away what I wanted most in the world. You might think you're okay with this, but later, when you think of the kids you might have had, you'll resent me. You need to find a woman who can be a mother to Ryan and give birth to those kids you want."

"I've found the only woman I want."

"No, Chris." She looked away from him and rubbed her eyes. She'd cried enough. "My answer is no."

"Come here, Bo." He pulled her close and

held her, his arms strong and yet so gentle. "I'm not giving up, but I won't argue with you anymore tonight." He held her in silence, stroking her hair, until some of the tension left her body. He kissed the top of her head. "May I still bring Ryan out after school tomorrow?"

"Of course." It was easy to see what Chris was up to. Dangling that adorable little boy in front of her like bait in a trap. It would be easier to maintain her resolve if she didn't have to spend time with Ryan, but this situation wasn't his fault. It wouldn't be fair to turn him away because spending time with him tempted her to believe in things she knew weren't true. Like happily ever after.

MARISSA THREW HERSELF into her chores the next morning, trying to outrun her doubts. In spite of their complicated history, she loved Chris. He was her first love, and her best. And now he was offering her exactly what she'd always wanted, a home and a family. But it was a mirage.

He may have been late to the party, but now that the urge to have children had finally hit him, it had hit him hard. She understood. It had taken her a long time to stop grieving over her lost opportunity and accept that she would never have children. If she were honest, maybe she was still grieving a little bit.

She wanted the whole experience. Coming together in love to create a real live person. Bonding as a couple, and over the course of a pregnancy, morphing into parents. When women she knew talked about morning sickness, swollen ankles and labor pains, she handed out sympathy, but an ugly little voice inside of her screamed, "Why not me?"

She would never experience becoming someone's biological parent, but Chris still could, and she wanted him to have that chance. Besides, there were other reasons this couldn't work. She had responsibilities. Jason was finally behind bars, but it didn't sound as though his victims would be getting their money back anytime soon, if ever. She needed a good job in her field to pay off the mortgage on the farm. She'd combed through every job listing in Alaska, but the only opening she'd found was a part-time position in a bear study. Actually, it sounded like a great study, but she needed a full paycheck, and that meant relocating. It wouldn't be fair to drag Chris away from his home and business, or to take Ryan away from his grandmother.

As usual, Chris was letting his heart lead

the way without a plan. He loved Ryan, so out of the blue, he'd announced he would give up fishing and take up some other yet-to-be-determined profession so that he could adopt him. He probably hadn't even checked if Ryan was available for adoption. He just assumed it would work out.

Chris loved her, and so without considering where they would live or how they would integrate their professional lives, he'd asked her to marry him. And even after she told him she couldn't have children, he'd persisted in believing it would all work out. Love conquered all, at least in Chris's mind.

But somebody had to face reality and plan for the future. Love was not going to pay off that mortgage. Love didn't cover the medical bills. Love wouldn't make her body work the way that it should. Marissa had responsibilities to her family, she had a career to salvage, and right now, she had a goat pen to clean.

She grabbed a pitchfork and started piling the soiled straw into a wheelbarrow. Willa waddled over, rubbing against Marissa's leg to get her attention. Since she weighed almost two hundred pounds, she was impossible to ignore. Marissa stopped shoveling to scratch under her chin. Stiff hairs poked against her hand, but Willa's blissful expression kept her scratching. Of course, the goats noticed, and decided to get in on the affection. Marissa had to sprinkle a little extra food into their trough in order to lure the herd away so she could work. No doubt Ryan would give them all the affection they could handle when he came later.

She smiled. That boy loved animals. She'd been the same way. Instead of watching television or playing video games, she'd spent most of her time hanging out with the livestock, or observing the wild animals. As a teenager, she'd raised several orphaned birds and once nursed an injured marmot back to health. Nobody was surprised when she chose wildlife biology as her major. Maybe Ryan would, too, someday. Or maybe veterinary school. He was smart enough, and so gentle with the animals. She could definitely see it.

She hoped with all her heart Chris was able to adopt him. Ryan deserved somebody like Chris to love him and take care of him, to give him confidence in his own abilities. Chris was always good at that. When she was in school and would become discouraged over a project that wasn't going well, or a disappointing grade on a test, Chris was always there to encourage her and let her blow off steam. He'd let her talk it through, organize her thoughts. Even though he teased her about her tendency to overplan, he never tried to change her. Ryan would thrive with Chris as his dad.

And maybe now that Chris was finally in settling-down mode, he'd quit dating women who were only passing through, and find himself a good wife. Someone who would be a good mother for Ryan and the children they would have together. Meanwhile, Marissa would be somewhere faraway, maybe studying pelicans in the Everglades or cutthroat trout in Wyoming. She wouldn't get to see Ryan grow up. The best she could hope for was that Chris would stay in contact with Oliver and Becky, although once they sold the farm, he'd have no reason to bring Ryan for visits anymore. Maybe Chris and his wife would send Marissa a Christmas card every year with a picture of their kids, and she would be happy for them. Even if it only made her more heartbroken.

Once she finished feeding all the animals and cleaning out the pen, she went inside for lunch. The machine blinked with a message to call her headhunter. She ignored her growling stomach and dialed the number. He got right to business.

"Great job on that interview."

"You saw it?"

"Everybody saw it. It's all over the country, and it's working. Now that they see how passionate you are about wildlife, several of the employers that turned you down have contacted me about possible positions. I'll send the details ASAP, but you may want to pack. I'm fairly confident you'll be interviewing in the next couple of days."

"That's great." It was exactly what she'd asked for, and if she wasn't as excited as she should have been, well, that was her problem. Still... "None of those positions is in south-central Alaska, by chance?"

"No." He paused and continued in an accusing tone. "You said you were free to relocate anywhere."

"I am. I just wondered. I'll check my email and get back to you right away. Thank you."

Good news. If all went well, in a week or two she would be doing the work she loved again, studying wildlife, and at the same time helping Oliver and Becky financially. They could sell the farm and move to town, closer to medical care. Finally, everything was going according to plan. But that realization wasn't as satisfying as she would have expected.

CHRIS WRAPPED THE glass he'd had cut to replace that broken windowpane at the farm
and packed it in the back of his truck, along
with a few extra tools and supplies. Last time
he was there, he'd noticed a dripping faucet,
and he suspected when he checked he'd find
a lot more.

Once he finished loading the truck, he
walked over to the fence to watch Ryan. Kimmik had a toy in his mouth, and Ryan was
chasing after him, giggling. After several
laps around the yard, he stopped to catch his
breath, his hands on his knees. Kimmik hurried up to present him with the toy.

Earlier that day, Chris had received word
that his background check had gone through,
and he'd made an appointment for an interview with the mentor service. He was almost tempted to cancel. He didn't want to
be a sometimes friend for Ryan. He wanted
to be his dad. But there were a lot of details
to work through before anyone was going to
let him adopt, and this was a good first step.

"Hey, Ryan. Ready to go to the farm?"

"Yeah." Ryan rubbed Kimmik's ears and
trotted over to the gate. "You think Marissa
will let me lead one of the reindeer?"

"I don't know. You'll have to ask her."

"I think she will. She's really nice."

"Yes, she is."

Ryan climbed into the truck and buckled himself into the new booster seat Chris had purchased for him. "She's pretty, too."

"Yep." Chris started the truck and backed out of the driveway.

"Is Marissa your girlfriend?"

He laughed, but there was a bitter edge to it that caused Ryan to look at him questioningly. Chris gave what he hoped was a reassuring smile. "No, not anymore."

"But she used to be?"

Chris nodded. "A long time ago. Before you were born."

"Why didn't you get married?"

"That, my friend, is a long story. But the short answer is because I'm a stupid man and it took me too long to figure out what I wanted."

"You're not stupid. You're smart." Ryan's quick defense warmed Chris's heart. But after a moment, he continued. "Not as smart as Marissa. She knows all about animals, but you're still smart."

Chris chuckled. "Thank you. You're smart, too. Especially about dinosaurs."

"I know."

When they arrived at the farm, they had to

wait several minutes before Marissa answered the door. "Sorry, I was upstairs, packing."

"Packing?" Chris suddenly felt the chill. He stepped inside after Ryan. "Where are you going?"

"Oregon." Her tongue flicked over her lower lip. "I have a job interview. I'm flying out tomorrow. I'll stop over in Seattle and spend the weekend with Oliver and Becky on the way back."

Reality hit Chris like a cannonball in the chest, making it hard to breathe. So this was it. He'd tried to convince himself that if he gave her a little time to think things over, she would change her mind. He should have known better. Marissa always stuck with the plan, and her plans didn't include him.

Ryan was looking up at him, with his eyebrows drawn together. Chris tried for a smile. "Congratulations. What kind of job is it?"

"Wildlife inventory. A multiyear project counting the different plants and animals in the management area and assessing the relative health of their populations and what might impact it. They need someone to head up the team."

"It sounds right up your alley."

"Yes. It's perfect." She answered a little too fast. "I want to thank you for encouraging me to do that television interview. According to my headhunter, that's why people suddenly want to hire me now."

"Great." So he'd managed to sabotage himself. If he'd left well enough alone, maybe she'd have stuck around a little longer. Maybe he could have changed her mind.

But he wasn't sorry. It wasn't fair for Marissa to be blamed for something she didn't do. Besides, he wanted her to marry him because she wanted to be with him, not because she had no other options. And he understood why she needed a paycheck. Still, he wished they'd had a little more time. "Who's taking care of the farm?"

"I have a call in to the farmer in Palmer who always does it when Oliver and Becky travel. He has a couple of teenage sons who don't mind driving over to earn a few bucks."

"No need to pay somebody. I can stay here and take care of the farm while you're gone."

She looked up at him, a wrinkle between her eyebrows. "I can't ask you to do that. You have your own business to take care of. And what about your sister?"

"Dana's fine, and Sam's home with her for another five days. There's no snow in the forecast until the end of next week. I can handle this. All I need is a list of chores and a schedule."

"I already have that."

Chris chuckled. "I'll bet you do. And I'll bet it's color-coded."

She rolled her eyes, but a smile sneaked through. "And what if it is?"

Ryan tugged on Chris's sleeve. "Can I live here, too? I can help."

Chris wrapped an arm around Ryan's head in a mock wrestling move. "Sorry, bud, you have school. But maybe you can come out and help one afternoon."

"Okay. Can we go see Willa and the goats now?"

CHAPTER EIGHTEEN

THE FACILITY SPARKLED. Nondescript on the outside, the gray-green walls almost disappeared into the forest, but the brand-new building housed a well-equipped lab, efficient offices, a conference room and plenty of storage. An adjacent building would hold a small fleet of trucks and ATVs. A huge map of the area covered one wall. Marissa traced her finger along one of the jeep trails following a ridge.

"We'd leave it to you to put together a team. We have a budget for four, not including yourself. The grant goes for five years, assuming you meet the benchmarks to insure the project will be completed on time. Let me show you the crew quarters." Nancy Lawson, the woman who would be her supervisor if she took the job, led the way.

Marissa was impressed. Nancy reminded her a little of Becky, organized and down-to-earth. In her waterproof boots and fleece vest, she could have been any random hiker on the trail, but after spending the morning with her, Marissa was convinced Nancy knew more about wildlife management than anyone she'd ever worked with. She outlined the project parameters and exactly what she wanted from the team. And Nancy made it clear she wanted Marissa.

They followed the path past a cluster of mountain ash to the crew quarters. Siding matched the work building and a green metal roof blended with the trees. Large windows flanked the door. The roof overhung the front of the house, creating a long sheltered porch. The front door opened into a spacious living area with a corner fireplace. To the left, the kitchen was divided from the rest of the room by a large island. A long pine dining table hugged the window with its forest view. A basket of fir cones sat in the center of the table.

Nancy took her down the hallway to show her the small, dormitory-type bedrooms, each with its own bathroom. At the end of the hallway, a washer/dryer combo shared space with a treadmill, weight machines and a rowing machine. Marissa and her team could be quite comfortable here.

They returned to the main room. A tapping sound led Marissa to the kitchen window, where she spied a red-breasted sapsucker pecking on the birch behind the house, drilling a row of tiny holes through the bark. She smiled.

This was Marissa's dream job. A beautiful location. Plenty of time in the field, observing the animals. A chance to choose her own team. And a generous paycheck that would go a lot further, since housing was furnished. Plus, they were only two hours from Portland, which was a three-and-a-half-hour flight from Anchorage, so she could get up to see Becky and Oliver more often.

She should be turning cartwheels over this opportunity. It was exactly the type of assignment she'd dreamed of when she first decided on her college major. The leadership experience she'd gain with this team put her ahead on her five-year plan. It was perfect. She just needed to get her heart on board.

"So. What do you think?"

Marissa turned to face Nancy. "It all looks fantastic." But somehow, she couldn't seem to pull the trigger. "When do you need my answer?"

Nancy frowned. "As soon as possible. We'd like to get the team assembled and ready to move forward by March 1. May I ask, are you considering other offers? Because there might be a little flexibility in the salary if that's what it takes to get you."

Marissa shook her head. "That's not it." She knew even as she said it she should have negotiated, but she wasn't used to approaching jobs as a mercenary. Still, it was a generous salary, and whatever they paid her came out of the working budget. There, she was already thinking like a team leader. "I just want to think it over before I commit."

"I understand." Nancy glanced through the front window. "It's a beautiful day. Do you have time for a little hike before we go back to town?"

"I'd like that. My flight isn't until seven tonight."

Nancy led her along a trail that cut through the trees. Marissa filled her lungs with the perfume of the forest: damp earth, leaf mold and fir needles. Winter was already on its way out, with a few seedlings pushing up from the earth alongside the trails. It would be months before spring arrived in Alaska.

The trail took a sharp bend. A series of switchbacks cut through the dense forest to the top of the hill. A Douglas squirrel chattered at them as they passed under his tree. Nancy was probably two decades older than her, but Marissa had to hustle to keep up. She was panting when they reached the crest.

They followed the trail a little farther to a clearing overlooking the valley below, and Nancy stopped. Marissa came to stand beside her. A rocky slope ranged downward to a deep blue lake surrounded on three sides by dense Douglas pines, with snowy peaks just visible over the treetops on the other side. At the edge of the water, two kayaks rested on the bank. Marissa felt an almost irresistible urge to scramble down to the beach, paddle into the middle of that mountain lake and just stare up at the majestic trees and the blue sky. If she took the job, this would be her backyard.

The sun shone warm on their faces. Nancy stood silent, letting the twitters and chirps of the forest birds surround them. After several minutes, Marissa turned to her and chuckled. "I see what you're doing here."

Nancy smiled. "Is it working?"

"You know it is."

"Good. Because this study is important to me. I want the best person I can get in charge, and I'm convinced that's you."

"THERE'S MY GIRL." Oliver held out his arms and Marissa let herself be enveloped. After a long hug, she stood back and looked at him. Good color in his face, no panting from the exertion of standing. The Oliver she remembered was back.

"We've missed you." Becky took her turn for a hug. "Tell us all about the job interview."

They settled onto the sofas in Becky's friend's town house, where they were both staying now that Oliver had been released from the hospital. He still had to check in often with the transplant center, so they needed to stay in Seattle for another few weeks.

"It went well." Marissa gave them the rundown of the facilities and the job, and showed them the pictures she'd taken. "The position is team leader for a wildlife inventory."

"Beautiful." Becky smiled at a photo of a western bluebird. "Do you think they'll offer you the job?"

"They already have." Marissa paused. "It's a great facility, and I really like the person I'd report to."

"But?" Oliver prodded.

"No but. It's a great opportunity."

"You haven't accepted?" Becky asked.

"Not yet, but think I will soon. It's really the perfect job. I won't be finding anything better."

Becky studied her face. "Then why don't you sound more excited?"

"I am excited. It's just…"

"Just what?"

Marissa sighed. "Just that I've been enjoying my time in Alaska, with you." She licked her lips. "I love my job, but I also love home."

"Are there no jobs in Alaska?" Oliver asked.

"One so far. A part-time position in a bear study in the Anchorage borough. It would be a step back, careerwise. This job in Oregon would be a huge leap forward. It's a beautiful area, and the pay is good." She didn't mention the salary would allow her to make payments on the mortgage and undo some of the damage her relationship with Jason had caused. Her aunt and uncle would just assure her it wasn't her fault. But it was.

"You make this Oregon study sound like your dream job, and yet you haven't accepted it." Becky cocked her head. "I have to wonder why."

"I don't know, exactly. I think I will take it. But I'll miss Alaska, and the people there."

Becky chuckled. "Any particular people?"

Marissa gave her a wry smile. "Chris asked me to marry him again."

Oliver broke into a grin, but Becky didn't even look surprised. "Oh?"

"I turned him down."

"Did you?" No judgment in her voice, but Marissa felt the need to explain.

"I had to." She stood and walked to the window. After a moment she turned. "He wants kids. He didn't before, but now he does. I wouldn't give up having kids for him ten years ago. How can I ask him to do the same for me now?"

"You told him about your accident?"

"Yes."

"And what did he say?" Oliver sounded ready to challenge Chris to a duel if he gave the wrong response.

She smiled, in spite of herself. "He said it didn't matter. He wants to adopt Ryan, anyway, and he says Ryan is enough. Only, before I told him about my accident, he'd been talking about little brothers and sisters for Ryan. He wants that."

"But he wants you more."

"That's what he says."

"You think he's lying?" Oliver asked.

"What? No. I don't think he's lying. Just that he doesn't realize what he'd be giving up by marrying someone who can't have children."

Oliver and Becky exchanged glances. *Oh, no. Open mouth, insert foot.* Marissa didn't know the particulars, but given how much Oliver and Becky loved children, they hadn't remained childless by choice. Her face grew hot. "I'm sorry. I shouldn't have said that."

Oliver took Becky's hand. "Sometimes we have to make difficult decisions. Think long and hard, weigh the choices, but don't forget to listen to your heart."

Becky smiled at him. "Mine never led me wrong."

THE FLIGHT FROM Seattle Sunday evening gave Marissa plenty of time to think, but her thoughts seemed to be going in circles. Finally, she opened her laptop and started a list of all the pros of taking this job. Financial stability, pay off mortgage, career advancement, pleasant environment, chance to lead a team, beautiful setting, gathering important wildlife data... It was a long list.

Then she listed the cons, and really, it came down to one thing: giving up a chance for love. Was it enough to outweigh everything else? She'd spent ten years angry with Chris, the man who wouldn't commit, but when it came down to it, she was the one who'd called off the wedding. He may have had doubts, but he would have gone through with it. Now she'd turned down his proposal again. Maybe she was the one who couldn't commit.

Chris loved Alaska. If she married him, she couldn't ask him to leave the state to follow her around the country, especially with Ryan in the mix. And she wanted Ryan in the mix. She adored that little boy. But if she stayed, she would have to take that part-time position, assuming it was offered, and hope once the study was done she could find something permanent. Her career might never recover.

If she took the Anchorage job, she could help Oliver and Becky around the farm, painting and fixing up the place once the weather warmed, but she wouldn't be able to help with the mortgage or replace what they had lost. If they couldn't make the payments, they might even lose the farm, and have to survive on social security and Oliver's small pension. And they'd do it. Cheerfully. Becky and Oliver would be the first to tell her she owed them nothing, and that they'd rather see her face than her money any day. Because they loved her.

Marissa jumped when the announcement interrupted her thoughts. "Please return your seats and tray tables to their full and upright position. We'll be landing shortly, about thirty minutes early this evening."

Early was good, especially since no one was meeting her. She collected her carry-on from overhead and rolled it through the airport, onto the shuttle and to her car in long-term parking. She drove east across the city. The five-pointed star perched on the mountain above Anchorage looked like one on top of a Christmas tree.

Before long, she left the city behind and followed the highway through the darkness. When she turned north, off the highway, a faint green light glimmered above the treetops in front of her. The aurora borealis, flitting by to welcome her home. More than once, she and Chris had watched the display together, his arms keeping her warm as the green light flickered and danced in the sky, sometimes for minutes, sometimes for hours.

An unfamiliar blue jeep was parked in front of the farmhouse beside Chris's truck. Marissa circled around back and pulled her car into the garage. Light spilled from the kitchen windows. She opened the door to the sounds of music and conversation, and slipped through the darkened mudroom to the kitchen.

Across the room, Chris and his sister

leaned over some papers at the table. He'd obviously been at it for a while, because he'd been running his hand through his hair until it was a mop of curls. Ryan and Sam sat on the window seat, playing with a couple of the toy soldier nutcrackers Becky had collected. The cat lay curled in Ryan's lap. No one noticed Marissa immediately as she hovered at the doorway.

Ryan walked the nutcracker across the cushion. "My dad was a soldier. He died."

Sam nodded. "I'm sorry. My dad died, too."

Ryan looked up at him. "Did you miss him?"

"Yes." Sam smiled. "But later I got another dad who was really great. His name was Tommy."

"Do you think I'll get a new dad someday?"

"I do." Sam ruffled the boy's hair. "And he's going to get a great kid."

Marissa's heart swelled. She and Sam had been so lucky, finding new families who loved them after losing their own parents. Ryan was lucky, too. Chris was going to be a wonderful dad. She stepped into the light.

Chris looked up, a smile brightening his face. "Hey, you're home early." He reached over to shut off the music. The voices stopped and they all turned her direction.

"Tailwind." She looked from one to the other.

Ryan jumped up, sending Tiger scurrying away. "Hey, Marissa."

"Hi, Ryan." She squeezed his shoulder and looked past him to the others at the table. "Did I miss the party?"

"I wanted to see the reindeer, so Sam and Ryan brought me out." Dana gave a hesitant smile. "I hope that was okay."

"Of course it's okay. Did you see them?"

"They're gorgeous. Ryan introduced us to all of them." Dana flashed a smile in his direction before turning back to Marissa. "You were so lucky to grow up here."

"Yes, I was." She shifted her gaze. "Hi, Sam. It's been a while." And the last time she saw him he'd had some harsh things to say.

"Marissa." Sam met her eyes, and slowly a smile crossed his face. "It's good to see you home again."

She smiled back in relief. "It's good to see you, too."

Dana jumped up from the table. "Look at the time. We need to go."

Sam glanced up at her in confusion, but Dana widened her eyes and telegraphed him a message. He chuckled and stood. "I guess you're right. Ryan, you have school tomorrow. We'd better get you home."

"Do I have to go?"

"It's time."

He gave a deep sigh. "Okay."

Chris gathered up the papers on the table, slipped them into a manila folder and tucked it under his arm. Sam laid a hand on Dana's back and guided her into the living room where he helped her on with her coat and adjusted her collar as though he were protecting her in bubble wrap. He dropped a kiss on the top of her head before he let go.

Marissa had to stifle a giggle. Who knew Sam had such a tender side?

Ryan shrugged into his coat and picked up his hat. "Bye, Marissa. Bye, Chris."

"Bye. I'll see you all later." Chris closed the door behind them and turned to Marissa. "How did the interview go?"

"Very well." Marissa tried to put some enthusiasm into her voice. "It's a great opportunity. Beautiful area. Excellent facilities. It even includes housing for the team."

His shoulders sagged just a bit, but he managed a small smile. "That's good. Are you hungry? I made chili."

"Thanks, but I ate on the plane." She shed

her coat and sat on the couch. Someone had left a pen on the coffee table. She picked it up and clicked the ballpoint in and out. "Why did everyone run away when I walked in?"

He shrugged. "I guess they noticed the time."

"What were you looking at?" She nodded toward the folder under his arm.

Chris rubbed the back of his neck. "Something I'd like your advice on, but I'm sure you're tired after traveling. You can see it tomorrow."

"What is it?"

"A business plan."

She raised her eyebrows. "For?"

"A business I'm thinking of investing in. And you're the best planner I know, so I'd like you to look it over before I make any decisions. Besides, it concerns you."

"Okay, now you've got my curiosity up." She reached out a hand. "Let me see."

"You don't have to do it now."

"Chris, show me the darn plan before I stab you with this pen."

He grinned. "Well, if you really want to see it." He handed her the packet.

She tucked the pen behind her ear and opened the folder. As she skimmed the first page, her eyes grew wider and she read more carefully. When she looked up, Chris was standing perfectly still, watching her.

"You want to buy the reindeer farm?"

"Yes."

"But why?"

He settled on the couch beside her. "I told you, I'm giving up fishing so I can be with Ryan. I was out in the barn, feeding the goats, and thinking about what sort of work I'd like to do instead, and it occurred to me the perfect place to raise a child is right here, where you grew up."

"Yes." It was a wonderful place to grow up, and Ryan loved it here. But Chris was a fisherman, not a farmer. "Can you pull it off?"

He gestured at the papers in her hands. "You tell me."

She turned the page. "You have no experience as a farmer. Can you get financing?"

"No financing needed. I've been saving ten years to buy a boat. I can cover this."

She flipped through the pages. Seasonal cash flow, estimated expenses, repairs needed. It was all there. Even bar charts. In color. "You put this plan together?"

"Yes, ma'am. Of course, the cash flow is an estimate. I'd need to talk with Oliver and Becky to pin those numbers down. And I have a few ideas for extra revenue I want to run by them. But I think it's doable, especially if I keep the snowplow business, too."

"But what do you know about farming? Or tourists? Or parties?"

"Not enough." He moved closer to her. "That's why I'd like to ask Oliver and Becky to stay on as live-in advisors. The house is certainly big enough. With a few bathroom updates, Ryan and I could move into the wing they're not using." He paused, studying her. "The question is whether that would be okay with you."

"Why wouldn't it be?"

"Because." He let out a slow breath. "Because this is your home. I've seen how much you love this place. I don't want to move in and take over if it means you don't feel comfortable coming home to see your aunt and uncle."

Even after she'd turned down his proposal? "Why are you so worried about my feelings?"

The corners of his eyes crinkled. "I thought we'd covered this the other day. I love you, Bo. I want you happy."

She met his eyes. Blue eyes, set under strong brows and bracketed with lines from his frequent laughter. Sometimes those eyes could look fierce, but not tonight. Tonight they were soft, forgiving. "You really do, don't you?"

"I really do. I think this could work for all of us. It would give Ryan the stability he needs, and of course he'd get to spend time around the animals. If Oliver and Becky decide to stay on, I'd be here to help them as they grow older, and they'd be a good influence on Ryan. They'd have the money from the sale of the farm to pay off their medical bills. That would leave you free to take this job without worrying about them or the farm. I know Oregon is closer than you've been in the past, but it's still too far to fly up for weekends."

"You've put a lot of thought into this."

"I have."

"But you love the ocean, love fishing. Are you sure this is what you want to do?"

A slow smile spread over Chris's face. "I do love fishing, but I love that kid more. And farming is growing on me. This morning, when I went to feed the goats, Willa started snorting and ran over to greet me. The fish never did that."

She laughed. "No, I guess they wouldn't."

He stood and nodded toward the folder. "Take a look at the plan. See if you find any obvious errors, and whether you're okay with the whole concept. If you think it will work, I'll put together an offer for Oliver and Becky."

She stood, as well. "I'll go over it and call you tomorrow."

"All right, then. Good night, Marissa." He started toward the door.

"Chris, wait."

He turned back toward her. "What?"

She stepped closer and wrapped her arms around him. "You're going to be an awesome dad."

MARISSA STAYED UP LATE, reading over Chris's business plan and checking his numbers. This could really work. Early the next morning, she put in a call to Oliver and Becky and outlined what Chris had in mind.

"I'm so relieved," Becky confessed. "I knew we'd have to sell the farm sooner or later, but I wasn't looking forward to moving to town. But are you sure Chris would want us there?"

"He's counting on your help, both to learn the business and with Ryan."

"It's a great idea. Ryan is a natural-born farmer," Oliver said. "He's got the touch with livestock."

Marissa went over some of Chris's revenue

and expense estimates with Oliver to make sure they were in the ballpark.

"That all sounds about right," Oliver answered. "But if you want to double-check, all our books are on the computer in the den."

"Are they password protected?" Marissa clicked her pen open. "Let me guess. Santa? Sleigh? Rudolph?"

"The password is Sweet_Marissa."

"Aw." She smiled. "Okay, I'll take a look and compare your numbers. If it's all workable, I think Chris wants to give you an offer sooner rather than later."

"We'll look forward to that," Becky said. "But sweetheart, what about you? Did you accept the job in Oregon?"

"Not yet. I'm still thinking about it."

"Well, whatever you decide is fine with us," Oliver assured her. "We just want you happy."

"Thanks. I love you guys. I'll talk with you later." She hung up the phone and brushed away a tear. They wanted her happy. Chris wanted her happy. Even after all the problems she'd caused, they loved her.

What would make her happy? The job in Oregon, counting wildlife in that beautiful setting, adding to her reputation in her career, sounded wonderful. It was what she'd worked toward, a continuation of the life she'd been leading for the past ten years. But was it truly the life she wanted?

CHRIS SAT AT his desk in the warehouse, ostensibly updating the books, but his gaze kept returning to the cell phone on his desk. It was midafternoon. Why hadn't Marissa called? Were his numbers so far off she didn't want to disappoint him with the news he and Ryan couldn't possibly live off the income? Or maybe she was having second thoughts about him sharing a house with her aunt and uncle. Would it be awkward in the future if she brought a boyfriend to visit?

His jaw tightened at the thought of Marissa with some other man, but he had to face facts. She'd turned him down. She didn't want to marry him. Oh, sure, she'd tried to soften the blow by pretending it was all for his sake, because he wanted children, but the bottom line was that she'd said no. One day she would fall in love with someone else, and there wasn't a lot Chris could do about it. And being right there in the house with her family when she brought the guy home wasn't going to make it any easier. But this was the right choice for Ryan and for him. Chris just hoped it was the right choice for her.

The buzzer sounded. Maybe that part he'd ordered last week had finally arrived. But when he opened the door, Marissa was waiting outside, holding the folder. "Hi. Can I come in?"

"Sure." She'd come to deliver the news in person. This might be worse than he thought. He led her to his office. "Coffee?"

She looked at the jar and wrinkled her nose. "Thanks, no. I've had your so-called coffee." She sat in one of the straight chairs and set the folder on the desk in front of her. "Let me show you what I've found."

Chris settled into the chair beside her. She opened the folder and flipped through a few pages. "I talked to Oliver and Becky this morning. They're thrilled with the idea, and Oliver gave me permission to look over his books. These are the corrected figures."

Chris ran his eye down the columns. "This actually looks a little better than what I'd estimated."

"Exactly. I think financially, you'll do fine."

"That's great." He turned to her. "But this concerns you, too. Can you live with this arrangement?"

She glanced down at the papers again and

took a breath. "You want to know what I think?"

"That's exactly what I want."

She looked into his eyes and rested her hand against his cheek. "I think that you are the most amazing man I've ever known, and that I'd be a fool to let you out of my life again." She smiled at him. "Will you marry me?"

He raised an eyebrow. "You turned me down when I asked four days ago. What changed?"

"I was scared. Now I'm not."

"Scared of me?"

"Never." She laughed. "Scared you might change your mind. That you'd grow to resent me because I couldn't have kids." She took his face between her hands. "But I'm not scared now. You love me. You love me enough to want my happiness even if it means giving me up. I don't deserve that kind of devotion, but I'd be stupid to let it get away. Because I love you, Chris." She tugged his head closer and whispered the words against his lips. "I love you."

He reached for her and pulled her from her chair into his lap, where he could kiss her properly. She giggled and put her hands to his cheeks. She was back in his arms, right where she belonged. One taste of those luscious lips of hers, and he knew he'd never get enough.

Eventually, of course, they had to breathe. He rested his forehead against hers. She stroked his beard and smiled at him. "You haven't answered me."

"You don't look worried." He chuckled. "Have I ever refused you anything you really wanted?"

"Only once. And I was a bit of a brat about it. So I want your answer. Christopher Allen, will you marry me?"

"Yes, Marissa Anita Gray, I will marry you." He pressed his lips to her forehead. "But what about that job in Oregon?" Would he need special permission to take Ryan out of state? How would all that work out?

"I turned it down."

"You did what?"

"Now, don't panic. I'll be a contributing member of the household. I interviewed this morning for a position in a local bear study, and they offered me the job. It's only part-time, but it sounds like a great study and might lead to something more down the road. I start next week."

"Are you sure? I'm almost certain a part-time study wasn't in your five-year career plan."

She smiled. "Sometimes you've just got to throw out the plan and follow your heart. I think we should go with your plan instead. Buy the reindeer farm and live here. Give Ryan the best childhood we can. I can be Ryan's mom—" she pushed a strand of hair away from his forehead "—and your wife. And maybe we'll decide to adopt more kids later."

"You're sure that's what you want?"

"It's exactly what I want. Someone else can lead that wildlife inventory in Oregon, but my place is here. With my family. With you." She laid her head against his shoulder.

Chris reached for her left hand. "So we're officially engaged. Tomorrow, we can go ring shopping."

"What did you do with our original engagement ring?"

"I still have it. But I thought you would probably want to start fresh."

"I love that ring. When you put it on my finger, I felt like the luckiest woman in the world."

"In that case, let me up."

She moved back to the other chair, and he stood and removed his wallet from his back pocket. On the surface of a small compartment meant to hold change, a circle had worn into the soft leather. He reached inside and slipped out the ring, a modest diamond flanked by two emeralds in a leaf-shaped setting.

Marissa took the ring from him and ran her finger over the smooth golden curve, a smile on her face as though she'd been reunited with an old and cherished friend. At the time, it had taken a huge chunk of his savings to afford that ring, but he'd seen Marissa admiring it in a jewelry store window and he wanted her to have it. He could afford a bigger diamond now, but judging by the look on her face, she wanted this one.

She looked up at him. "How long have you been carrying this around?"

He shrugged. "Ten years." Ever since she'd returned it to him. Every once in a while, he'd notice it in his wallet and tell himself he should sell it or something, but he never did. And now he knew why. He'd been waiting all this time for Marissa to come home to him. And she finally had.

He took the ring from her and knelt on one knee. "Will you marry me, Bo?"

She laughed. "I think we've already established that I will."

He slid it on her finger. It still fit, just like they still fit together. Better than ever.

CHAPTER NINETEEN

RYAN RAN AHEAD down the hall. A nurse frowned, but he dodged around her and waited at the door to the gathering room, one hand on the knob and the other clutching a plastic pterodactyl as he waited for Chris and Marissa to catch up.

Chris reached for Marissa's hand. "I don't know why I'm nervous," he whispered.

"Because we're being interviewed for the most important jobs of our lives?" she whispered back.

"Oh, that's why. I feel better now."

Marissa laughed and squeezed his hand. "Come on. Ryan's waiting."

As soon as they arrived, Ryan pushed through the door into the room. It looked more or less the same as it had at the party two months ago, but with Valentine hearts decorating the walls rather than Christmas shapes. Residents clustered in front of the television or over at the big table, working on a jigsaw puzzle. At another smaller table, two men played checkers, one in a wheelchair.

Ryan scanned the room. "I don't see her. I'll try the sunroom."

One of the checker players looked up. Martin, from the Christmas party. Chris waved. Martin's eyes went to Marissa's hand in Chris's and he gestured for them to come closer.

Chris tugged Marissa with him. "Hi, Martin."

"Well, if it isn't Santa and his elf." He winked. "Any news you'd like to share?"

Chris held up Marissa's hand with the engagement ring. "How's this?"

Martin grinned. "Told you so. Persistence. That's the ticket."

Marissa looked from one to the other. "Now what are you two talking about?"

Chris nodded toward the old man. "Martin had to ask his sweetheart six times before she agreed to marry him."

"Is that so?" Marissa grinned in turn. "I only had to ask once."

Martin's gaze whipped back to Chris. "She asked you?"

"Yes, she did." Chris gave Martin a smug smile. "And I said yes before she could change her mind."

"Wise man."

Ryan came running in. "She's not in the sunroom, either."

An aid came to them. "Are you looking for Mrs. Mason?"

"Yes."

"They're waiting for you in the conference room. I'll show you."

They said their goodbyes to Martin and followed the woman through a side door and down a hallway. Once, she turned back to whisper, "Winnie's doing much better now that the doctor changed her medication."

When she opened the door, Ryan ran to a tiny lady sitting at a table with Marigold, Ryan's social worker. "Granny!" At once, Chris recognized her smile. The dove lady he'd sat beside at the Christmas party.

"There you are, Ryan." She reached out and hugged him. "My goodness. I think you've grown in the last two weeks."

"Maybe. I'll ask Marissa to measure me again. She marks it on the doorway at the house on the farm."

"Hi, Ryan." Marigold smiled at him. "Aren't you going to introduce your granny to Chris and Marissa?"

Ryan nodded eagerly. "This is Marissa. She takes care of the animals on the farm, but Chris and me are gonna live there, too. Chris drives trucks and fixes stuff. This is my granny."

"Winnifred Mason." She held out a shaky hand. "Please, call me Winnie."

"Hello, Winnie." Marissa shook her hand gently.

Chris followed suit. "So nice to meet you."

"But we've met before, haven't we?" The old lady's pale blue eyes regarded Marissa for a few moments until her face lit up. "At Christmas. Yes, I remember seeing your pretty face at the party." She turned to Chris. "I don't remember seeing you there. But your voice seems familiar."

Chris glanced over at Ryan. Judging from the puzzled frown on his face he was taking all this in. "I have one of those voices. So, Ryan says you raised chickens when you were a little girl. We have chickens, too, at the farm."

"Ryan told me all about them. We had plain ole brown hens, but he says you have all kinds of fancy breeds. Do they really lay blue eggs?"

"Just the Ameraucana hen," Marissa said. She, Winnie and Ryan talked chickens for a few minutes. Chris sat back and watched them interact. When Ryan tried to imitate the sound one of the hens made, Marissa laughed and laid a hand on his head. Winnie smiled. So far, so good.

He and Marissa were already taking classes required to become licensed foster parents, but it wasn't an overnight process. In the meantime, Sandy and Brent were keeping Ryan. If all went according to plan, Ryan would remain with them to finish out the school year and move to the farm this summer, after the wedding.

In the meantime, Chris had been spending most of his spare time remodeling the bathrooms in the old wing at the farm, often assisted by Ryan, who particularly enjoyed the demolition phase. Give that kid a pair of work gloves, safety glasses and a hammer, and he transformed into a human wrecking ball. Marissa and Becky had picked out all the new bathroom fixtures, repainted the walls in the bedrooms and ordered new mattresses and furniture for Ryan's room.

Best of all, Oliver was back. He hadn't completely recovered, but he seemed to grow stronger every day. He credited the fresh air at the farm. He and Chris had formed the habit of making rounds together, discussing things like how many reindeer would calve this spring and whether Chris should get Ryan a puppy or an older dog once he moved to the farm, because it was clear the boy needed a dog of his own.

Between the wedding, the remodeling and the farm chores, there was a lot to keep track of. Fortunately, Chris was engaged to a master planner. Marissa had set aside a small room in the old wing as her office, and covered the walls with charts and calendars. Her new boss on the bear study was highly impressed with her organizational skills, and had all but promised a full-time position as soon as something opened up.

"So, when is this wedding I've been hearing about?" Winnie asked.

"June 2," Marissa said. "At the farm. My aunt Becky is making my dress. I'll show you the sketch." Marissa pulled out her phone. "Chris, don't look."

"Wouldn't dream of it." Chris sat Ryan in the chair beside him and they played with the dinosaur while the women, including Marigold, drooled over the pictures on Marissa's cell. The dress didn't matter to him; he'd seen Marissa in everything from an evening gown to fishing waders, and she was always beautiful.

Marissa ran an eye over Winnie. "I'm thinking a soft rose would be good for your dress. Maybe in chiffon? We'll have to get together with Becky and get her advice."

"I'm invited to your wedding?" Winnie's eyes sparkled.

"Of course you are." Marissa beamed at her. "You're Ryan's grandmother. One of our most honored guests."

"Snowflake is coming, too," Ryan volunteered. Chris was learning that while Ryan appeared to be completely engrossed with a toy, he was often listening closely to the adult conversation in the room. Something to keep in mind. "I'm gonna lead her in. Becky's making her a new halter, for the wedding."

"Who is Snowflake?"

"A reindeer. She's old, and she likes carrots and apples. She's Marissa's favorite."

"Well, my goodness. A reindeer at a wedding. I'll look forward to seeing that."

"Maybe you can come out to the farm next week so Becky can measure you and talk about dresses," Marissa said. The three ladies once again put their heads together and murmured about fabrics and fashion.

Chris nodded in satisfaction. This was going to work out fine. Marigold had told them Winnie was apprehensive about letting them adopt Ryan, afraid she wouldn't get to see him anymore if she gave up her rights.

Chris couldn't blame her. If he were in her shoes, he'd feel the same. But once Winnie realized she was part of their family and always would be, she'd come around. After all, they all wanted the best for Ryan.

They talked for almost an hour. When it was time to go, Chris bent to kiss Winnie's cheek, and spoke in a low voice. "Thank you for sharing Ryan with us. He's a special kid."

Winnie gasped. "Santa Claus!" She clasped her hand over her mouth.

Marissa stifled a laugh. Chris looked over at Ryan. The puzzled frown on his forehead suddenly gave way to clarity. You could almost see the pieces click into place in his brain: Marissa's presence at the party, his granny's recognition of Chris's voice and the time Ryan had spotted Chris dressed as Santa in the cul-de-sac on Christmas Eve. Chris raised a finger to his lips.

Ryan grinned. "Chris isn't Santa Claus, Granny." He slipped his small hand into Chris's large one. "He's my new dad."

* * * * *

Get 2 Free Books,
Plus 2 Free Gifts—
just for trying the Reader Service!

Get 2 Free Books,
Plus 2 Free Gifts—
just for trying the
Reader Service!

YES! Please send me 2 FREE Love Inspired® Suspense novels and my 2 FREE mystery gifts (gifts are worth about $10 retail). After receiving them, if I don't wish to receive any more books, I can return the shipping statement marked "cancel." If I don't cancel, I will receive 4 brand-new novels every month and be billed just $5.24 each for the regular-print edition or $5.74 each for the larger-print edition in the U.S., or $5.74 each for the regular-print edition or $6.24 each for the larger-print edition in Canada. That's a savings of at least 13% off the cover price. It's quite a bargain! Shipping and handling is just 50¢ per book in the U.S. and 75¢ per book in Canada.* I understand that accepting the 2 free books and gifts places me under no obligation to buy anything. I can always return a shipment and cancel at any time. The free books and gifts are mine to keep no matter what I decide.

Please check one: ☐ Love Inspired Suspense Regular-Print ☐ Love Inspired Suspense Larger-Print
(153/353 IDN GLW2) (107/307 IDN GLW2)

Name _____
(PLEASE PRINT)

Address _____ Apt. # _____

City _____ State/Prov. _____ Zip/Postal Code _____

Signature (if under 18, a parent or guardian must sign)

Mail to the **Reader Service:**
IN U.S.A.: P.O. Box 1341, Buffalo, NY 14240-8531
IN CANADA: P.O. Box 603, Fort Erie, Ontario L2A 5X3

Want to try two free books from another line?
Call 1-800-873-8635 or visit www.ReaderService.com.

* Terms and prices subject to change without notice. Prices do not include applicable taxes. Sales tax applicable in N.Y. Canadian residents will be charged applicable taxes. Offer not valid in Quebec. This offer is limited to one order per household. Books received may not be as shown. Not valid for current subscribers to Love Inspired Suspense books. All orders subject to approval. Credit or debit balances in a customer's account(s) may be offset by any other outstanding balance owed by or to the customer. Please allow 4 to 6 weeks for delivery. Offer available while quantities last.

Your Privacy—The Reader Service is committed to protecting your privacy. Our Privacy Policy is available online at www.ReaderService.com or upon request from the Reader Service.

We make a portion of our mailing list available to reputable third parties that offer products we believe may interest you. If you prefer that we not exchange your name with third parties, or if you wish to clarify or modify your communication preferences, please visit us at www.ReaderService.com/consumerschoice or write to us at Reader Service Preference Service, P.O. Box 9062, Buffalo, NY 14240-9062. Include your complete name and address.

Get 2 Free Books,
Plus 2 Free Gifts—
just for trying the
Reader Service!

Get 2 Free Books,

Plus 2 Free Gifts—

just for trying the Reader Service!

READERSERVICE.COM

Manage your account online!

- Review your order history
- Manage your payments
- Update your address

*We've designed the
Reader Service website
just for you.*

Enjoy all the features!

- Discover new series available to you, and read excerpts from any series.
- Respond to mailings and special monthly offers.
- Browse the Bonus Bucks catalog and online-only exculsives.
- Share your feedback.

Visit us at:

ReaderService.com